Pipeliner

Shawn Hartje

Enjoy + thanks for reading!

Reviews are much appreciated...

Helen Springs Press
San Bruno, California

First Print Edition

ISBN 978-0999854105 (Helen Springs Press)

Cover Design by EbookLaunch.com

Book layout by https://ebooklaunch.com

Pipeliner/Shawn Hartje. — 1st print ed.

For their excellent editorial assistance, I would like to thank:

Paul Samuelson http://storywrangler.com

Bobby Bradford of Dominican University of California
http://www.dominican.edu/academics/ahss

Ashley Gillespie Rich https://www.linkedin.com/in/ashley-rich-851aa92

Oh, and also thanks to everybody who was, is, or ever will be…you people rock!

"If this world is but a shadow of the next one,
then imagine how bright is the future?"

—Author unknown

Chapter 1

In the Trail King parking lot, Jason Krabb saw his friend Isabel Perkins's brown Dodge Aries sedan parked between giant pickups, a good sign since she'd lately been hanging with Shelly Stewart, whom Jason had been flirting with in algebra II. He found Isabel by herself in a diner booth, smoking Camel Lights and acting older than she was.

"Hey Jason." Isabel looked happy to see him. "Did you cut your hair?"

Jason shook the long blond hair from his face and sat close beside her, making sure his hips pushed into hers.

"Watch it!" Isabel smiled, pushed him back, and combed a lock of hair behind his ears.

Jason had known Isabel since back when her mom ran a home daycare on their small ranch directly across the interstate from the Trail King Truck Stop. Isabel had long straight hair that she was always dying in various patterns. Today it was blond up top, black at the ears, and maroon-tipped. She was quite pretty, with a tanning-bed complexion, a seductive smile, and sporting a huge chip on her shoulder.

"Where's the party tonight Izzy?" Jason asked.

"You think I'm sharing that with high schoolers?" Isabel sounded disgusted.

Like Jason, Isabel was fiercely independent of anything to do with high school. As a freshman she'd been mocked for being too country, favoring embroidered getups with horses and lariats and her name stitched golden upon sharp blue denim. Jason remembered how Becca Black, queen of the top tier girls, used to bully Isabel, pushing her into the lockers and pulling on her fringes and tassels.

Isabel was now more ambiguously outfitted, playing to whatever scene she was currently interested in. Today she wore a men's V-neck shirt in winter camouflage with black Capri pants above white slip-on Vans. Her skin looked too lustrous, as if coated in caramel.

"Your new boyfriend in town?" Jason asked.

Isabel turned serious. "Ben's partying with his crew up in the Black Elks. He just bought a camper trailer. It's badass, has a TV with a VCR above the bed."

Jason laughed at this. "Sounds like a nice fuck pad."

Isabel winked at him. "We call it the stabbin' cabin."

Jason loved this about Isabel. He could relax and be his horny teenaged self around her, could talk about anything sexual and she'd gamely jump in the conversation.

"How'd he buy that?" Jason was curious about her latest boyfriend, Ben Stone, who'd graduated high school last year. All Jason remembered about him was that he'd never talked and wore Metallica T-shirts.

"Pipeliners make serious money," Isabel said. "His parents don't like me at all. So he bought the camper and moved out. Now we don't have to put up with them anymore."

"What a stud," Jason said. "Dude's hanging around poaching high school girls."

Isabel was into older guys. When Jason started hanging around the Trail King as a depressed freshman, she'd been dating one of the clerks, a mustachioed guy in his twenties who bought her cigarettes and let her wear his worker's smock.

Isabel blew smoke at Jason. "You high school boys aren't up to snuff."

"Whatever," Jason said. "Hooking up with older guys doesn't change the fact that you're stuck in Idaho. Just like me."

Isabel shook her head. "I'm like from the Trail King anyways. It's an embassy of the open road, doesn't belong to any one state."

The Trail King was indeed full of travelers, and Jason liked seeing strange license plates from all over the country. He watched a big rig gunning it up the westbound entrance ramp out the window, no doubt bound for glory in Portland and Seattle, exotic places where he planned to become a famous rock guitarist—once he escaped from Helen Springs, population 58,000 and hub town of southern Idaho. He ordered a beef sandwich from the skinny, gum-chewing waitress and then went into the convenience store. Sitting among the cheap sunglasses, air fresheners, and Corn Nuts was the holy grail of tape racks. Full of greatest hits anthologies and themed compilations, the truck stop tape racks had culled the vast world of music for him. The huge selection at the Musicland store in the mall overwhelmed him and it was hard to find good stuff among so many duds. The King's racks were ever-changing and spanned the decades and genres. It was common to find Lynyrd Skynyrd next to Marvin Gaye, and Waylon Jennings beside Steely Dan. He loved buying tapes here and would go home and pick out the easier songs on his guitar by working the rewind button on his Sony tape deck.

With high expectations, Jason ran his fingers down the rack and was thrilled to find Bobby Womack's greatest hits, which looked like a winner. It was as if he needed to hear this; obviously, the cool people running the scenes in Portland and Seattle would be concerned to learn he wasn't up on Bobby Womack.

He paid for the tape with a twenty he'd snatched from his mom's purse and got seventeen and change back. Shelly Stewart was sitting next to Isabel when he returned to the diner. Aside from a severe case of acne, Shelly was otherwise flawless. Jason stalled, taking in her black tights worn under pink jogging shorts and her yellow-laced L.A. Gear high tops. Her lycra shirt silhouetted breasts that he imagined were firm, like the boneless hams he'd recently and unabashedly felt up in the supermarket cooler.

Shelly's auburn hair was crimped back and looked fresh from a workout. Her parents owned the South Idaho Gymnastics Center and had been touting her older sister Marjorie as a hopeful for the 1996 Olympics, which was three years away. Jason liked that Shelly had something going on other than high school, just like he wanted to be a rock guitarist. She flipped around on mats or something and he strummed three-chord-deals in his bedroom. His stomach tingled at the good fortune of running into her outside the confines of high school, and at the start of spring break to boot.

Ron Devry, the new kid in town, walked up and caught Jason ogling Shelly.

"Yup," Ron said knowingly. "Don't go for trophy fish if you want to catch a lot. The pizza faced ones are easier to catch and just as fun."

A Wisconsin-to-Idaho transplant, Ron was potbellied with a pale goatee, and always likened chasing girls to fishing. Jason took Ron seriously and wanted to learn things from him.

Jason shrugged. "She's cool though, not into typical high school bullshit."

The waitress walked past with Jason's hot beef and he followed the smell of gravy back to the booth. Shelly grabbed a spoon and ate gravy off his plate like it was chocolate pudding. Jason bared his teeth and playfully growled at her. Then he flipped the hair from his eyes and looked wronged until she reached over and mussed his hair. Her flirting seemed to be half-joking or half-serious, and not knowing made his stomach do back flips. They'd had plenty of practice flirting in the back row seats of Mr. Ebbett's algebra II class, a subject they both struggled with and commiserated over.

"What the fuck happens around here for Spring Break?" Ron sounded angry.

"Isabel knows about a bonfire up in The Black Elk Mountains," Jason said.

"A shitkicker? Jesus Fucking Christ! I wish there were some shows to see. Haven't been to a concert since I moved here."

Ron always bragged about the concerts he'd seen in the Midwest. Aside from his potbelly, Ron was a rather spindly boy with a gaunt face and a deeply gruff voice. His pale goatee seemed bleached—or something—and didn't match his long brown hair. Jason thought Ron's cool-guy concert act was desperate, since none of the bands he liked came anywhere near Helen Springs.

Jason pressed Isabel about the party in the woods, but she remained guarded. "It's way the hell up there. I'm staying in Ben's new camper, and you'd freeze your ass off."

"Fuck camping then." Ron sounded remorseful. "I hate this redneck town. Garth Brooks can suck my dick." He grabbed his crotch for effect and they all laughed.

Shelly looked mad at Isabel. "If you're going to be with Ben, then why am I going?"

"They said you could go?"

Shelly nodded and Jason's heart did a flip turn.

Isabel explained the situation. "Shelly's parents don't like me at all. They treat her like a stepchild. She's been totally back-seated by her sister Marjorie."

Shelly glared at Isabel until she gave directions to the bonfire. They were complex and confusing, but Ron kept a pen in his fanny pack and sketched a map.

"When you hit this gravel road," Isabel pointed to his map, "you go forever, seriously like twenty miles or something, and that ends at a forks where you head up the biggest mountain."

"What's a forks?" Ron seemed dubious.

Isabel snapped, "It's where the fucking road forks."

"Where do the other forks go?" Ron drew a large mountain and looked concerned.

"I expect they'll get you lost."

Everyone laughed but Ron. He had no idea of the vast boonies surrounding Helen Springs.

Chapter 2

Doug Stills lived on State Street in a tiny rental house on a weedy lot next to the train tracks. It hadn't always been this way. Jason fondly remembered the Stills' nice spread along the Black Elk River north of town. It had pastures, stables, ATVs, tractors, and a long asphalt drive that was pitch-perfect for traveling wheelies on a BMX bike.

Best buddies since diapers, Jason and Doug had recently formed a band, but Ron clearly didn't want Doug in on the camping trip. "Jesus Christ, let's split already."

They were going far from town in Jason's hand me down Toyota Camry. Jason liked the idea of having Doug along since the Black Elks were a bad place for a Toyota Camry. Doug could fix things and stuff always came up in the boonies.

Doug answered the door before Jason could knock, not surprising since Doug was embarrassed about his house. The few times Jason had been inside, he'd tried too hard not to notice the cracked plaster, stained carpets, and that the whole place smelled like a leaky sewer pipe. Having a pasty-white face splattered with brick-colored moles, Doug was a trim boy. His thin dark hair was cropped and his upper lip sprouted some fledgling whiskers. On weekends, he usually delivered pizzas in his battered Ford Escort, but complained tonight about not getting a shift. Jason produced Ron's fancily drawn map with its roads coursing between pine trees and up craggy mountains.

Doug pointed at the map, frowning. "It'll be freezing up there tonight."

"We're getting beer from Ron's house." Jason knew this would get Doug's attention. Ever since his dad lost the ranch, Doug had been breaking out of his Mormon shell, something Jason loved to encourage.

Doug licked his whiskers. "We could see if Marty wants to go."

"No way." Jason didn't want Marty Bachmann along tonight. Marty was their band's know-it-all bass player who, like Doug, was into advanced placement courses and over-achieving. Worse still, Jason's mom Leah was friends with Marty's mom. Leah had long used Marty's superbness to torment Jason.

"He tells his mom everything, and she'll tell my mom."

"I'll tell him it's top secret." Doug guarded the door even closer.

Doug had been pushing Marty extra hard lately. Marty had a music studio in his basement that was loaded with rock and roll instruments, all of which Marty played expertly. Marty had taught Doug how to play drums. Marty had the highest test average in trig class and he was obviously going to an Ivy League college. Jason was sick of all the straight A aggressiveness at his high school. He'd never been impressed by good grades, especially not since his older brother Robert had written the book on over-achieving while at North Helen. Jason shrugged. "I'm sick of Marty. Are you coming or what?"

Doug looked hurt. He was extra sensitive these days—especially when Ron was around.

"Hi Jason." It was Marty Bachmann, pushing open the door from behind Doug. "Going drinking in the woods?"

Having been at odds with Marty for a long time, Jason had no qualms about talking behind his back. Marty knew the score between them. The worst part about this sneak attack was that Marty was allowed inside and Jason wasn't.

"Don't worry Jason, I'm not interested. I'm doing trig homework tonight."

While Jason was tall, Marty was even taller, with pale skin and curly red hair. He was both the most confident and the most uncoordinated person Jason had ever known.

Giving Jason a forlorn look, Doug escorted Marty over to a fancy touring bicycle resting against the house. This was an expensive toy and Doug adored it. Marty clipped on a helmet and explained the bike to Doug, who nodded approval at everything Marty said. They all watched Marty pedal away down State Street, wobbling and shifting heavily as if on the verge of crashing. Doug whistled and shook his head. "Okay, let's go camping."

* * *

Leaving Doug's house, Jason drove the boys beneath the interstate exchange; one branch flowed north and south through Montana, Idaho, Utah, Nevada and Southern California, and the other started (or ended) in Helen Springs, heading northwest to Boise and onto Oregon, Washington, and Jason's hoped-for nirvana. Overlooking the interstate exchange—and the whole town—was Jason's neighborhood of Stone Bluff, a decade-old conglomeration of sprawling ranch homes built on a breeze-catching rise full of sagebrush and lava rock.

The Krabb's prominent home was clearly visible from down below, but Jason avoided looking at it. All was not well on the home front. His poor midterm grades had sent his parents on a tirade, especially his failing status in algebra II. This subject was most dear to his father Curtis, a physicist by training and director of the federal nuclear lab just outside of town. With the rest of Jason's courses, it was easy enough to memorize the glossaries in order to pass quizzes and bullshit through his essays. Algebra wasn't like this, and it sucked that math book glossaries weren't at all helpful. Now his algebra teacher, Mr. Ebbett, was gunning for him, dragging him up in front of class to solve equations that looked entirely fake to Jason, if not downright otherworldly. Because he came from a smart family, it seemed to Jason that Mr. Ebbett viewed him as a frozen dinner kind of student—something pre-cooked that a teacher could just pop into the oven. A badly cooked TV dinner kid must be embarrassing for him.

Traveling south along the foothills of the Black Elks, they passed through desert, pastureland, and over irrigation canals carrying the Black Elk River's clear, dam-fed snowmelt. Irrigation canals were so prevalent in and around Helen Springs they often marked the school district boundaries. The April evening's warm air rushed in the open windows, smelling sweetly of cow manure and sage. Drinking a Lowenbrau beer stolen from the bar at Ron's house, Jason sang along to The Little River Band playing "Help Is on Its Way" on Z-93 IDAHO ROCKS. The station was celebrating the year 1993 with a promotional blitz of uninterrupted classic rock blocks every weekend. Instead of commercials, an anonymous announcer dispensed rock trivia between song blocks. Jason was surprised to learn that the Little River Band was from Australia, surprising since their music sounded right at home in this far corner of Idaho. In the rear-view mirror, he watched Doug air drum with a beer between his knees and was glad to see him relaxing, especially after being cagey by hiding Marty in his house.

Ron was fed up listening to the radio. He opened his carrier case full of artfully marked and carefully curated tapes from various concerts.

"No way," Jason protested. "I want to hear my Bobby Womack."

"Who the fuck is Bobby Womack?"

"I don't know. Looks like a black guy."

"What's with you and your truck stop cheese?"

Jason shrugged.

Ron only listened to concert bootlegs and liked to overload Jason with information about each show. Ron also didn't seem to care that they sounded like something recorded with kids using soup cans and strings.

Picking a Grateful Dead tape that he snottily claimed best represented the band's disco years, Ron placed it in the tape deck and hit rewind. "This is Shoreline, '77."

His skinny fingertips stopped the rewind just before "The Music Never Stopped." The bass came on murmuring, the guitar plinked over a clip-clopping drumbeat, and Ron scrunched his face in a conceited smack. He raised up his bony elbows and flapped them lazily at shoulder height, index fingers outstretched, half drumming and half pointing out the windshield, eyeglasses sliding down his greasy nose. "That's Donna Jean Godchaux singing backup. Disco Donna. Yeah baby."

Jason tuned him out. For how much Ron loved his music, it was strange how he always talked over it.

"Check *this* out." Ron pulled a squat bottle of amber liquor from a grocery bag between his legs. The odd-shaped bottle was unopened and looked beautiful. "It's Damiana, a potent extract."

Jason was in awe. This was why he loved hanging out with Ron. "What's it taste like?"

"I don't know." Ron grew serious. "I smuggled it back from a family vacation to Mexico. Been saving it for a special occasion."

Ron cradled the shapely bottle. "They were lining up for it down there. Girls on vacation are, like, obligated to hook up. I was with a different girl each night from all over the place."

"Like you had sex with them?" Jason loved thinking that sex was uncomplicated—was just two horny people coupling for relief and pleasure.

Ron laughed. "You could fuck all fifty states down there. It'd be easier than actually going to all the states and trying to score. Let them come to you man."

Doug finished his beer, burped rudely and murmured under his breath. He was light years behind Ron and Jason where girls were concerned and was embarrassed whenever they discussed sex.

Ron turned to the backseat. "How about it Dougie, know what I love about Mormon girls?" Ron loved chiding Doug about girls, about being Mormon, about anything really.

Jason smiled but didn't laugh. Defending Doug while maintaining status with Ron was tiresome for him. It usually played out this way because Ron viewed Mormons with malevolence and blamed them for all sorts of problems.

Ron snorted, "I love how they won't let you past second base, but they'll take a stiff one in the poofter."

Doug was too smart to take the bait but Jason was horribly curious. "What the hell?"

Ron was all over Doug. "Come on Doug, tell us about the poop-hole loophole!" Ron laughed low and long and explained it to Jason. "How else do you think those Mormon girls keep their virginity for so long?"

Doug, blushing, pouted and looked out the window.

"That's insane!" Jason wondered seriously if there was any truth to it. He knew plenty of Mormons but actually little about them. Ron certainly knew things and had done things. The way in which he discussed sex—always bringing up oddities like this—led Jason to believe he was a seasoned veteran.

Ron passed around fresh beers. "Kate needs to stock up on beer," he joked. "We cleaned out Ray's stash!"

Ron always referred to his parents by their first names, making it sound as if he lived with roommates instead of parents. Ron's dad Ray was a bigwig at one of the firms contracted by the nuclear lab, and Kate spent most of her time at the country club playing cards and indoor tennis. The boys had met last summer, just before starting junior year, at a Welcome Wagon dinner party hosted at the Krabbs. Jason was thrilled to meet another guy with long hair which was a rarity in Helen Springs. While the adults socialized downstairs over white wine and Bud Light, Ron bragged about concerts where he'd eaten magic mushrooms and smoked pot with hot college chicks. Jason liked that Ron came from a place where boys had long hair and also drove imports; Ron's white Nissan Maxima made Jason less sensitive about his peach-colored Toyota Camry. Wisconsin sounded cool and Jason planned to check it out after making it as a guitarist in Portland and Seattle.

Turning off the highway onto the well-marked road leading up to the Black Elk Reservoir, they were stopped behind a pickup truck at a rail crossing while a freight train slumbered past. Ron checked their progress on his map. "I don't see a reservoir."

"It's not in your directions," Jason said. "Everyone knows how to get to the lake."

Jason stepped out to piss and was annoyed when a fifty-something ranching couple climbed out of the rifle-racked Ford F-150 as if solely to scrutinize him. The man wore smudgy bib coveralls and a tattered baseball cap, his face weathered from years of dusty, alkaline winds and Intermountain sunshine. The woman wore black jeans, cowboy boots and a flowery blouse. She was built similar to her husband—both like gas pumps—and her ashen, range-bleached hair was crimped back into a messy ponytail. They considered Jason and his Toyota Camry humorously, as if they'd stumbled across some exotic species of teenager.

Jason hated being judged by these hard-looking people and was suddenly embarrassed to be wearing the crisp new Levis his mother had just bought him at the Desert Crossroads Mall. He was the post that didn't hold up their rails. Too much fancy-pants shopping with Mommy in her gold-trimmed Lexus and not enough backroads bouncing and fence post pounding. Too much salad at home and not enough pork butt in the crock pot.

Like with his algebra teacher, Mr. Ebbett, it seemed personal with these people, as if Jason had somehow dashed their hopes for a decent future. The state was going to shit because of pampered dandies like him who were bad at math. Ranching was all math-based—he knew this was the case since the ranch kids at school talked about slaughter weights versus transport costs and fence post diameter versus gauge of barbed wire. He hated Idaho and Idaho hated him. For relief, he imagined this couple had a daughter in town at South Idaho State who studied range management and dressed like her mom. One of those cute cowgirls with the kind of legs that could grab a guy's ass and pound home some fence posts. Somehow he'd win over these people and prove he could fill the shoes of any buckaroo in Idaho. As the train cleared the tracks, Jason rudely zoomed around the truck, dusting the couple, and which only made them more amused.

Soon the boys passed an overlook of the Black Elk Dam where there was a memorial plaque dedicated to a wayward wagon party that had briefly settled this stretch of river before vanishing without a trace. The plaque blamed the disappearance on a marauding tribe of Sheepeater Indians. Supposedly there was a boneyard of dead pioneers lost in the river bottoms, but the only remnants ever found were bygone wagon wheel ruts and some log cabin ruins. Jason had visited the memorial site on a grade school field trip and found the mystery disturbing. Indeed, the mountains rising ahead looked bigger and more shadow-streaked than he remembered. He chugged his beer and chucked the bottle out the window.

Ron packed his lip and spit tobacco juice into an empty beer bottle. Chaw, as they called chewing tobacco, was easily purchased at the Trail King. Ron went through Kodiak like candy and Jason, of course, had picked up the habit, too. Having tossed his empty bottle, Jason dug under the seat for an old spitter, a plastic Mountain Dew bottle containing a week's worth of rotten spit, which made the car smell like fish guts.

Aside from a few switchbacks above the dam's tail waters, there was no high pass to climb or remarkable transition into the Black Elk National Forest. The scenery just evolved upwards and outwards from the road, gradually changing from brushy foothills and unremarkable rangelands into piney mountains ringing a large reservoir. The lake's waters were choppy near the dam but glassy up at the tree-ringed headwaters, the water reflecting the snowfields hanging over the lake like icy banners.

Their directions started above the lake where the narrow river meandered alongside the road with water dark and clear. Jason stopped the car and watched the heavy aquatic growth bent over in the current and waving green, as if the river had grown hair.

"Twenty miles from here?" Ron clutched his map.

"Twenty miles to the forks." Doug said "forks" just as curtly as Isabel had done, and Ron looked annoyed just the same.

Jason opened his new tape and relished that freshly unwrapped cassette smell that was oddly perfumed. Ron carefully ejected his bootleg before Jason jammed Bobby Womack into the slot. There wasn't any reason to fast forward since "Lookin' for a Love" was on top and right off Jason knew he'd found a new cheese anthem. It had all the elements: sexualized lyrics, wah-wah pedal guitar, and plucky drumming, which had Doug pounding the air again. Ron seemed to ignore the fun but Jason knew it was just a matter of time before he started singing along.

Fingers of setting sun lit the high westerly ridgelines with alpen-glow and the sage green valley was dotted with distant black blobs of grazing cattle. Jason thought it strange to see cows far away from any ranches, but the Black Elk was a hard working national forest, traveled daily by cattlemen, sheepherders, miners, and loggers. By night it was deserted, and he comfortably sped his Toyota down the gravel road, drinking beer and jamming tunes. There was nothing around for miles but sweet freedom.

Chapter 3

At the forks, the river branched off into trickles draining the high country through thick-timbered canyons. Jason got out and examined deep-looking puddles that guarded the web of forest roads veering off into No Man's Land. The air was frosty and steam wafted up from the moist ground into a star-filled sky. Jason was hoping to smell a campfire, but sage and pine dominated the air. Nor were there any sounds of a campfire. The tree tops were still and yet a low hum rang above them like wind. Having sensitive hearing, Jason was concerned until he realized it was just the eminent, echoing breath of the mountains: sound of running water, shifting rock, and god knows what else.

Doug marched up and pissed in the largest puddle. He seemed flat-out drunk after two beers. "Fresh tire tracks heading from this puddle," he said. The track quickly disappeared up the mountainside into the woods, much like all the others did.

"Careful Jason!" Doug was excited. "Driving through these puddles is like driving through puppy poop. Roll up the windows and punch the gas. C'mon now, let's get after it!"

Jason had been buzzed a few times from previous home bar raids but didn't remember acting like Doug was, breathing heavily and stumbling around.

Ron held a lighter next to his map for consultation but up here it was useless. Jason studied the map's cartoonish route up a lone, prominent peak to a nifty looking campfire, all drawn in the same style as the homemade concert T-shirts Ron liked to wear. The kid was talented but in reality every peak out here looked prominent. Funny how from town the Black Elks looked like just a few peaks, while up here they were a vast-reaching mountain range.

"What if Isabel and Shelly aren't there yet?" Ron was concerned about everything. "What if we show up to a bunch of rednecks?"

Jason was most scared of getting lost or stuck in No Man's Land. The cowboys and Mormons who so intimidated Ron weren't a problem for Jason. He liked sticking up for Ron with the sons of the Intermountain West, guys who gave no credence to hacky sack and country club sports. Jason liked having this edge over Ron and imagined himself as the cool-handed local Sheriff who teaches the hard-ass, big city cop about the sticks in one of those fish-out-of-water action movies.

Again pointing the way through the largest puddle, Doug bugged Ron to crack his special bottle.

"Uh, no." Ron scowled at Doug. "The party will appreciate an untouched Mexican import sticker. Stop being a lush."

Doug got pushier. "C'mon, gimme a swiggie."

Ron glanced at Jason, who shrugged. This wasn't the Doug he'd known since diapers.

"The trick tonight," Ron said in his lowest voice, "is to let these hicks have at this stuff. We souse them and keep the women in sporting shape."

"Dang it Ron! You're such a flipping lech!" Doug's words had that certain sting only a Mormon on the verge of cussing could muster. "Acting like you're gonna waltz into this party and have your pick of girls. It takes serious effort to get girls this far from town and I'm sure a lot of planning went into this. Nobody's gonna fold over for you because of some fancy booze."

"It's no fun with you two bickering." Jason got everyone back in the car and center punched the ominous puddle at thirty miles an hour.

The first twenty yards were shallow but firm-bottomed and the car easily planed. A wave dingy with sediment and cow dung fanned up over the hood as they skipped across the puddle's surface. They banged into the far side with the front wheel drive churning and miraculously climbed out. With the engine block steaming, they hooted and celebrated the awesomeness by cracking the last of the warm Lowenbraus. Jason rewound "Lookin' for a Love" and even Ron sang along now.

Going fast uphill on a roadbed covered in pine needles felt great.

The Camry's wheel felt every contour and rut but there was no slowing Jason down. The road roughened with rock outcroppings and he just rallied around them, thinking about Doug calling Ron a lech. He didn't really know that word, but guessed it was like being a pervert. At least if you were a lech, then a girl knew what she was getting into—kind of like doing business with the mob. He figured Shelly knew what she was getting into after he'd ogled and flirted with her all semester.

Up ahead warm firelight danced across a clearing and he slowed down. A fleet of sleekly-finished fiberglass campers and pickups were circled up like wagons around a bonfire. Five guys sat in plastic lawn furniture on the smokeless side of the flames, facing the road and stirring now, obviously surprised to see a dung-splattered, wayward Toyota Camry.

* * *

Jason's first and only kiss was with Margo Mullen in his freshman year. She was a junior he didn't know who'd suddenly developed an interest for him. Margo was energetic and cute with freckles, blond hair, a skinny nose, and flat lips. She'd approached him at his locker and said, "Let's go out." Like most things in his life, she more or less fell into his lap.

In late September on the first chilly day of the year, he rode his bike down from Stone Bluff to meet her at a park. They walked holding hands, shuffling through leaves and talking silly kid stuff, like how they'd be famous and live on private islands some day. They sat on a bench with a fine view of the Black Elk Range, which dominated the town's southern horizon and where groves of Big Leaf Maples rusted upon the lower slopes.

Margo said she was cold, snuggled against him, and put her arm around him. He faced her and she came for him like a horse going for an apple, grabbing his head and forcing her tongue deep into his mouth. Nothing in his world had compared to the sensation of her finely grained tongue twirling against his. He tasted her breath when she sighed and thought it was like tomatoes and honey. She released him and stared at him, looking pleased to see him completely flummoxed.

Pedaling up the long grade to Stone Bluff had never been easier.

His stomach did loops for days. He phoned her at night from his teen line and followed her around at school. She showed him off to her friends, which was a big deal because they were juniors and seniors. Seeing her in the hallways between periods made him want to dance. Nothing else mattered but Margo. She was the past, present, and future. Even Doug, his best buddy, got the cold shoulder from him when Margo was around.

Also at this time he was on the ill-fated North Helen Swim Team. His older teammates had jealously teased him over Margo. They called her a "hottie" and said nobody had gotten anywhere with her before. He told them about their kiss, not so much in bragging but because he hadn't told anyone and was bursting with exuberance.

Margo got wind of it, phoned him that very night and said, "I'm breaking up with you." Then she hung up on him.

His mouth went dry and tears flowed. It was the scariest thing he'd experienced. It got worse when she completely ignored him at school and looked through him like he was a ghost. High school had started with a fantastic bang, but by semester's end Jason was in full social retreat, save for the swim team guys who propped him up, appreciating his fast breaststroke and for nearly cracking Margo's code.

While a lot of snow fell in the mountains, the high desert around Helen Springs usually didn't get that much. But that freshman winter was frigid, with a blizzard blowing through town every week, drifting over the wide streets and causing hardship. Coinciding with the epic winter were updated state athletic mandates and the school district flared in conflict, holding many contentious meetings. The axe fell upon the North Helen Swim Team and it was controversially and spitefully eradicated midseason. Now just another boring freshman with no identity or social status, Jason kept late hours learning guitar from the complete Led Zeppelin guitar manual—or at least the easy songs—on his black Fender Catalina, a birthday present from the Musicland store in the mall and which sounded awesome.

* * *

"Isabel's not here!" Ron appraised the bonfire and was scared. "No girls at all. Kill your lights."

Jason turned off the lights, but he wasn't going to cower like Ron.

He'd come up here to escape all the nonsense of being a teenager in a sleepy town. Jason stepped from the car and called out, "You guys order the pizza?"

He felt solidly connected to the mountainside, like it was a part of his future. The campfire guys murmured with confusion and Ron groaned fearfully from the Camry. Jason felt sublime, in a heart-chugging, stomach-fluttering kind of way.

The shortest of the campfire guys stood up, belched and happily said nobody had ordered a pizza, "But we was supposed to have some girls coming up here. You seen anybody out there?"

"Just cows. We saw Isabel in town, surprised she isn't up here yet." With the guts of the matter exposed, Jason waited to be welcomed or shunned.

The happy short guy invited the boys to join the fire and offered them cold Busch Beer from icy coolers. "That's right boys, head for the mountains." He nodded assuredly, as if he had a great loyalty to the brand.

Ron laughed like a desperate hippy at a shitkicker. It didn't matter though since the pipeliners seemed bored with their own company and welcomed the distraction of three wide-eyed high schoolers.

Short Guy rolled his eyes and tipped his beer. "Yeah, Mr. Ben's been waiting on Miss Isabel to show but some girls can't find the sun in a bright blue sky. We're also expecting college girls and thought we'd be seeing them by now."

The short guy's name was Ross Early and he hadn't stopped moving since the boys arrived. He was unfamiliar to Jason even though he'd graduated last year from North Helen. Sitting farther back from the fire than the others, drinking beer, bottom lip fattened with chaw was Sean Patt, a dull-faced giant from an outsized Mormon family. Jason remembered Sean as a straight-edged, quiet footballer, though now he barely recognized him with a shaved head, full beard and stud earring flickering in the firelight. And there was Bruce Simpkins, one of those know-it-all ranch kids who'd gone through high school dressed like an L.A. cowboy, always bedecked in snazzy, overdone western gear. Bruce had considerably toned down his dress: instead of bun-snuggling Wranglers, snap-buttoned plaids, and roper boots, he had on baggy Levi's, a zippered sweatshirt, and basketball sneakers.

Ben Stone was still black-clad and had a pierced left ear and a greasy ponytail. He looked muscular and mean, drank whiskey from a bottle and stayed quiet.

Hardly believing his eyes, Jason recognized Allen Heber. Thick, tall, mallet-fisted and famously hot-tempered, Allen had been kicked out of North Helen for kicking ass when Jason was a freshman. This expulsion had coincided with Allen's older brother Stewart going to jail for assaulting a state policeman, which greatly intensified the Heber legend around town. Like most of North Helen, Jason had feared Allen and was grateful for his expulsion.

Allen tilted back his plastic chair and balanced his sandal-clad feet on a pine stump. He wore fuzzy blue socks and patchwork pants. He had a colorful serape draped over his massive shoulders. But most astonishing was the rainbow-beaded fanny pack resting on his lap. It seemed that Allen had become playful, even peaceful. His once furious scowl was now a lazy smile, his once buzz-cut hair was now an oily wave not quite covering up enormous ears. Allen's transformation reminded Jason that things never turned out the way he imagined they would. He too hoped to grow out of his high school self and take on some new persona.

Playing ambassador for the boys, Jason asked with genuine curiosity about pipelining. The guys worked four days of twelve-on and twelve-off out in the BLM desert, building a transmission system for delivering natural gas to the West Coast from the booming gas fields of Wyoming. This information was mostly provided by their foreman, a talkative older guy named Ferdig who seemed pleased with Jason's interest in pipelining. Ferdig was balding, goateed, heavyset and drank vodka from a Dixie cup. He smoked a tattered cigar that he kept relighting with a matchbook.

Jason had no concept of energy production and said it was crazy that gas could be piped across the state of Idaho.

"You get good compression," Ferdig said, "and gas goes easy. Come next year, we'll be keeping the lights on in Portland and Seattle, and for a lot cheaper than they do it now."

Imagining that guitar amps in Portland and Seattle clubs were somehow connected to natural gas floating through his backyard made Jason's stomach lurch. Whatever magic occurred to make this happen surely had to do with lots of math, but it was exciting nonetheless. These pipeliners were crucial to the awesomeness happening over the hills and far away and he was hanging out with them drinking beer. "That's so fucking cool. I wish I was building pipelines instead of going to high school."

Ferdig shook his head and waved his stogie at Jason, "Ain't all fun and games anymore. The Exxon Valdez changed that. Now we get our piss tested. One guy fucks up and we all suffer. Least they give us fair warning. See they know it ain't wise sneaking piss tests on your field crews, be nobody left to work." Ferdig struck another match and chuckled. "That's 'cause everyone tokes, from Thomas Jefferson to Bill Clinton."

This speech anticipated a meaty joint being rolled by Allen, who'd pulled a small Tupperware of weed from his fanny pack. Allen licked the finished product and notched it in a tree-stump to dry in the firelight.

Jason had already made up his mind to smoke weed or "ganja" as Ron lovingly called it. Like sex, he'd yet to experience marijuana and not for any moral or health reasons, but because it was scarce around Helen Springs. Ron had unsuccessfully hit up all the rumored potheads at school. The pipeliners pulled their chairs close as Allen lit the "*bambalacha,*" which he pronounced with overdone Latin flair. Jason wondered where Allen had acquired these affects. Busting out Spanish words was a fascinating development for an ass kicker, as was the serape. Allen's signature garb in high school had been a faded jean jacket with a huge Guns N' Roses patch.

The joint smelled sweetly familiar to Jason, kind of like when sage grass got stuck in the Camry's wheel wells and heated against the rubber. But this was heartier, like someone had thrown an onion into the bonfire.

"Y'all take the weed?" Ferdig asked the boys.

Anticipating the joint's direction, Ron had favorably repositioned himself in front of Jason and Doug. He took it from Ferdig and handled it with gentle authority (similar to how he handled his bootleg tapes), prudently pinching it between his lips until it fired brightly. It churned smoke out both ends when he passed it to Jason. The guy knew things.

The joint felt hot and wet on Jason's lips, and its smoke scratched his throat all the way down into his lungs. Strangled by a sudden urge to cough, he barely managed to pass it to Doug before succumbing to painful convulsions. These continued involuntarily and loudly while the pipeliners laughed. Ross Early joked, "Gotta cough if you wanna get off."

Doug erupted coughing moments later. He nearly dropped the joint before Ron swooped in to rescue it.

"First time?" Ferdig asked.

Jason nodded. Doug spat in the dirt, still coughing and drooling, hands on his knees.

Ron launched into a curricula vitae of toking, "Wow that's some good shit. I'm from Wisconsin and used to puff the skunk when I lived there." The pipeliners ignored him.

The pipeliners turned up the music and partied on while Jason's thoughts bounced around the years. His mind felt hotter than the bonfire and it *was* good. It was like his memory was taking itself for a walk, out getting some exercise. He thought about his Grandpa Krabb's windowless basement in his ranch house outside of town. Grandpa had a dartboard down there and always tuned the radio to AM talk shows. Though he hadn't been down there in many years, Jason vividly remembered the cool awards and certificates from the war: Grandpa was a lucky bastard, said one, a hero and a leader, said others. There was a black and white picture of a young Grandpa in his bomber jacket, smooth-skinned and with eyes expectant, and also pictures of him with Grandma Krabb, whom Jason had never met. And there was that strange picture of Grandpa alone in the desert with barren, sun-drenched mountains rising sharply behind him. Grandpa was posed in coveralls, thick-soled boots and wearing a belt with an exotic array of tools. With his skin creased, lips rigid, and eyes boring through the glare, it seemed now like an advertisement.

Grandpa's house was out near the diversion dam where an irrigation flume crossed the Black Elk River. In summer, kids floated across this flume and Jason loved jumping in on a hot day. Summer was coming and he'd be sure to take Ron down there, since nothing in Wisconsin could compare to it. The flume was an open-top tube of chest deep water that emerged from a black hole in the canyon wall and bridged the river's deep gorge. Its bottom was slick with algae and he remembered gliding by at ten miles per hour, shimmying or doing the moonwalk, feet frictionless against the tube slime and how it tickled like a foot massage. The flume finished with a fast plunge down a cement ramp into an irrigation canal on the other side of the river. One time, a girl much older than him had lost her swimsuit bottoms in the turbulent backwash. Jason had seen her pubic hair as she rolled around fighting for a breath and now the sight of it glinted in his memory—wet and shiny like flume moss.

Chapter 4

Ross Early raked some coals away from the bonfire with a stick. He picked up a baseball-size coal and juggled it from hand to hand.

"Hot coals! *¡Qué divertido!*" Allen shouted. He hopped up and took a pass from Ross, catching the coal behind his back before launching it up again. His feet shuffled, his bushy hair flopped, and sparks trailed from his hands. Jason was astonished. Allen got more awesome every second.

"Holy shit, you guys are nuts!" Ron did his deep laugh—the idling motorboat—but backed away from the action.

A circle formed as Sean Patt joined in. The coal jumped orbits among them, like an electron skipping between atoms, or was it the proton that did this? Jason couldn't remember which one, but it didn't matter, positive and negative charges had no bearing up at the shitkicker bonfire. The only trick was to keep the coal jiggling around on a bed of air in order to not get burned. Jason stepped into the circle and intercepted the coal. It was shrunken now from contact and he rolled it around his palm before passing it. The searing hotness of the coal, he knew, was the secret sauce behind everything. This was a force that the smart kids in algebra class missed by following all those rule-bound formulas; they were so afraid of getting burned that they missed the point entirely.

"*¡Caliente!*" Allen caught the pass from Jason. "*¡Flujo libre!*"

Allen caged the coal between his hands and rattled it above his head like a set of maracas, hips swaying and feet stomping up a cloud of forest dust. He opened his hands and blew on them, but nary a spark remained: hot coals was over.

Jason accepted a hand-slap-finger-pull-to-fist-bump gesture from Allen. This must be a thing guys did wherever Allen had gone to become so cool. Feeling pleased, Jason sat on a pine stump to reflect. He was glad Shelly hadn't arrived, thinking about girls all the time was tiring and he relished the break. Ross's pickup was parked close to the bonfire and a music mix blared from the open doors: Tom Petty, Damn Yankees, The Clash, Van Morrison, Guns N' Roses, Chicago, Tesla, The Beastie Boys, Jane's Addiction, Nirvana, and Metallica played on the high-end speakers. Jason thought everything sounded great and was thankful Ron wasn't in charge of the music, had heard enough Grateful Dead for one night. What kind of band needed two drummers anyways? It was like dancing on a trampoline or rolling down the windows in a convertible, how much enhancement did a guy need? A joint came around and Jason took another hit.

Beers and potato chips were passed around and hot dogs were roasted on sticks. Jason ate and drank plenty but never felt full. The pipeliners were generous in their sharing and nothing was in short supply. The trash went into the bonfire and the plastic flared with entertaining flashes. The conversation turned to concerts. Ross and Bruce Simpkins had seen the Beastie Boys in a Portland arena. Ross described an accident they'd witnessed in the nosebleed section. "Some dude snuck in through an air vent twenty feet above our heads and asked us to catch him. The crowd shouted, 'jump, jump' and that dude jumped, actually flapped his arms like a bird but everyone scattered. I did too, but then I hadn't been egging him on. Birdman crashed into the seats and broke his leg."

While Ross made it sound like a joke, Bruce was still concerned. "The security guards came up there and just carried him off, leg dangling all weird, head lolled off to the side. They were too pissed off to care if he was injured. We never did find out what happened to him."

Last December, Allen had seen the Grateful Dead in Tempe, on his way down to Mexico. "Got some peyote from a parking lot shaman and spent the first night's show on top of a van staring at the sky."

Ron informed everyone they'd played "Me and My Uncle" at that show, a favorite song of his, and he asked Allen what that was like. Allen smiled and shrugged, "I remember a lot of pretty skirts twirling by." Allen was so different. Jason guessed the old Allen would've kicked Ron's ass just for wearing a fanny pack and now they were fanny-packed brethren.

Ferdig stopped the show for Jason by revealing that he'd seen Led Zeppelin. "Seventy-seven, out in Cali. Houses of the Holy. Goddamn." Ferdig refilled his cup from a plastic vodka jug. "There's a song to make your hair stand up. I met a girl at the show who called me Moby Dick. She kept that up for days," he said luridly.

The pipeliners assaulted Ferdig then with old guy jokes and Jason imagined the shit Ferdig had seen over the decades. Pipelining and going to concerts had obviously kept him young. The pipeliners were so cool and the night just kept getting better. Jason walked into the woods for a pee and wished he had a concert story to share. He'd never been to a real concert but thought he might still share some insights. Like how music flowed like water, down from the mountains in rocky streams rolling over stones. Whoa, being stoned had him feeling poetic. It was like seeing the world through a new set of eyes that gave everything a more favorable impression.

Ron joined him and Jason said he should bring out the Damiana. Ron peed softly upon the pine needles and spent shell casings that littered the forest. "I don't know about that."

Jason hated how stubborn Ron was. "But they gave us beer and got us stoned. I'm so high man!"

Ron frowned and acted like this was in bad form—seasoned potheads didn't discuss their stonedness. "They can afford it. Bruce told me they make thirty dollars an hour!"

Jason wasn't concerned about money. It was the gesture that counted and Ron was being stingy. Ron laughed and pointed out that Doug had been silently staring at the fire since smoking the joint. "Turned his brain to Rice Krispies."

Jason watched Doug crouched alone by the campfire, biting his lips and twisting his hands together.

Jason went and knelt down by him. "I'm so stoned. Isn't it wild?"

"I'll not be having anymore," Doug said. "I keep seeing stuff. Not actually, you know, but I'm imagining things, like history and stuff."

Doug stared at the fire as his fuzzy lip moles shimmered with spittle.

"I know what you mean." Jason laughed. "I'm all over the place. I'm remembering stuff that..."

"No!" Doug grabbed Jason's arm. "You don't understand. I'm

looking backwards and imagining forgotten things. We remember nothing, everything is imagined, and we start from scratch every time we think!"

Doug's hand hummed like an appliance on his arm and Jason knew he was scared.

"I'm sorry Jason, that must sound crazy to you."

"You're not crazy." Jason laughed again. "Just stoned."

Doug was brilliant but he didn't get the silliness of the moment. It was strange thinking about smart kids doing drugs, like maybe they really popped on them. Jason didn't know what Doug had been talking about but something was clearly off with him. Jason's own reaction to pot was like acquiring a superpower where his brain crackled with possibilities. This awesome new world was full of serape-clad jesters who kept the lights on in Portland and Seattle. He patted his loyal friend on the back and hoped Doug would soon be in a better place.

The truck stereo had stopped and another bag of hot dogs made the rounds. Jason ate his straight off a scorched stick and seared his mouth. Allen pulled a battered guitar from his camper and played it poorly. Jason's fingertips tingled like they were on the frets, almost like they were inviting him to play.

Ben Stone wanted to mount a search for Isabel. He held a spotlight and aimed it into the pines for show. "She's probably stuck down at the forks. I'm sick of waiting. I'm gonna drive down, have a look." He was serious compared to the other pipeliners, who were all slack-eyed and in no shape for going anywhere.

Thinking to be helpful, Jason spoke his two cents. "I know her, like really well. She didn't bail on you."

Ben glared at Jason and then ignored him. Bruce theorized law enforcement was involved. "Rangers stake these roads out at night. You drive up on that scene, they'd know you were complicit."

"We're in the middle of butt fuck nowhere." Ross drunkenly bobbed his head. "Nobody got pulled over, they got lost. Or else they found better happenings. Wouldn't that be our luck boys?"

"They're stuck at the forks." Ben headed for his truck. "God-damned puppy poop this time of year."

Sean Patt volunteered to go with him and Jason was glad to see Ben drive off, the guy had been fuming all night and Jason sensed it was because of him.

* * *

Intermittent echoes came from Ben's truck descending the twisty road. It faded until they couldn't hear it for awhile and then it started again. Bruce claimed Ben was headed back up the mountain.

Doug sat squarely in the dirt and broke his silence. "He is. And so's another truck, a much older one with an engine wobble."

The pipeliners all watched Doug and cocked their ears at the forest.

"He's right," Allen said. "I hear it now."

Doug nodded. "Diesel truck, 1970s probably."

"No way!" Allen jumped forward. "That's Betsy's truck. *Amigo*, that's some crazy hearing you got."

Headlights panned across the clearing as the two trucks roared into their space, tearing apart the crackling-fire serenity. Indeed there was an older Ford pickup with three long-haired heads bouncing around the cab as the driver swiftly and expertly parked the huge truck. Sean Patt bounded down from Ben's truck and flashed a thumbs-up at the guys. Ben killed his engine and remained seated, tipping back his bottle of whisky.

This truckload of girls hadn't been lost but was stopped for a pee break down at the puddle-strewn forks when Ben found them. Allen introduced them to Jason. Krissy and Joey were in college at South Idaho State, but he pointed out that Krissy's little sister Betsy was a junior at South Helen.

Jason didn't know any South Helen girls and so Betsy was exotic right from the start. She was a fierce-looking hottie with sunken cheeks, a cutely upturned nose and deep-set eyes the color of the stained cherrywood in his parent's library. Her long black hair was wavy and an eye-catching braid ran down between her shoulders like an appendage. She wore a black denim jacket and tight faded jeans with lace-up black boots that looked well suited for logging or firefighting. Her older sister Krissy was also short with long black hair, but had a puffy, trashed-looking face that wasn't nearly as striking. Joey was raven-haired and shifty-eyed, with purple lipstick and black clothing. All of these girls seemed hard core to Jason—the kind of girls who spoke their minds and fought real fights.

Allen pulled Krissy down onto his lap for a loud welcome kiss. Of course the coolest, most awesomest guy brought in the chicks. Betsy twisted open a beer and tossed the cap into the fire. She took a deep swig and then one-handedly snapped a match to light her cigarette. Jason thought this was all for show and that she must be hamming it up for him.

South Helen was the other high school in town and rough rival of North Helen. It pulled students from the leafy, wide streets south of State Street where the community's plumbers, carpenters, security guards and tractor salesmen lived in single story, low-slung bungalows and also the trailer parks hidden in the river bottoms.

North Helen was a mix of suburban kids from affluent housing developments like Stone Bluff and also rural kids from the Black Elk River Valley, which was prime agricultural ground and home to many well-off ranchers and farmers.

The students from both schools had long perpetuated stereotypes about each other. South Helen students claimed North Helen was full of snobby, import-driving doctors' kids and spoiled farm kids with new pickups. North Helen students claimed South Helen was full of bologna-eating trailer trash who rode the school bus. Missing from both schools was serious poverty. Helen Springs was an agricultural hub with a large federal government presence and the nuclear lab alone contributed millions of dollars to the local economy.

Ross played a solemn, urgent-sounding band with raspy vocals. They were the Stone Temple Pilots, a new band out of San Diego, and he sounded proud to be up on such things. Jason liked how the new faces got a fresh soundtrack. It was so cool being here with college girls and pipeliners while his classmates back in town had already bored themselves to sleep. This was the life for him.

Little Betsy fit right in here. She guzzled beer, smoked pot and talked shit. Krissy complained how Betsy's driving up here had made her carsick. Betsy gave her the finger and boasted how the big Ford was her sweet sixteen present, a hand me down from their daddy. "Once I put a couch in the bed she'll be the best party rig in town. No more riding around in your puke-green Fiesta."

"At least I bought my Fiesta myself and Daddy can't take it away from me. You think it's your truck alright, go put a couch back there and find out whose truck it really is."

"You're just pissed your car ain't fit for these roads."

Jason thought having a couch in a pickup bed would be awesome, especially around here with miles of empty roads and good scenery.

Betsy removed her coat and warmed her bare arms above the fire. They popped with veins and muscle, like a small weightlifter's arms. As if extracting magic from the fire, she snapped at the wall of flames and started dancing with her eyes closed. Jason—and everyone else—watched her tank top lift over a flat tummy. Jason had never seen a girl blatantly showing off her body before and the sight of her breasts, showcased front and center like cupcakes at a bake sale, was hide-raising. She opened her eyes and returned his gaze and this was the way things worked for him with girls. Like a porch light on a buggy evening, he just drew them in.

Chapter 5

Something stalked the dark forest around the bonfire. Pine branches snapped with sharp cracks and Jason was startled, but it was only Ben Stone, gathering firewood in a mild rage. He walked up and rudely dropped an armful of wood at Jason's feet. Jumping out of the way, Jason went over to his car for another pee and stared up at the Milky Way looking like a thick-spun web of electricity. With an excessively expanded mind, he found the starry view more imposing than ever and worried he might see something he didn't want to. Recently his parents had ordered the premium cable package and he'd been watching creepy UFO specials on the high-numbered channels. While these shows scared the living shit out of him, he still watched them obsessively with the hope of learning how to avoid being abducted.

Betsy though came from the fire and not the sky. She looked to be out for a stroll, shuffling confidently toward him in her lug soled boots. She smiled flatly and laughed a smoker's laugh, congestion gurgling deep in her chest. "That your car?"

He nodded and patted the Toyota defensively.

"You know it ain't fit for these roads? It's fancy, like your pants. You buy those jeans new today?"

Jason was thrown and twice flipped the hair from his eyes before responding. "So what? I'm growing a lot."

"Yep, you're just a big puppy."

What the hell was her deal? Jason struggled to respond.

"It's okay babe. I like fancy stuff just fine."

She lit a smoke, took a draw and walked off into the piney woods beyond the Camry. Jason stayed put, unsure of what to do. She turned back, "These woods are full of scary things. Can't let a girl go in all by herself."

Indeed feeling like a puppy, he followed her. They stopped in a clearing with just enough starlight to see their breath in the cold air. Nothing about the moment was uncomfortable as Betsy seemed to have already made a decision concerning him. He got that giddy feeling, when both people know physical contact is imminent, and thought to kiss her but instead started talking in order to extend the feeling. "You're a showoff. Dancing like that around the fire."

Betsy smiled. "Wanna know a secret? I don't even need music."

She grabbed his waist and danced, pulling her hips into him. This was happening fast and it felt incredible. Close up, she smelled like beer and campfire smoke and not shampoo and lotion like Margo Mullen. She ran her fingers inside his shirt, sending out warm, shivery currents. He did the same to her and she hummed the song playing in her head. Her back felt strong and he felt her muscles flow across her spine like waves.

"How about kissing?" Jason looked down at her through his hair. The low roar of the mountains, the chirping crickets and the shitkicker bonfire all went silent. "You got secrets for kissing too? Probably show off when you kiss."

She brushed the hair from his eyes, let it fall back and did it again. She whispered, "Whenever you're ready."

Jason bent and kissed her. Her lips were soft and alive but her tongue led the way. It drifted from his mouth, worked on his ears, tasted his neck and then was back in his mouth. She tasted smoky-sweet, like a mild barbecue sauce, which he thought was awesome. In the two years since kissing Margo Mullen, he'd forgotten how gloriously soft and wet kissing was. His nerves short circuited with sensation and his knees wobbled. Her hands grabbed his butt and pulled him in tight. Impulsively, he squashed her butt cheeks between his fingers. They were like a pair of waterlogged baseballs: firm, lively, and a wee bit squishy. It felt ridiculous to be doing this and he couldn't believe it was happening. She had to be aware of his erection, burrowing out the front of his fancy pants like a groundhog. Betsy caught her breath and kneeled in the pine needles. "Ready to get down?"

Things were happening and he had no control. It was like a force had come for him. What did "get down" mean? He tried sitting down but the new Levi's didn't have much play and he toppled clumsily on top of her. He kissed her again and painfully crunched his new jeans against her. She rolled her eyes, pushed him onto his back and unzipped him. "I got a better idea."

Next thing he knew, his pants were around his knees and his legs were immobilized. Hog-tied with pine needles poking his ass, his cock soared up between the pines and felt the cool air. Whatever she planned to do, he was ready and adrenalized from being on the edge of something that promised to be delightful.

It was hard to establish where her soft hands stopped and he started. One moment he was harder than the granite countertop in his Stone Bluff kitchen and then he was a candle melting around its stick. It was as if her hands were inside of him and pulled him outwards. His buttocks involuntarily quaked and a low, white noise came into his ears. When he came it wasn't the grand passage he'd imagined but it was tight and jerky, like something pinched out through a kinked hose. The moment was so embarrassing that he was unable to relish it. He sat up and sorrowfully tried to wipe himself, but Betsy pulled his hand away and dabbed the mess with her fingers. "Uh oh, got some in your hair. Who's the showoff now?"

She poked him in the chest and gave him a gentle kiss, which was sort of the last thing he wanted and the only thing he wanted. The night's sounds had returned but everything sounded different. It was like his ears had cleared and were sensitive to every noise for miles around. He picked out an engine climbing the road, steady and high, which he knew was Isabel's car. Indeed, her headlights flashed the trees around them and he curled up to conceal his cock, perplexed how it seemed bigger than ever, especially after just having melted down. It had obviously gone nuclear, its molecules were whipped into a frenzy and nothing would ever stop it.

Grabbing his wrist, Betsy pulled him back to the party like something caught in the woods. She rudely considered Shelly, who'd changed into jeans and a purple sweater and had brushed out her hair. Jason had never seen her wearing anything but gym clothes and guiltily realized that effort had been made on his behalf. Aside from an initial hurt look, she ignored Jason. Isabel also seemed displeased with him, lighting a smoke and cooly blowing it toward Betsy.

Jason hated being the center of so much posturing. He'd felt in control while driving up here, looking forward to seeing Shelly away from school. This was so far from what he'd imagined that nothing about it seemed real. He'd set out with wolflike fervor and now he was a puppy on parade. Allen whistled and Krissy laughed at them. Ron made a heinous catcall.

With everyone being so muddle-faced and squinty-eyed, Shelly seemed to be the sharpest person around for miles. She looked hip and adult in that sweater, which looked like something from one of his mother's mail order catalogs. Ron swooped in like a vulture and offered her a cold Busch, which she gamely accepted.

What a cruel twist that all of their paths had collided this evening. It was as if the universe had strict rules about this type of thing and Jason figured that if Betsy hadn't shown up then neither would've Shelly. Shelly explained how Isabel had been afraid to drive through the big puddle at the forks. Isabel stepped out to pee and Shelly had commandeered the car and blasted through the puddle.

"Right on!" Ron sounded much too agreeable.

Isabel sounded tired, "Real funny. It almost swamped the engine."

"That's because your car ain't fit for these roads," Betsy said, not looking at her.

The trashy twang appeared on Isabel's face before she even spoke. "Hon, what's your problem? Why are you acting like a little bitch? Did I do something to you? Think I just got here and you're getting in my face."

Isabel had been a fearless child and Jason remembered her breaking horses in the pastures below Stone Bluff, speeding around with her hair fanned out and range dust trailing up a stormy cloud behind her. But these days her pastures were full of cattle and her only exercise was chain-smoking at the Trail King. Jason feared that Betsy would tear her to pieces.

Betsy sounded amused, "Just offering my advice."

Isabel seemed thrown and Jason sensed they might be on similar bandwidths.

In his deepest foghorn voice, Ron talked gymnastics with Shelly. It happened that she was going to Milwaukee that summer for a national meet. Ron knew all about the coliseum where Shelly's meet was and had seen the Spin Doctors there, "before they got all cheesy on the radio."

Shelly licked her lips. "This one's only me. Marjorie's got her olympic trials that weekend. I'm flying there all by myself." She nodded into the fire and seemed to be making her mind up about something.

Ron went on about all things Milwaukee, which was impressive since he was from Madison. He mentioned oddities and cool places to eat and Shelly was captivated, blinking her eyes too frequently and glowing in the firelight. Jason tried to act indifferently about all of this, considering he'd just been milked in the woods by another girl, but having Ron involved just plain sucked. Betsy eased the sting by sitting down on his lap with Busch Beers, black braid falling on his chest and reminding him that he'd won the jackpot, though one he had no idea how to spend.

Allen came over and teased them, "Look at *you* guys." He hand-slapped-fist-bumped Jason and passed a lit joint down to Betsy. She puffed and then held it to Jason's lips, who smoked even though he didn't need anymore. Betsy got up and danced again and he wondered where she came from. He imagined the wallpaper, furnishings and carpet in her home, wanted to know what she'd been soaking in.

Ben whisked Isabel away to his camper without either of them saying a word. Jason again feared for Isabel. Despite her always acting older than she was, it looked scary being hauled off like that—presumably to have sex in a camper. With a shiver, he wondered if Betsy would come and lead him off similarly.

Full of Busch Beer and hot dogs and sated by weed, the pipeliners staggered from the bonfire to their campers. Sean Patt struggled to get his shoes off and packed his lip with a giant bedtime chaw. Ross killed the music and offered to bunk with Bruce so that gloomy Joey could sleep in his camper. Joey hadn't spoken a word all night and looked freezing cold and pissed off, probably some *guy* hadn't shown up for her.

This left Allen, Krissy, Jason, Betsy, Shelly and Ron around the fire, couples it seemed. Ferdig snored in his chair and Doug was still curled up like a Lab in the dirt, staring at the flames as if trying to memorize them. Krissy snuggled into Allen's serape. Shelly told Ron that there were sleeping bags in Isabel's car, "Don't want anyone to freeze tonight." She walked soberly to the back seat of the Aries K and

Ron feigned a shiver at Jason on his way to join her.

Betsy pulled Jason away to her spacious Ford crew cab and they kissed lazily on the broad backseat. But she wasn't leading him anywhere, this was a goodnight kiss and he was relieved. Weird how he'd been on edge about possibly having sex, had thought it was like eating, that when you were hungry you just ate and you didn't think much of it. She laid her head on his lap, stretched out and went to sleep.

Within a moment his thoughts seemed to overtake him. Possibly he'd smoked too much weed and had too many Busch Beers. His heart thumped in his ears and he couldn't stop swallowing. The evening's strange course had been more eye-opening than he cared to think about right now. Betsy's hair formed a black mass upon his lap and he ran her long braid through his fingers. Its diamond pattern was like an illusion that grew smaller or larger depending on how he looked at it. Someone had likely helped her with it, time spent with her sister, mother, a friend, someone working patiently behind her to create what felt like a velvet bullwhip. Who was this creature? Did she have posters on her wall, trinkets on her dresser, a shoebox full of awesome tapes? It was weird to know so little about her and it seemed like the world had arranged this ripple in his fate.

Funny how some weed, a hand job, and too many beers had him thinking about god, or something like god anyways. His parents had never professed any religious beliefs to him. Leah had been raised Jewish out in Santa Monica but rarely acknowledged it anymore. He'd gone to Mormon church with Doug a few times, but couldn't recall anything from the sermons, just remembered coloring high top sneakers on Jesus's feet in a Sunday school classroom.

Outside the dark pines swayed below the fiery stars, a bad sign since there was no wind. On the edge of nausea, his spinning eyes found Allen's guitar. It was left outside in a chair and the dying embers twinkled red across the laminate surface. He slid from under Betsy, leaving one jackpot to claim another.

His playing sounded different tonight. What normally pleased his ears sounded simple and sloppy, something put together by a boy up in his room. His new persona didn't care for this sound, and obviously neither would the pipeliners, or the gods who doled out hand jobs.

This new persona was more demanding and it called for skills he didn't yet have. This was a massive and painful gain in perspective. Frustrated at knowing only simple chords, he began growling notes as formative, chanting lyrics and chopped at the strings. His fingertips blistered and his nails bled, his throat was raw and his eyes stung. He exhausted himself and then passed out, clutching the guitar in his arms.

At daylight he woke up freezing under a frosty blanket that someone had tossed over him. The fire was dead and no birds chirped; he imagined they were all frozen solid like his face and ears. Ron and Shelly emerged from Isabel's car, shivering and wrapped in sleeping bags. They crowded around Jason, taking in his frost-glazed head.

"That's so freaky," Shelly said of his frozen head. She sounded hoarse and frazzled, like maybe she'd also had an eye-opening.

Ron immediately wanted to go home. Jason looked for signs of Betsy in the big Ford. The sun hitting her truck was an eye-piercing laser that throbbed into his head. It was over, the night he would never forget was over and done. He kept popping his ears and the world still sounded amplified. But where had all the wax gone? He wanted to say goodbye to Betsy, but this thought hurt his head and he couldn't imagine pulling this off in any way at all.

Ron and Shelly piled into the Camry's backseat with Doug asleep in the front seat. Jason drove down the mountain road to the forks where the large puddle steamed in the morning's rays. It looked ominous, though not as ominous as what awaited at home for pushing his curfew so far. He charged forward and water fanned over the hood, but this far side was steeper and not conducive to skipping across. The Camry's tires mired deep in the soggiest part. Sadly, the path he'd followed last night didn't allow backtracking.

"Jesus Fucking Christ," Ron said. "What the fuck now?"

Jason shrugged. He was okay with not going home right away. He jumped over the water into the sagebrush and peed. The car was hopelessly stuck and would need to be pulled out. Ron scowled at him but Jason would roust Doug, who'd know what to do. Then there was engine noise coming down the mountain. Betsy drove her big red Ford with one hand and didn't even slow down, just veered around the puddle into the sagebrush, which crackled beneath her tires. Krissy sneered down at him while Joey clung scared from the handle in the crew seat. Betsy backed up to the puddle and climbed down, pulling on rawhide gloves. She looked every bit as alluring as last night, which lifted his spirits considerably.

Betsy flicked a smoke into the puddle and hopped up into the truck's bed. "Said that car ain't fit for these roads." From the toolbox she produced a dirty, yellow tow strap and sloshed out in her black boots to connect it to the Camry, and then to her hitch, doing all of this quickly and with little grunts.

Jason watched dumbfounded until she ordered him back behind the wheel, "you gotta steer it out."

He mucked his way back behind the wheel, felt the truck engage, steered for a moment and then he was free with the Camry caked but none the worse. Betsy hurried to disconnect their vehicles and shook the mud from her gloves. "Goddamned puppy poop."

Krissy climbed out and peed immodestly in the middle of the road, yelling at Betsy to get moving. They loaded up and Betsy put the truck in gear. She looked down at Jason and slipped her muddy boot from the brake so he had to walk alongside the truck. "Krissy has to wait tables today. If she's late she'll kick your ass and I don't want that." She winked at him, slammed shut the door and the big truck rumbled off down the road.

Leaving the pee-strewn forks behind, Jason shuttled his sleeping crew across the empty forest roads. The driving energized him and he played his favorite cheese tapes. They sounded different, as did the wind across the hood, the gravel chinking the wheel wells, and his heart thudding in his ears. The world was smellier too: road dust, pine, sage, and cow dung had never smelled so rich. If nothing else, the hand job had turned out to be a powerful, full-bodied decongestant. He witnessed the morning sky fade from pink to blue above the black forest and snowy peaks. A rising mist clouded the reservoir like steam from a hot bath and drifted across the road to Helen Springs.

Chapter 6

Jason's older brother Robert was coming home from Princeton for spring break and Leah Krabb prepped a large Sunday meal for his homecoming. She dashed around her kitchen, trailed by an unruly swath of blond-going-gray hair. On the menu were smoked salmon, beet salad, and herb-crusted potatoes. Grandpa Krabb was coming, which made the meal extra special since Curtis's father was a hard man to pin down. Mindy Smith, Robert's high school girlfriend, was home from nursing school in Salt Lake City and would attend as well. Leah was unsure of their status, but Robert had seemed pleased about this over the phone.

Moping around the kitchen while Leah cooked, Jason foraged through the healthy snacks and complained. "Why can't you buy me some hot dogs or potato chips?"

Failing to come home the night of the bonfire had cost him his driving privileges. He'd finally shown up late the next morning, zoned-out, smelling of cigarettes and beer and caked with muddy debris. He claimed that his curfew had been extended. She said, "Give me a break," and lamented her night of fretful waiting up, asking him if he really thought it was okay to stay out all night. What had he been doing all night? Camping, he said. Did you bring a sleeping bag or tent? No. Then where did you sleep? In a chair by the fire. He said he wanted to go to bed. Who were you with? Ron and Doug and some others. What others? Just some guys having a bonfire. She told him to shower first and then go to bed, couldn't stand her child looking like a zombie.

The meal's centerpiece was a fresh Sockeye salmon that Leah had mail-ordered from an Oregon specialty catalog. She'd also bought a bag of alder woodchips and a custom-made smoking pan for her oven.

Robert was a healthy eater and had complained how bad the food in New Jersey was, "Everything is fried Mom, and heaped with pickles." She worried her fruit from the Fred Meyer supermarket wasn't fresh enough for Robert, probably should've mail-ordered that, too. When Robert left for college, she'd ramped up her pediatric practice and cooked less but kept the kitchen stocked with enough fruit to feed a family of chimpanzees. She bought real bread and encouraged Jason to eat it with peanut butter and whole fruit jam. While Robert had taken her lectures on healthy eating seriously, Jason had little concern for nutrition. When she dared look inside of his Camry, it was full of junk food wrappers and empty soda cans.

Outside it was like winter again. The temperature was in the low forties and the budding shrubbery and trees around the Krabb house were lively in a chilly, northwest wind. This was typical for April. Last night it had snowed in town, a couple of inches of slurpee snow already melted, with much more falling on the peaks of the Black Elks. Today, viewed across town from her kitchen windows, their stark summits sparkled with the fresh accumulation drifting in the alpine bluster. Curtis had left at three in the morning to fetch Robert after a red-eye flight from Newark. Thankfully there were no high passes on the interstate from Salt Lake and she wouldn't worry too much. A day in the car with his non-combative son would hopefully be good for Curtis, who'd been a ball of stress lately.

Leah's kitchen had a professionally installed sound system with speakers recessed into the ceiling. She rarely used the CD or cassette players but had made the technician snake the antennae wire through the ceiling, out the roof, and several times around the chimney flashing until the reception for Idaho Public Radio was crystalline. Whenever he had the house to himself, Jason would hijack this stereo and blast rock music, and she'd always know because her hanging artwork had shifted in the vibrations.

A Prairie Home Companion was on Idaho Public Radio. Leah enjoyed Garrison Keillor's deep voice, liked how it was windy and full of nose. On these bitter days, the tales of strong-backed women cooking through blizzards and men besieged by snow and ice helped her to appreciate life as a transplant from L.A. to Idaho. She felt fluidly in step with America and spaced out into her own narrative with an

Idaho backdrop: *While the resolute Mormons attend church in the town spread out before her dual-paned, picture windows, Leah chops beets and seasons a wild Pacific salmon. Her day is similarly dedicated to family, a celebration of nutrition and reunion with loved ones. Her peaceful meditation is aided by Idaho Public Radio on the hifi and savory Arabica coffee beans brewing in a lavish Krups brewer that she'd guiltily had air mailed to her office. The machine gurgles out smells of nutty froth, filling her soul with warmth and glee.*

Having grown up in a big city full of beautiful people made Leah's daydreams all the more potent. She'd never imagined herself in a starring role, and as a girl she'd been bookish, pragmatic, far from the center of attention. Now she was a figurehead in this town and couldn't go anywhere without running into people who made a big deal of her. It helped that Leah was stunning and overloaded with charisma. She had pert cheeks, a button nose, and smooth tanned skin. That she obviously put little effort into her appearance, especially her abundant and gravity defying hair, made her seem all the more captivating to the people of Helen Springs. While it was thrilling to command so much respect, she felt increasingly self-conscious around town, and the respite of her kitchen—alone with her thoughts and gadgets—was particularly relaxing. The coffee maker chimed that the coffee was ready and she'd no sooner poured her first cup when the doorbell rang.

Jason answered the door and Mindy followed him into the kitchen, greeting Leah with a crescendoing "Hiiiii!" It was evident Mindy wanted to bounce over for a hug. Leah had never accepted physical affection from her son's girlfriend and quickly opened the fridge to divert herself. Mindy just laughed giddily and to no one in particular, as though she were being tickled by an invisible hand. Her teeth glistened white between giant red lips that, as usual, were coated in a healthy layer of fruit-scented balm.

"It's good to see you Mindy." Leah needlessly managed the contents of the crisper drawer. "How's your family?"

Mindy was the eldest child of a dutiful Mormon family, all of whom were "doing fantastic."

"I just couldn't sit around waiting for Robert. I thought you could use some help?"

"That's so kind, but everything's under control."

Mindy had long doted on Jason and started into a fresh appraisal. "Jason, Holy Cow! You've grown like a foot since I've seen you. And your hair's so long. Good thing I brought my scissors!"

Mindy loved giving haircuts. She'd grown up cutting her four younger brothers' hair and had cut Robert's and Jason's whenever she could. Leah thought this business of cutting hair was childish, odd that it hadn't gone away now that Mindy was in nursing school.

"How are your classes Mindy?"

"Oh my goodness! Chemistry is like sooo much harder than high school but I have more time to work on it. I had like no time in high school, just with like everything. Hmm, I smell coffee. Coffee places are like everywhere in Salt Lake now. That smells sooo good!"

Leah offered her some and Mindy seemed tickled. "Nooo," she chuckled, "but thank you sooo much!"

"Well you've got the right attitude about school." Leah turned to Jason. "Hard work will see you through anything."

Jason shrugged and looked bored. When did he get so smug? Since losing his car he'd done nothing but play guitar and fume at the world. She feared his grades had slipped beyond repair. At least she planned to have him finish algebra II at the I.L.C. with the more accommodating Mr. Chakrabarti, so she needn't worry about that grade. The I.L.C. stood for Individualized Learning Center and it was where the bad kids got a GED after being booted from regular high school. Jason had completed all of his previous math credits at the I.L.C., though he'd been there not because he was disruptive or had a learning disability, but because it was a savvy loophole for privileged kids who were bad at math.

Mindy again offered to help in the kitchen and Leah suggested watching TV downstairs.

"Jason knows how to work it. We have literally hundreds of channels."

"Maybe later, but right now someone's got a hair appointment."

Leah watches Jason disappear from the kitchen, knowing he will submit to careful trimmings from his older brother's most jubilant girlfriend. Leah dislikes this practice, possibly because she doesn't manage her own hair well—let alone her son's hair—and she tries not to fault

Mindy for it, knowing that it's her nature to do such things and it will make her a better nurse. Finally, her coffee is deliciously sublime on this day when winter has returned to Idaho, just as the scissors have returned to Jason's hair, which falls like snow onto the bathroom tile where Mindy sweeps it up in a sisterly fashion.

* * *

Sitting on the toilet lid, Jason warned Mindy about removing too much. "I want it long."

"I know. This will be perfect Jason. You're being sooo steady. Good posture is key for haircuts."

Jason smelled her breath on him while she trimmed. It was clean and fragrant, like she'd eaten flowers for lunch. She was strong, her hands felt powerful and smoothly in control.

"Robert told me that you lost your car staying out all night?" Mindy wasn't incriminating, just looked confused. "I told him he needs to check in with you. That's what brothers are for."

"I'm a real trouble maker these days Mindy." Jason smirked. "Even though I was only camping."

"You should try scouting. My brothers go camping with their troop like all summer. They have tooo much fun!"

Mindy's brown dress pressed against her legs and revealed the outline of her super-garment underwear, bringing on an instant boner. She wielded the scissors with a surgeon's precision and Jason imagined that her skilled, slightly chubby paws were well suited for hand jobs. Throughout his puberty, Jason had been afflicted by painful erections. Waking up with them was painful, and playing with his prick so far hadn't helped matters, only made it harder. He imagined that flaming acne like Shelly Stewart had was preferable to a case of chronic raging boners. He focused hard on the floor, trying to get it under control. This constant sexualizing was exhausting, like suffering from allergies and always fighting back a sneeze.

Having a stiffy certainly didn't make for good haircuts and he finally stifled it by acknowledging that Betsy had disappeared in the two weeks since the bonfire. He had no basic information on her, like even her last name. With each passing day his heartbreak worsened and his memory of her grew hazy with fantasy; he kept coming up with a slightly different looking person each time he tried to picture her. It was dreadful thinking that one awesome night was all he was going to get.

"I love working with your hair." Mindy fanned it with her sprightly fingers. "What do you think?"

It was still over his ears and eyes, but the bulk was gone from the back. She was clearly thrilled with her work and Jason agreed it looked good. It was proportionate, a tad more together and not as thatched-looking. This boosted his confidence. His hair was like kryptonite, all he had to do was get in front of Betsy and his hair would do the rest.

* * *

Leah cranked the volume for a swinging number on *A Prairie Home Companion*. She scrubbed Idaho Russets in the stainless steel sink, shoulders bobbing to the piano and wayward hair aflutter.

Mindy returned leading Jason like a show dog and Leah stopped. It had been awhile since she'd seen his face without hair obscuring it. Who was this strange young man with a woman's haircut? He didn't look anything like Curtis or Robert, whose faces were colorless and featureless in comparison. Jason's stern face was tanned and wide with a man's rigid jaw line and puffy red lips. Stubble sprouted from his chin and cheeks, growth she hadn't ever noticed. His blue eyes were curious, shifty, wanting of something. His movements seemed to be under direct strain from growing. This was her son and puberty was really dishing it out to him:

Leah remembers Robert skipping puberty altogether, like he went to bed one night a serious, sweet boy and woke up a serious, pleasant man, having bypassed whatever has blown up in Jason. She fears that her increased call schedule and the lack of nutritious home cooking has exacerbated Jason's hormonal state, recalling from medical school how complicated is the stew of pubescent chemicals. Maybe Curtis will talk with him, man to man, like adults, over a cup of coffee perhaps. Hopefully, her husband is better at handling their son's transformation than he is at tutoring him in algebra.

Chapter 7

The bronzed salmon was centerpieced on the polished elm table. Roasted with cider-soaked alderwood chips, its smoky scent permeated the house. The Krabb family commenced eating without a prayer and Mindy was clearly uncomfortable. Robert noticed this and briefly clasped hands with her. He took a small bite of fish and then set his fork down to chew. Robert's hair was silky like Jason's but darker and short enough that it never feathered. His lean face was accented with a boniness that looked unhealthy under most lighting. He wore stylish wire-framed oval eyeglasses, a sharp blue polo shirt and Eddie Bauer khakis. This preppy outfit was from Leah's attempt at a makeover before sending him off to Princeton. Formerly, he'd worn square-frame glasses and tucked Izod shirts into blue jeans.

Grandpa Krabb said the salmon reminded him of California and specifically addressed Robert. "Before the dams went in, the rivers ran so thick you'd get knocked over wading. Your great-grandfather hated eating fish, would curse while picking the bones from his teeth."

It was customary for Bill Krabb to yarn out stories to Jason and Robert specifically, as if his memories would be lost on his son. Stocky, lean of face, sincere and bespectacled with cropped brown hair, Curtis Krabb looked more like chief of police than scientific honcho. Curtis loved it when his father reminisced and added his own memories. "I remember you had me tear down Grandpa's smokehouse. I smelled like smoked fish for weeks."

Bill Krabb ignored him and turned to Jason, already on his second plate of food. "Jason, I saw the baseball team out practicing at your high school the other day. You playing any baseball?"

"Not since Little League. Probably forgot how to play Grandpa." Jason clearly appreciated the attention.

"That's a shame. Say, the football team could use a strong lad like you next fall. These Idaho boys seem small to me."

Leah spoke up, "We like Jason the way he is Bill. We don't want him concussed or with a broken neck. Besides, he hasn't had any interest in sports since the school district did away with the swim team."

Jason acted hurt. "If you guys cared about anything other than grades, I might be more into sports."

The longstanding family joke was how much Leah loved swimming and hated football, and Grandpa Krabb winked at Jason. At seventy-five years old, his hair was still streaked with brown as if old age hadn't won him over entirely. He had an alert, sun-wizened face and looked like he could leap from his chair and quickly clear away the dishes without undue strain.

Curtis shared his own football days. "I made varsity and you were concerned I wouldn't get my chores done."

Bill Krabb ignored him and turned back to Robert, "Tell me about college out east. Have you settled on a major yet?"

Curtis had asked the same question on the drive home and Robert had brushed him off with the skill of a weathered politician.

Caught off guard, Robert swallowed and glanced at Mindy who blushed at him. "My professors are all so amazing. Every subject could become a lifelong interest, but I'm especially fond of this modern religion course. It's a broad survey of Christianity, Judaism, and Islam. The professor is a rabbi who's also a poet. He's hilarious and academically top notch."

Curtis heard in Robert that whining intellectual tone used by Leah's sister Judy, an associate professor of something or another at some Podunk state school somewhere out west. He wiped with his napkin and looked down at his plate, frowning.

Bill Krabb said, "I didn't know rabbis could be professors. So he has two jobs?"

"Along with his rabbinic ordination, Rabbi Gross holds various degrees in religious pluralism," Robert stated matter-of-factly.

Curtis had received little direction from Bill Krabb on his own important adult decisions. The day after taking his physical to go to Vietnam, he'd driven from Berkeley out to his boyhood home in Livermore. When he said he was likely going to war, his father had casually responded, "Is that right?" It was perplexing that his father, a man who was clearly haunted by his own service in World War II, could be so apathetic regarding this news.

"My legal reasoning course is another favorite," Robert continued. "The basis of law is rooted in a complex mix of philosophies. Sort of how math is the basis for science." Robert looked at his father, who still frowned at his plate.

Grandpa Krabb nodded and leaned back his chair. "That's where the magic money is. These days, lawyers can make money appear from nothing."

"Hey now," Mindy said, "my dad's a lawyer."

Robert again clasped hands with Mindy. "Mindy's dad is suing the BLM on behalf of energy providers for withholding oil and gas reserves. I'm helping with the legal research in my free time. The federal government is inexplicably against opening up the empty wastelands of southern Idaho for energy production. It seems that the people in charge would rather keep on fighting overseas wars to secure our energy. If he's successful, it will bring revenue to Idaho and a jobs boom developing the fields."

Jason surprised everyone by jumping into the conversation. "Did you know they're building a pipeline through here to take gas from Wyoming to Portland and Seattle? It's gonna lower power costs out there."

Curtis was floored by the swing in conversation but kept his eyes downward. He was sick of hearing the woes of the oil and gas business, had spent a career shaking his head at them. A single reactor (the one he would build anyway) could safely power Idaho and most of Utah. But that was beside the problem as Curtis was already familiar with this lawsuit and had enacted a plan to make it go away, which was highly classified. Nobody at the dinner table was aware of his involvement nor ever would be. The empty desert of southern Idaho was full of problems and there was no way anyone was getting access to drill in an area that was best left alone. Even the new president was being kept in the dark and the task of deceiving the Commander In Chief rested squarely upon Curtis's shoulders—no doubt a test that would determine his future with the Department of Energy.

Robert grinned at his younger brother. "Have you been reading the news Jason?"

"No I'm just friends with some pipeliners. Did you know they make thirty bucks an hour? I'm thinking about doing it to make some money, before starting my band in Portland and Seattle."

Curtis shot a confused look at Leah, who seemed helpless with this new information. What the hell was going on with the world that both of his sons had a stake in this business he'd rather forget?

"That's dangerous work Jason." Bill Krabb seemed amused. "You want to work, I could use a hand this summer. I'm breaking ground on another unit."

Grandpa Krabb referred to his storage units, the first and only facility in Helen Springs and his sole enterprise since retiring to Idaho. Curtis had long puzzled over why his father, who'd had a lucrative career with the Energy Department's Lawrence Livermore Lab, had moved to southern Idaho to live alone and build storage units. Even with his top security clearances, Curtis hadn't been able to learn what his father had worked on for all those years as there was no record of him in any files.

"How's the storage business, Dad?" Curtis didn't hide the sarcasm in his voice.

"Well it's booming," Bill Krabb answered. "People have too much crap and they keep buying more!"

Leah served fat free angel food cake with sliced fruit and ice cream. Robert declined cake and ice cream and picked at the fruit. The peaches and pears were indeed on the mealy side, as was the cake. Jason ate four scoops of ice cream and then claimed the leftover cake nobody wanted.

Robert turned to Jason and frowned. "A wise woman once told me that poor diets sneak up on a body like termites eating a house. Things look fine for years while the inside falls apart."

Leah nodded her approval and Jason shrugged. "I'm not feeling bad about eating cake."

Curtis had no appetite for dessert. The conversation had him stressing, and now he was stressing about all the stressing he'd been doing these days. Was this how life was going to be for him? Was being a stressball the price of knowing things? He considered opening up to his sons about what he knew, but, classifications aside, this still wouldn't be an easy thing to do. If nothing else, his conundrum perhaps shed some light on why his own father hadn't discussed Vietnam with him.

Grandpa Krabb thanked Leah for dinner and said he needed to go check on Ted, the Vietnam vet who bunked in one of his empty storage units. He provided Ted with electricity, a sink, and a porta-john, and also spent time hanging out in Ted's unit, drinking instant coffee with him, talking about the weather, baseball, and the country's growing demand for storage. When the family teased him about this charity, he claimed that Ted was like an employee and was not just getting a handout. But Curtis was uncomfortable thinking about his father vicariously reincarnating his dead son Stevie with a homeless stranger and Curtis, for one, never joked about it.

Curtis followed his father out to his car. The driveway was fully exposed to the north breeze and he braced against it, wearing just a shirt. "Dad, you're welcome to hang around the house tonight. Probably can find you a baseball game on the TV to watch. Leah's been making popcorn lately in the dutch oven. It's really good."

But his father was already seated behind the wheel of his Crown Victoria LTD. It was the same model he'd been buying for years, upgrading it every couple years and always in maroon red. The only way Curtis would know that his father had traded in again was when Lincoln changed the model.

"I better check on Ted, these north winds go right through those walls. Hey listen, you got some great kids in there."

Curtis nodded, shoved his hands deep into the front pockets of his pants and put his head down. "I don't know about Jason. Leah and I are worried about him. He didn't come home the other night. Showed up the next morning hungover. He's got bad grades. I doubt he'll even go to college."

Bill stared at his lap. "Some kids are gonna buck the system. Trick is to let them buck, for better or for worse," he broke off as if he'd said too much.

Curtis was shocked, couldn't recall the last time his father had given him advice. He didn't know what to say and simply shivered as his father backed out of the driveway and was gone. Shutting himself into the warm house, Curtis wished he hadn't laid out his problems to his father. Despite being chummy with his grandsons, it seemed his father wanted to forget the past and retreat somewhere no one knew him. When Curtis accepted his first job at the nuclear lab, he'd called Bill in Idaho to inform him they'd be neighbors, which had elicited the same response, "Is that right?" Curtis moving to Idaho probably reminded his dad of everything he'd already lost in life, two brothers in World War Two, his son Stevie in Vietnam, his parents and finally his wife, taken by a stroke at fifty-five watching Johnny Carson on the couch. Curtis felt horribly naive now, following the footsteps of a man who kept covering them up.

Tearing up, Curtis struggled to compose himself. His worst fear was that someone, especially Leah, would learn how vulnerable he'd become. If word got out that he'd taken to blubbering around the house, well, he could kiss it all goodbye. The smell of fresh coffee steeled him. He thought he might have a cup and take another crack at tutoring Jason on some good old algebra, which would surely cure this bout of sappiness.

Chapter 8

The Krabbs had a large library, used as a home office. Lots of paperwork and dictation occurred here but not much leisure reading. It had high ceilings with built-in cherrywood shelving from floor to ceiling. There were plenty of scientific texts, natural history and photography books, and a meager collection of fiction. Most dominant on the shelves were Leah's out-of-print, giant volumes of CIBA Medical Illustrations. Regularly missing from the collection was "Volume 3: The Reproductive System," with its life-size vagina portraits and likely to be found in Jason's room by the weekly maid service.

The fiction was paperback novels by John Updike and Michael Crichton and some raggedy looking classics like *The Odyssey*, *The Inferno* and *The Canterbury Tales.* These were the creased remnants from required literature courses at Berkeley, where Leah and Curtis had been college sweethearts.

The room's large windows overlooked the front yard and the neighborhood, but Curtis had closed the drapes in order to minimize distractions. He and Jason sat on straight-backed chairs at a desk and worked on squaring binomials, which Jason didn't seem to be following. In the three weeks since his last attempt at tutoring, Curtis had been bombarded with complexities at the lab and now it looked doubtful he could make up for the lost ground.

"So if the binomial has a minus sign, then that sign appears only in the middle term of the trinomial. Therefore, doubling up the positive and negative signs, like this," Curtis slowly showed his work, "and you can state the rule like this."

He watched Jason, waited, and then wrote some more. Jason clenched his jaw and stared intently at the paper in front of him. Curtis thought he might actually be trying and hoped that he was.

"How about this one?" Curtis wrote something else and tried not to leer. "Is this a perfect square trinomial?"

Jason looked confused. "I thought we were squaring *bi*nomials?"

Curtis answered calmly that a perfect square trinomial *is* the square of a binomial.

"Wow! How could I forget that?" Jason pouted and dropped his pencil.

"Jason, the rule is the square of the first term, twice the product of the two terms and the square of the second term. Now these are stated in trinomial products, but that's the lesson. Come on, let's try it again. It works."

Jason boiled over, "I love that algebraic way of doing something just because it works. So boring. It's like flushing a turd down the toilet with no respect for the plumbing, it just disappears somewhere below and then you wash your hands."

Now Curtis dropped *his* pencil. What the hell was his son talking about? "Jason you're not impressing me. You think you're brilliantly working backwards or something, after some deeper logic?"

"What I want to know," Jason poked the textbook with his index finger, "is who came up with this stuff? If this thing's present then you can do this, but only if you haven't already done this without doing that. Sounds like a bunch of space alien mumbo jumbo."

Great, here come the aliens again. Where did he get this crap? It must be all those high numbered channels available on the new cable box. Curtis was tired of hearing about aliens, black ops, and top secret government programs. He'd been trained to say nothing about these types of things, which only fueled Jason's imagination. Curtis explained that the nuclear lab's focus was energy production and toxic waste cleanup, but security classifications required that specifics were never discussed, and Jason had been trying to use this against him lately, like it was open season for conspiracies.

Curtis sighed. "I've no idea what you're trying to achieve Jason. Everything's right there in the rules. Start using them and you'll see the proof is in the process. Seems to me you haven't been paying attention in class."

Jason looked wronged. "But Mr. Ebbett goes too fast. Mr.

Chakrabarti has more patience. When I get stuck like this, he just does…" he paused, "well it's like he shows me what to look for and then I can figure it out again."

Curtis sat back, shaking his head. He couldn't rightly blame the boy. It'd been his idea to yank Jason out of the I.L.C. for his junior year and get him back into a proper classroom, thinking he'd have the time and patience to work with him. But even when he'd found time, it seemed he lacked the ability to teach him. Meanwhile, Mr. Chakrabarti had the magic touch, had shown Jason what to look for—whatever the hell that meant. It sounded like spotty procedure to Curtis.

Leah had warned Curtis that Jason was too accustomed to the ways of the I.L.C. "It'd be a lot easier to keep him there," she'd told him. "We're ensured a passing grade and he gets the credit."

Still, this I.L.C. business had never sat well with Curtis, especially the monthly checks they wrote to Mr. Chakrabarti for private tutoring services. The man probably steered Jason's pencil across the exams.

Leah had no qualms about paying the teacher. "Mr. Chakrabarti is an institution in this town," she'd said. "The good news is most liberal arts programs only require one higher math credit for admission. And he won't have to do any math once he gets into college, foreign language is where it's at for electives anymore."

Curtis hated to think she'd already written Jason off to the humanities. He cringed thinking about his son being educated by someone like Leah's sister Judy, who was always going on about inconsequential matters.

Curtis saw Jason's biggest problem as being lazy, likely because many things came easy for him—like music. He remembered giving Jason a guitar for his fifteenth birthday and it seemed that overnight he'd figured out the thing, sounding good even to Curtis. But sounding good didn't cut it in the real world. Math never came easy for anyone. Curtis knew that even people with a mind for it just saw harder and more complex problems the more they figured out. This didn't seem the case with musicians, they just knew what sounded good and didn't care how they knew this.

"At this point," Curtis openly sneered at Jason, "it's probably best you went back to Mr. Chakrabarti. Might as well keep funding his retirement."

Jason said okay.

Curtis raised his voice, "And I'll tell you something else. Being a smartass won't get you anywhere in life. Talking about aliens and other garbage. What do you know about anything that's real? Want to talk about flushing the toilet? If the world were left up to people like you there'd be shit all over the place."

His main objectives in working with Jason today were to keep his cool and concede nothing. But here the kid was waltzing back to his beloved tutor and Curtis was ranting about turds.

"Chill out Dad." Jason triumphantly closed his algebra book. "You're acting like I'm dropping out of school." He rolled his eyes as if worrying was silly.

Curtis shook his head. How could the boy be so careless with his future? Curtis had always worried enough to stay far ahead of the pack. He'd grown up working hard and had thus made every important cut in life, especially that last minute cut in 1965, a token internship with the Energy Department to keep capable minds out of Vietnam and working toward Ph.Ds.

Jason seemed desperate to escape the library. "Look Dad, I don't understand this stuff. Even when Mr. Chakrabarti shows me how to do it. It just seems pointless."

Pointless? Curtis didn't say anything, afraid he might just lose it. He hated not being in control of his emotions. A few weeks ago up in their bedroom, Leah had jokingly diagnosed him as depressive after reading new medical literature that called for family care physicians to start looking for depression and anxiety disorders. She rattled off some symptoms, "fatigue and loss of interest in sex," and nudged him with her cold toes under the sheets. Fearing she was onto something, he defensively rolled over and screwed her just to prove her wrong.

Jason lingered by the desk. "Are you serious about me going back to the I.L.C.?"

"It's your future. Go ahead and play your guitar."

"That's not fair," Jason whined. "Playing guitar is hard work. Why are you so against me playing guitar?"

Curtis looked away. Growing up in California, his younger brother Stevie had always skipped out on things to play guitar. Stevie had dropped out of Chico State as a freshman and started a band called

Motherlode. In May of 1968, Curtis went to their first and only gig in Berkeley, had filtered into a smoky hall with the longhairs and watched a shirtless, eighteen-year-old Stevie play electric guitar up on a plywood stage. Stevie sounded good and looked at ease in front of all those dopers and hooligans.

"I'm not against it." Curtis was barely in control. "I'm against you putting so much faith in it."

Curtis had long struggled to recall his last memories of Stevie but now they came in flashes so real it was unsettling. His memory jumped back so hard he actually smelled the drug smoke and body odor at that concert.

"Mom says Uncle Stevie played guitar, was good at it too."

Curtis grew short of breath and straightened against the chair. It was like living it over again. When Stevie had been called up for Vietnam, Curtis was sure he wouldn't go, was convinced he'd go north, south or AWOL. But Stevie showed up at Curtis's apartment in June, drunk and stoned with hair down to his shoulders and said, "They could probably use a guitar man over there."

Curtis remembered the glint in his brother's eye and heard the syrup in his voice, nearly forgotten details that seemed important after twenty-five years gone by.

"I'm sorry he died in Vietnam." Jason backed out of the library. "But that doesn't have anything to do with me."

* * *

Downstairs in the TV room, the kids watched "America's Funniest Home Videos," on which a string of hapless dads were repeatedly tagged in the nuts by all sorts of things. Mindy whooped and gushed over the babies and toddlers who said cutesy things, sounding wise beyond their years. Leah delivered bowls of dutch oven popcorn that she'd prepared with Robert's low sodium tolerance in mind. It wasn't nearly salty enough for Jason, but he stuffed his face with it anyway.

Robert was engrossed with the show and nibbled a lone kernel for a whole minute before swallowing. During a commercial, Jason switched stations to a paranormal show on a high channel about haunted burial grounds.

"This is garbage TV," Robert protested. "Please go back, I want to see the results of the video show."

The show seemed genuine to Jason. "People don't go on national TV and make this stuff up. I know you've always been scared of ghosts."

A haggard-looking mother bitterly recalled ghostly apparitions of young Indian braves hell-bent on massacre appearing over her sleeping children. Mindy stopped chewing and froze. Jason thought it was the first time he'd seen her without a fairy tale smile.

"How would you even know if your house is on a burial site?" Mindy was concerned. "Can you like check with the city or something?"

"That's enough Jason." Robert was annoyed. "You're upsetting Mindy."

Jason turned to Mindy, "Do you believe in ghosts?"

"Totally." Mindy wedged herself close to Robert. Jason noticed her face was tinged with color, like she'd been exercising, and again realized how sexy she was. Robert seemed put out by the affection; having a girlfriend to snuggle with wouldn't trouble Jason in the least.

On the way back down the channels, Jason found the steamy George Michael music video "Freedom" playing on VH1, the one where supermodels lip-synced the words and fondled themselves in a shadowy mansion. He stalled at the sight of flesh and listened to Mindy sing along.

Jason appraised her sideways through his bangs. She was barefoot and scrunched her long toes into the plush carpet. They looked powerful and smooth, like her hands had felt cutting his hair. Her dress was partly caught beneath her legs on the couch, revealing the dangling arc of cream-colored, firm legs. She knew all the lyrics and sang them well.

Watching a nice girl like Mindy sing along to George Michael was enchanting and she nearly glowed with hotness. Robert stopped snacking and placed his hands carefully atop his knees. A supermodel grimaced with pleasure in the video. Robert stared red-faced at Jason, obviously wanting the channel changed, but too embarrassed to say anything with Mindy clutching his arm, grooving to the song. Jason loved irking Robert and so did Mindy, who sang softly in Robert's ear. Jason thought maybe she knew things, like Ron and Betsy knew things. Maybe Joseph Smith had received the blueprint for sex from God himself, a sort of Mormon Kama Sutra, and passed it down through the generations. This better explained to Jason how Mormons saved themselves for marriage. They'd been told that sex was like plugging into heaven and, well, the church had to back it up with something.

Leah believed that Robert was going to convert soon, and Jason agreed. Back in high school Robert had joined the predominantly Mormon Boy Scouts and acted like he'd won heavenly approval. He wowed his troop with a mastery of complex projects, like a homemade weather barometer and scrambling Leah's pager to open garage doors. He was also strangely fascinated by Velcro and had stitched military grade Velcro patches onto his clothing in lieu of buttons and zippers, claiming it was far superior. Jason remembered the grating ripping sounds coming from Robert's room whenever he undressed. Robert already seemed more like a Mormon than any Mormon Jason knew and it was likely that he'd long been in recruitment talks with Mindy's parish. It was only a matter of time before Mindy's father gladly passed down the family's copy of the Mormon Kama Sutra.

Jason stood and tossed the clicker at Robert, who made no effort to catch it. He went upstairs to his room, locked his door, and grabbed his guitar. He strummed some chords but was soon bored, plagued by self-doubt, and thought his playing sounded dumb. Ever since playing Allen's guitar up at the bonfire, a little voice inside his head kept telling him he wasn't up to snuff. He wanted it to shut up, being a guitarist meant everything to him, and he couldn't stand sucking at it. Grabbing his Led Zeppelin guitar manual, he flipped the pages, trying only the craziest looking chords, and the ones he'd always avoided. The F6 made his fingers ache, and the Csus2 by itself wasn't too hard—that is until he tried switching to it from another chord. The harder he tried nailing difficult chords, the more tired and useless his hands became, and the less flow he had.

Strangely, he pictured Shelly Stewart flying across the mats, a whir of flips and skips under stark gymnasium lights. He figured she must be good and wondered if her coming from a family of gymnasts had made learning to tumble easier for her than it was for him learning these masochistic chords. Gymnastics was her thing, and because of it she seemed content coasting through school in the back row, getting by. Guitar was his thing, but it seemed he was just coasting through school in the back row for the sake of coasting. When his left hand started working again, he went back and forth between the Csus2 and F6 until his fingers were too cramped to continue.

Feeling better for having tried, he removed his jeans, plopped down on his bed, and found that his right hand still worked fine—twirling his prick in his fingers felt awfully nice, especially with all those glistening supermodels fresh on his mind. While his previous attempts at masturbation had left him sore and frustrated, it seemed that Betsy had opened a door. Twirling turned to gripping and that became stroking, and the supermodels had Mindy hands and then Betsy hands and they were steady upon him. His ears and nose unclogged just as he dribbled across his belly. The release wasn't anything like with Betsy, but was deeply pleasing and full of promise.

Chapter 9

Health II met after lunch in a windowless classroom. In lieu of a teacher's desk was a broad black counter equipped with a deep washbasin. The class had already covered brushing, flossing, nail-clipping and, of course, CPR. Now they were poised to dive into the darkest depths of human physiology, Coach Billy Sags having saved sex ed for the semester's end. The overhead projector displayed diagrams of male and female reproductive anatomies and, for a change, the class waited attentively for Coach to get started.

Coach sat ramrod straight behind the counter, looking bored and staring down. With a strong background in physical and driver's education, Coach Sags was as qualified as any to teach sex ed. Tall, thick-chested with sandy hair and muscular legs, he was a man who never joked and who tucked golf shirts into polyester athletic shorts. Jason had seen him around town running errands and he habitually dressed as if sports might occur at any moment. Ron had spoonerized Coach's first and last names into the now obvious Silly Bags, which the boys used endearingly. Having been teacher's pet in Coach's famously rigorous driver's ed course, Jason liked him the most of any teacher at North Helen. The man put on no airs and seemed to practice what he preached: pushups every morning after a wholesome, grainy breakfast, then brushed his teeth and drove to school with his hands at ten and two.

Jason and Ron exchanged looks regarding the diagramed penis on display. It was unusually oblong, fat, and labeled only as "Glans."

The boys were in the back corner behind Becca Black and Valerie Smith, who'd gladly shunned the front row for lowly health II. Valerie and Becca were popular and perpetually honor-rolled—the benchmark of attractiveness and personality for the junior class and fantasy fixtures in the minds of every boy. Earlier in the semester, Jason had partnered with Valerie to perform CPR on Resusci Anne dolls. She had curly blond hair, a snaky body and a gentle face with wide, hazel eyes that didn't seem entirely focused. Getting to know her was easier than he'd imagined for a top-tier hottie.

Valerie whispered to Becca, "This is weird. Nobody uses these words."

Becca slouched deeper into her seat and hugged herself. She looked cold to Jason, wearing a skimpy white blouse, a black denim miniskirt and lace-up sandals. Her glistening legs and feet were unseasonably tan and smooth.

Jason tipped his desk toward the girls. "What's up with that glans?"

Becca unexpectedly laughed out loud and Coach glared at their corner. Once the heat was off, she turned and flashed Jason a flirty, daring look. While he and Valerie had a history flirting, Becca had mostly been impartial toward him—it must be the new haircut.

"That glans looks like a potato," Ron whispered.

"That's because it's an Idaho glans." Jason made sure both girls heard him. "Famous taters dude."

The dam cracked and the girls erupted into the kind of contagious, strained laughter that only happens under strict supervision.

Silly Bags stood, clapped his hands as a warning and seemed thrown. It was unusual for top tier girls like Valerie and Becca to cause trouble.

"Quiz time!" Coach switched off the whirring overhead and passed out papers with unmarked diagrams. "Label the parts and put them in my basket."

This quiz was delightfully easy for Jason, having long ago memorized these terms while poring over his mother's CIBA medical illustrations. In a nice flourish, he wrote "Glans" directly inside of the chubby cock, seeing as there was plenty of room for this. He finished first but waited until Valerie got up and then followed her up to the counter, staying close behind her so she had to playfully push him away on her way back to the desks. From behind his hair, he leered at her spiky breasts, which popped like traffic cones from her blouse and seemed to strain the fabric.

With the quiz over, Coach placed a condom diagram on the projector and then sat down without saying anything.

"Okay this is getting weirder," Valerie whispered critically to Becca.

Coach bent down and rummaged under the projector. Positioned beside the projector, Jason reached out into the projector's stream and shadow-stroked the condom with his forefinger, which elicited laughs from the whole class. Silly Bags was mortified by the ruckus and rose up to his full height. Jason coolly watched him pace the classroom, red-faced and looking for culprits. The trick was to look a tad concerned, but not too much, and Coach was none the wiser.

White sneakers squeaking and keys tinkling, Coach was agitated beyond anything the class had ever seen. He raised his blocky hands as if stopping traffic, a wry look spreading across his face. "I got news for you knuckleheads. There's nothing funny about sex."

Hoisting his shorts beyond what looked comfortable, Silly Bags squared up to the front row. "Now I'm going to talk about condoms, and since you're clearly lacking in maturity, the only thing I'm gonna say about condoms is that they block semen. None of you knuckleheads are ready to be parents so just steer clear of semen. Okay?"

Half the class stifled laughter and the other half looked queasy. Jason was reminded of driver's ed; "steer clear of semen" was akin to Coach's favorite safe driving mantra, "steer clear of distractions," and indeed it seemed like some solid advice.

* * *

Springtime was in full force in the hallways of North Helen High School. Jason and Ron darted between denim-skirted girls in colorful tops and T-shirted boys in many-pocketed cargo shorts. The doors and windows were open and Jason was overloaded with high school smells: greening athletic fields and flagpole flowers mixed with soggy fries, hairspray, and bubble gum. His newly improved sense of smell wasn't something he expected to fully understand but it was clearly related to his recent hand jobs.

Banners and printed fliers were stuck throughout the building announcing Saturday's Spring Social. The theme of this year's dance was "Ropin' the Wind," a tribute to the chart-topping Garth Brooks album, and Printshop graphics depicted lariats, cowboy hats, and bull riders. It was only for juniors and seniors and the student council had hired a DJ to spin music in a carpet-walled ballroom downtown at the Black Elk Hotel.

Ron mocked the social to Jason, "Juniors and seniors only, but exceptions made for cute sheep!" He laughed low and bleated softly.

Jason knew that the Spring Social wasn't about having serious country swagger. It was the pet project of girls like Valerie and Becca—student council stalwarts—who loved themes and a chance to wear costumes they wouldn't dare otherwise. There would certainly be some authentic cowpokes in attendance, snap-buttoned and swinging around on shiny boots, but they'd be outnumbered.

Ron continued bleating but shut up as they passed a crew of rich farm boys. Amused by Ron's skittishness, Jason was thankful that an ass kicking seemed unlikely for himself. Walking the halls, there were few heads at his own level. He sized himself up against the larger farm kids, not with a mind to fight them, but just to see where he stood as a specimen. He was taller, in better shape, had veins poking through his arm muscles and a flat stomach that was boner-hard. He felt like a nimble panther amongst a herd of paunchy, slow-moving cattle. These guys did chores and hit the weight room religiously while his only fitness was playing guitar and, lately, masturbating. Just another mystery of the world to be grateful for. If only he had a girlfriend, someone to watch VH1 and cuddle with, then the world would be totally in his favor.

As if on cue, Betsy's abandonment of him settled over him like a black mist. That is until Valerie strolled past, trailing flowery scents and hugging a load of textbooks with velvety arms. She smiled at Jason like she anticipated another joke and he was directly lifted from his gloom.

Ron claimed Valerie was a waste of time for Jason, because she was Mormon and because she was too hot. He shook his head. "Best case scenario with her is a dry hump. Dry humping is like skateboarding on the lawn. You don't get anywhere."

Jason was still keen for worldly advice from Ron. "But it still works?"

"Forget her man. You heard from Betsy? That guy Allen had some primo ganja."

Jason sadly shook his head. "When I was a freshman Allen scared the shit out of me. He used to terrorize this place."

It was hard to reconcile, but Jason remembered that Allen had been expelled from these hallways for throwing a kid headfirst into a cinderblock wall, and for no good reason. The Allen from the bonfire seemed anything but a thug. Perhaps it was Krissy or maybe the hard labor on the pipelines that had broken him. Whatever had happened, Allen was currently the coolest guy on the planet and Jason agreed they should find him.

Shelly Stewart was at her locker, looking incredible in pink lycra shorts and high tops.

"Hey there." Ron's voice went much higher than normal.

Jason had no idea what had happened between these two the night of the bonfire. Ron was being uncharacteristically tight-lipped where that was concerned. Jason noticed her chronic raging acne had eased up—maybe Ron did something to her like Betsy had done to him, something that had cleared her complexion like his nose and ears had cleared.

"Can I get a ride home?" Shelly asked Ron. "Isabel's been in a bad mood. I can't stand riding with her anymore."

"Absolutely!" Ron grew a dorky smile.

"Wow! Cool." Shelly sounded excited and Jason was jealous. Ron was also his ride home and now he couldn't even look forward to the day's end.

* * *

The day's last period was American literature with Mr. Ebbett, who'd opened the windows overlooking the sun-blazed student parking lot. The vast array of pickups and sedans intensely refracted the sun's rays, blinding anyone who dared staring directly. Jason sat in his usual back row seat and interrogated Isabel about the pipeliners. He sensed that she was trying to exclude him from something.

Her hair was loosely crimped into a ponytail and hadn't been dyed for weeks. She'd been putting little effort into her appearance and today wore jeans and a horsey shirt that beckoned to her country girl past.

"Ben's getting sick of his crew." Isabel had a know-it-all tone and nodded to herself.

"Allen's gonna be around though?"

Isabel seemed to know where he was going and raised her voice, "I can't help you find that trashy girl."

From the front row, Becca Black turned and shot Jason a disapproving look.

Mr. Ebbett wore an untucked western shirt, khakis and old loafers with fuzzy white socks. Sets of equations remained on the chalkboard from Mr. Ebbett's algebra II class and Jason shuddered at the sight of them, thankful to be back on easy street with Mr. Chakrabarti.

The class had been reading *The Great Gatsby* and Mr. Ebbett brought up war. "I'd like to point out that, again, we have some flawed main characters. Having witnessed the brutality of the Great War is no excuse for Nick and Gatsby's behavior. No way Jose. The real world doesn't give hall passes for suffering."

Mr. Ebbett so constantly referenced Vietnam that everything they'd read, no matter the historical period, was contextually framed by war, and especially Vietnam. The only other person Jason really knew who'd been to war was his Grandpa Krabb, who at seventeen had flown in bombers over Germany, but he'd never talked about it.

Mr. Ebbett paced angrily around his cluttered desk. "Now their flighty antics make for a good tale, but thankfully they were the exception. Instead of causing a full-time ruckus, our country's veterans have done wonderful, inspiring things for this nation and the world. Just think of all we've accomplished since World War Two." He paused as if overwhelmed. "It's mind-boggling! And by God, *that* progress had nothing to do with minty liquors and lusty dance floors."

Isabel shook her head in disagreement and interrupted. "Nick and Gatsby are suffering from more than war. They're on the cusp of America's great malaise, ushering in a new century of crimes." She went on describing the evils of the industrial revolution, using the word "malaise" no less than ten times. Mr. Ebbett grudgingly listened and seemed poised to cut her off. Jason liked how her snotty tone and big words irked Mr. Ebbett. His Aunt Judy used words like "malaise," which similarly annoyed his father.

"Whatever caused their *malaise,*" Mr. Ebbett spoke sharply, "is no excuse to languish. Fortunately, others picked up the slack and we now have cable TV, microwave popcorn, and ATVs."

The front row crowd approved of this and laughed politely. Mr. Ebbett sat victoriously upon his desk, loafers dangling, gazing at the class with renewed authority. He picked up his paperback copy of *Gatsby* and tapped it rudely with long fingers. “I keep asking you to consider how the American dream plays into our literature. The American dream is hard work. It’s how you fight a war and how you fight its miserable aftermath—you do it one day at a time and it only gets harder the more you learn and the harder you work.”

Now Mr. Ebbett shook the novel, tearing the cover and scaring the class. “Look what happens to our flawed characters, they dissolve like ice cubes in a Mint Julep on a hot summer night.”

Short of breath and chest heaving, Mr. Ebbett pointed in Jason’s direction with a zombie translucence. “Now Mr. Krabb will pick up the slack. He sure looks like *he* has something to say about all this.”

Jason hadn’t read the book, but being singled out in English class was way easier than in algebra. “The people in this book,” he blurted, “they had no unifying aesthetic.” Aesthetic seemed like a word he could use without knowing its exact meaning. It made him sound intelligent, especially if he whined a tad when saying it.

“Nothing happens in this book,” Jason continued, “they were distracted and everything else that you just said.”

“I’m not following you Krabb. Please fill us in on your idea of a unifying *aesthetic*.” Ebbett spat out the word “aesthetic,” showing a clear distaste for it.

The entire room watched Jason and he loved it, continuing with, “Well, you know like with Vietnam? It seems that war led to expanding consciousness and peace and hippy stuff. You appreciate microwave popcorn and four wheelers but I’m glad for sex and drugs and rock and roll.”

The class laughed. Mr. Ebbett hopped to his feet, snapping his fingers. “Your idea of a unifying *aesthetic* of the sixties has been popularized in movies and on TV. I assure you, Mr. Krabb, it wasn’t so lovely. It was rife with conflict and class struggle. The hippies I crossed paths with were wealthy children from families that were immune to military service. For most of us, the only choice was to go fight a war or break the law. I went to work at the beef plant upon returning from Vietnam in order to pay for college at South Idaho State, and I was up to my neck in student debt and cow guts.”

Jason had heard this story before. His father described the sixties as a time of hard work and focus and it was the most boring thing he'd ever heard. He countered, "But look at how Woodstock brought all those people together. They were just dancing and singing together, all in the pouring rain."

"How so?"

"I don't know." Jason felt his edge slipping. Becca stared back at him as if what he said next would somehow forever affect her opinion of him. Even the egg-colored cinder block walls seemed to await Jason's response. "Um, it's just like, cool music doesn't start wars, but you know the world's gonna fight over microwave popcorn and four wheelers."

Mr. Ebbett's eyes suddenly cleared, as if after all these years one of his war tangents had finally delivered something. "I'll remind the class that drugs and sex are dangerous distractions to a well-functioning society. And I've seen those fleshy bottoms on your MTV. It seems to me that sex is the unifying *aesthetic* of your generation's music, but maybe I'm just old-fashioned. It's been said the context evolves but the song remains the same."

Did Mr. Ebbett even realize the mega Zeppelin reference he'd just dropped? Jason thought he was being toyed with. Just when it seemed he had these adults figured out they confused him by knowing things.

Mr. Ebbett summoned Jason to his desk after class. Close-up views of teachers always made him uncomfortable. Mr. Ebbett had a ruddy, crooked nose with veins branching out into sallow, sagging cheeks. The math teacher unscrewed a battered thermos and poured something resembling tea or weak coffee into a chipped mug imprinted with a bull elk bugling into a frosty Rocky Mountain morning.

Jason avoided eye contact while Mr. Ebbett lectured him about leaving his algebra II class. "I warned your parents during conferences about the dangers of Mr. Chakrabarti teaching you math down at the I.L.C. Your father especially should know better. Spoon fed math won't prepare you for out there."

Mr. Ebbett jerked a thumb out the smudged windows behind him to the parking lot.

Jason enviously watched his classmates stepping among the vehicles and making their getaway into the sunny day.

"Out there, nobody holds your hand."

Mr. Ebbett stared at him until Jason was compelled to speak.

"I don't like being dragged up to the chalkboard, in front of the whole class." Jason kept staring out the window, wanting to escape.

"People learn best under fire."

Jason dropped his head, realizing he was in for another mawkish war metaphor.

"Marching through the jungle, my mind grasped things with unparalleled thoroughness. Imagine catching hornets with your bare hands." Mr. Ebbett spread his chalky hands and abruptly clapped at Jason, trying to rattle him. "That's how I learned about war. And let me tell you, the buzzing and stinging made my brain swell with knowing things."

Mr. Ebbett creaked back into his chair, rubbing his milky eyes. "You'll never get to knowing anything if someone's always holding your hand." He shook his head and jabbed his thumbs back at the chalkboard. "As long as you're in one of my classes, Mr. Krabb, I'll be gunning for you."

He offered a chalky palm for Jason to shake, offering a fresh start or perhaps an apology. Jason didn't care, had thoroughly tuned him out. He shook his former math teacher's surprisingly hard hand and left.

Chapter 10

Ron's car had already left student parking when Jason arrived. He needed his wheels back, but unfortunately, other than acing that day's sex anatomy quiz, his grades were horrible, and good grades were the only way to leverage his mom.

He hit the vending machines at the gym and wandered the halls eating a bag of chili-dog corn chips. The student council types were still about, taping up banners for the Spring Social. Valerie squatted daintily over a pair of Printshop cowpokes. She smiled at him with glitter stuck on her face and her hair in golden curls.

"It's going to be sooo much fun! Tell me you're going!" She handed him the poster and applied tape to the corners, licking her lips in concentration.

Jason flipped his hair. "I asked Resusci Anne to be my date, but she hasn't gotten back to me yet."

"You probably took her breath away!" Valerie laughed; Resusci Anne jokes were a staple of their flirting.

Jason hung the poster for her above a drinking fountain. He didn't want his helping to seem like an expression of class spirit, so he explained that Ron had ditched him. She offered him a ride home.

Becca Black interrupted them at the double block of doors to student parking. "Where are you going with *him*?"

Valerie jerked up a glittery hand. "I'm giving him a ride home."

Jason hid behind his hair, which seemed like the safest place to be.

Becca smiled, "I'm going that way. I'll take him home."

Valerie turned to Jason. "Your decision." She said this without any bias, as if he should give Becca fair consideration.

"Your mom took your car away Jason?" Becca's eyes lasered right through his hair armor. "I heard something about a wild night in the woods. What happened? Who were you with?"

Being squeezed between the pinnacles of the top tier required a cool answer. "You ask more questions than my mom. I was camping with some pipeliners."

"Were you drinking beer?" As she asked, Becca watched Valerie. She was trying to paint him a sinner!

"Yeah."

Now Valerie knew he was all mobbed up.

"Sounds cool," Becca said. "I'd love to go to a real party sometime. It's been so boring this year. We're the next senior class and we're so lame. Enjoy the minivan ride." She huffed away, the soles of her feet flapping against her designer sandals.

Valerie's Chrysler minivan was full of lotion, wet wipes, and booster seats. "Check out this mix tape, it's so flipping good!" She jammed down the rewind button and nearly peeled out of student parking. Her traffic-cone breasts popped out so sharply Jason feared they might snag the steering wheel.

They rolled through town listening to Boyz II Men and Mr. Mister while Valerie gushed on about how cute all of her younger siblings were. George Michael's "Faith" played during the long grade up to Stone Bluff. Valerie knew all the words and sang along in perfect pitch a full octave above the recording.

Like antennae picking up a signal, Jason's neck hair raised. What was up with George Michael hogging all the bandwidth lately?

"George Michael is sooo my favorite," Valerie gasped. "He's like a total hottie."

Jason thought Valerie was a total hottie: big tits, smooth skin, and a top 40 voice. She was like a VH1 value meal. Knowing which house was his, she parked in the driveway and mocked Becca. " 'So how was the minivan ride?' Becca's my friend, but she's a bully. It's because she's spoiled."

"I got asshole friends too. Ron left me stranded in student parking."

Valerie frowned at the mention of Ron. "I know you're like best friends with him, but he seems creepy."

Jason had never thought of Ron as creepy. "I suppose he's no worse than Becca. Ron's cool, there's just a fine line between creepy and cool."

From the way Valerie watched him, it seemed he'd misspoken. In an attempt to break the heaviness, he pulled a wet wipe from the center console and carefully wiped her lips with it, as if prepping a Recusci Anne doll for mock CPR. She was dazed and her eyes were as lifeless and doll like as he'd ever seen them. He kissed her softly and felt bad for having chili-dog corn chip breath. He pulled away and neither of them spoke, a strange situation to be in after a semester of joking and flirting. Stepping from the minivan was like jumping into another dimension.

Valerie turned it into another joke. "I guess you'll pick me up on Saturday for the Spring Social then?"

Jason shook his head. "And break Recusci Anne's heart?"

* * *

Jason suffered through another healthy dinner and passed the evening on his bean bag, idly strumming his Catalina and feeling good for the first time since the bonfire. The sad truth of his situation was that replacing Betsy was obviously the best way of getting over her. Being courted by the top tier was eye-opening and Valerie certainly seemed a sunnier path than the one he'd been on. Therefore he decided to proceed cautiously, lest he get caught up in her top tier, teen spirit, start cutting his hair and wearing khakis.

The teen line rang in his room, someone dialing him direct.

"What are you doing?" It was a girl's voice.

He'd been pranked by mystery crushes before and liked to confuse them by pretending to know who it was. "Nothing. What's going on with you?"

"We're gonna have a keg in the garage."

"Um, that's cool." What the hell?

The voice laughed and he heard a familiar wheezing. "Betsy?" He nearly levitated from his bean bag. "How'd you get my number?"

"Ain't many Krabbs in town, especially with fancy teen lines."

Jason didn't recall mentioning his last name to her, or sharing anything in particular about himself, for that matter. These details hadn't come up between them and here she'd called him up out of nowhere without identifying herself, acting as if they talked every day.

Holy shit, she was still into him.

"The party's at your house? Where do you live?" Jason wished his car wasn't off limits.

"Don't worry about it. I'll pick you up on Saturday. We'll get started early."

"Sweet." Jason suddenly remembered his manners, "Should I bring anything?"

Betsy laughed sexily and the phlegm sounded devious in her throat. "You can sort that out yourself, babe. See you on Saturday." She smooched into the phone and hung up on him.

Had she meant to bring condoms? Of course she did, the way she'd laughed and called him babe. She wanted him prepared. His stomach churned and his face grew hot.

As great as this news was, the timing sucked and there was much uncertainty in it. The party would probably be crawling with South Helen guys who would inherently dislike him. He'd have to dress down and look poor, maybe go find some old sneakers. How did she know where he lived, and why did it seem anymore like this was common knowledge? Worse yet, she'd probably assume he could stay out all night. Having a curfew wouldn't fly with someone like Betsy. Probably she'd call him back to hash out some details.

He paced his room, high from adrenaline, plotting his next move. Earlier today seemed like a fantasy world; the high school hallways and Valerie's minivan had happened on another planet. He needed a friend to talk to, and Doug Stills answered on the first ring.

"Wanna come pick me up?"

"Jason?" Doug sounded guarded. "It's a school night. I'm doing trig homework."

Their friendship had taken a backseat since the bonfire. After determining that Ron wasn't involved, Doug agreed to come get him. Jason leapt down the back stairs and into the pantry, where he stole a twenty from his mom's purse.

His parents worked separately in the library, Leah dictating medical records on the phone and Curtis reading a thick report in the stuffed chair. Jason said he was going out. Leah shook her head, muffled the phone and whispered, "It's a school night."

Curtis lowered his glasses to stare at Jason, and then did the same to Leah.

Jason felt like he'd been asking permission his whole life and was sick of it. "Well I'm going out or else I won't be able to sleep tonight."

Leah was a huge proponent of a good night's sleep, and he left her considering this while he slipped out the front door.

The interior of Doug's Ford Escort smelled like pizza and Doug's cassettes were neatly arranged in their cases below the tape player. Jason popped in a Garth Brooks tape and played the song "Rodeo." He liked the bluesy keyboards and sang along to it with as much gumption as he could muster. Doug had always been a Garth fan and Jason knew that Garth posters covered up the cracked plaster on Doug's bedroom walls.

"Got any chaw?"

Doug squirmed. "No, I quit."

"Since when?"

"Doesn't matter. I'm not doing that stuff anymore."

"You back at church too?"

"Yeah. So what?"

Jason shrugged. "Nothing man, I don't care if you're religious again."

"I never stopped!"

Jason hadn't meant to put Doug on the defensive. "Whatever. I'm just bummed. We were finally having some fun this year."

"Maybe you're having fun, but I won't ever take pot again. I was cross-eyed for like a week, and it's been taking me forever to do my trig homework."

"Dude, that was like a month ago." Jason remembered being high at the bonfire, thoughts scattering, cheeks tingling and everything making sense. "You got stoned straight."

Doug approved of this and smiled. "I guess I did."

Best friends again, they rolled between the entrance pillars that delineated Stone Bluff from the otherwise empty range. Down at the Trail King, a row of waylaid big rigs rumbled in the oil-splotched parking lot, engines running to heat the cozy pleather interiors and power VCRs. Jason saw a compact screen glowing through a tinted window, looked like a Schwarzenegger or Stallone movie with lots of explosions happening. He always hoped to catch truckers watching porn tapes and assumed they all did since the Trail King was the only place in town that sold them, from behind a special smut counter that required ID to purchase.

Inside, Jason grabbed a Squirt soda and Corn Nuts before browsing the tape racks. With so many big happenings in his life, it was time for a fresh soundtrack. There was a selection of compact discs, locked behind glass doors in a fancier rack. Leah's kitchen stereo had a disc player, but Jason didn't care for the technology. He was hard on his music; tapes cost less and held up to the abuse. Twenty bucks was enough for two greatest hits compilations, snacks, and chaw with change leftover for the men's room condom machine, where he planned to stock up. Choosing *The Best of Crosby Stills and Nash* and *The Best of Protest Rock*, he approached the checkout counters and saw boxes of brand name condoms on display behind the special smut counter. Might as well buy the fancy kind, Betsy had said she liked fancy things.

"Yeah, um, can I get some Kodiak and a box of those Trojans?"

The smut counter clerk was a scruffy, smock-wearing guy with "Carl" on his name tag, and a cigarette hanging from his lips. He handed over the chaw but squinted at Jason through chocolate-tinted aviator eyeglasses and scowled as if he shouldn't be selling rubbers to a youth.

"Which ones? We got all kinds." Carl placed his smoke in a tinfoil ashtray on the counter and smoke streamed around Jason.

"How about that light blue box?" Jason clenched his stomach, hoping Carl would just grab the box without another word.

Carl smirked. "Them extra small ones? That the size you looking for?"

He'd seen cocks before, mainly in the locker room after swim practice. Some were low-hanging and other guys only had a button down there. How the hell did a guy measure himself for sizing a rubber? Betsy had fit both of her hands on his prick with room to spare, but then she had small hands.

"Just give me whatever's the most popular." Jason noticed a trucker waited in line behind him.

"I wouldn't know buddy. You gotta pick 'em yourself." Carl seemed irked.

Jason chose a bright red box, which Carl rang up along with his snacks, chaw, and tapes. The rubbers cost twelve bucks for a box of six, pushing the total over twenty bucks. He left with everything but *The Best of Protest Rock.*

"You don't have to buy me things." Doug cautiously accepted the Squirt soda in the parking lot. "I got a job."

"Whatever. It's my mom's money and she's got plenty."

Doug was ultra-sensitive about money since his dad had lost the ranch. Jason generally avoided thoughts of money and found it strange when sharing it made people uncomfortable. They listened to Lenny Kravitz on Z-93 and drove around. Doug savored his Squirt, smacking his furry lips after each swig and tapping beats on the steering wheel. "Marty's been teaching me how to play the double bass drum. It's like having drumsticks for feet!"

"Is that right?" Jason didn't hide his sarcasm.

"There's this one beat," Doug turned off the stereo to demonstrate. "It's a double bass kick on the *one* and a triple kick on the *and three*… it goes *BODOOM and two BODOOM-BOOM and four and BODOOM and two and four and…* and then you hit your snare on the two and four… *BODOOM and RAP BODOOM-BOOM and RAP and BODOOM…* with high hat on every beat."

Of course Doug had the beat all mapped out with numbers. Jason preferred grooving over counting. Amused, he added the high hat with his tongue against his teeth, "*tss, tss, tss, tss, tss, tss, tss, tss…*"

Doug was thrilled for the accompaniment, "*BODOOM and RAP BODOOM-BOOM and RAP and BODOOM…*" Amped up on Squirt and beat boxing, Doug was like a Mormon metronome. Back in the Krabb's driveway, Doug took a complex steering wheel solo that impressed Jason. "Nice groove man. We should start jamming again."

Doug frowned. "Marty's really busy, you know being in all AP classes."

"That's never stopped him before." Jason sensed he was being excluded.

"Marty wants to submit a demo for the Z-93 Band Battle." Doug looked uncomfortable. "He doesn't think you're, um, serious enough."

"Whatever. That's cool." Jason picked the callouses on his fingertips, newly hardened from his attempts at learning advanced chords. "I got some other stuff going on anyway."

"Like what?" Doug gave him an eye roll. "It's not like you ever study."

Jason hated when people assumed he had nothing going on. "Well I just bought a box of rubbers and I don't even know how to put one on."

Doug was concerned with this and changed the subject. "Look, I'll try to arrange another jam session, but you'll have to make an effort."

Jason shrugged off the hurt, got out and watched Doug drive away. Playing in Marty's band was stupid child's play. There'd be plenty of time to get up to snuff once he was a pipeliner.

Leah intercepted him at the front door. "Have you been smoking?"

"No. I bought some tapes at the truck stop. That place is full of smokers."

"Let me smell your breath." She leaned into him and he breathed up her nose. He held up *The Best of Crosby Stills and Nash*, hoping to distract her from his other purchases.

Leah recognized the band. "Oh, I know them."

Safely behind his locked bedroom door, Jason packed a chaw and unwrapped his new tape. The new tape smell was particularly sweet. Or was it? It seemed that something else was sweetening the air, something like candy.

"What the hell?" He examined his twelve-dollar box of rubbers. "Raspberry flavored!"

Why were these even for sale at a truck stop, and what kind of truckers bought fruity condoms? Carl must be down there laughing at him. Betsy would think him foolish, or possibly kinky, either way this wasn't the message he wanted to send.

Chapter 11

Shopping at the Desert Crossroads Mall, Leah was thrilled to find four tables piled high with blue jeans. Finding a decent selection of boys' jeans was surprisingly hard for a town with so many big families.

"Hello Dr. Krabb, can I *please* help you with something?" This eager sales clerk was also the mother of several boys, who were now or had been patients of Leah, pediatrician extraordinaire.

"Oh hi Jeannie. *Yes*! I'm desperate. Jason's already outgrown the thirty-two lengths I bought just last month. Robert never grew like this."

Jeannie took command selecting jeans, clearly relishing the role reversal and expending her vast knowledge accrued as a full-time mother and part-time clothier. She also informed Leah that her oldest son was going to be a Mormon missionary in Los Angeles.

"If he needs anything my parents are in Santa Monica. They live on Idaho Avenue."

Leah always played up this coincidence and she laughed with Jeannie.

"Missionaries aren't allowed outside contact." Jeannie's voice wavered. "I'm having a hard time with that. So young to be cut off from his family. His father says the isolation builds up character. Oh, well. I suppose anything worth doing is hard."

Professionally at ease with motherly plights, Leah assured Jeannie with the half-smile half-frown thing she did when mothers broke down around her. "Well I'd still be glad to help him. I know all the hot spots to see movie stars."

Her next stop was the Coffee Bonanza. Dressed up, liquid stimulants were a rapidly blossoming trend on the West Coast and Coffee Bonanza was the first specialty shop to open in Helen Springs. Its owners hoped to ride the coffee boom into the Mormon Belt with western-themed décor and 80s soft-pop music. Branded onto every disposable cup was their logo of a cowboy posed against a rail with his hat tipped low, holding a steaming mug of joe. The joke around town was to call it the speakeasy, due to the Mormon abstinence of caffeine, but business was booming. Even the Mormons loved the place; despite their strict rules, they weren't as intolerant as people thought, especially when an exciting business trend was involved.

Leah enjoyed a coffee, tapping her foot to Huey Lewis and Don Henley on the speakers, and watched the place fill up with lunchers. She recognized Dr. Kurtz, a mild-mannered oncologist with whom she served on the hospital board, dumping copious amounts of sweetener into his coffee. Diane Black, the mother of front-row Becca, beamed at Leah from across the room and immediately walked over, struggling to manage her coffee and many shopping bags.

Diane talked using her hands; with painted purple nails and fingers glittering with rings, they reminded Leah of dancing showgirls. She discussed Becca's upcoming summer trips to visit prospective colleges, all private and West Coast. She shifted her hips at Leah and her dark eyes flickered. "What about Jason? Is he looking at any schools?"

The question made Leah squirm. College was hardly on Jason's radar.

"We've just started that discussion." Leah tried changing the subject by reaching for her Motorola pager.

Diane mentioned that they were installing a pool and the Krabbs would be invited to a pool party when it was complete.

"We're shooting for Fourth of July but my fingers are crossed. You know the weather around here and how contractors can be—I certainly do, I married one!" Diane laughed as if this was the most hilarious thing ever.

Leah thought Diane liked to appear more stressed than she actually was, as if she hardly had the time to stop and chat. Leah imagined herself at a pool party, sitting in deck chairs munching from plastic bowls of sodden corn chips while being splashed by erratic pool games. She didn't have a swimsuit anymore, let alone the time or patience for summer fun.

"I need to run," Diane said. "I should get back over to the hotel. It's so much fun decorating the ballroom with the girls. I'm chaperoning tonight and look at these fun boots I bought at the western store!"

Leah squinted up from her Motorola pager, pretending to know about the Spring Social. Even if Jason were involved in student affairs, Leah wouldn't be hanging banners and streamers at the hotel. She was on call and the hospital was maxed out with newborns—springtime in Idaho was the high human birthing season. But because of Jason's outcast status, this wasn't even an option for her, which irked.

* * *

Like a rat sniffing out a Cheeto, Ron showed up at Jason's on Saturday, sensing a party was in the works. Over a chaw, he squeezed the info from Jason and was convinced that Betsy's party would be full of hippie-hating cowboys.

"Cowboys? I doubt it." The only place Jason regularly encountered authentic cowboys was at the McDonald's near the interstate exchange. They had tanned arms and faces, smelled like dung, and tipped their dusty hats at the counter girls. The older ones posted up in the corner booths all day long, drinking coffee and socializing. "But I'm hoping the pipeliners will be there."

"That'd be cool." Ron spit into a murky Dew bottle. "She better not live in a trailer park though. Those places are ground zero for getting busted."

Betsy hadn't called back to firm up their plans and his imagination had been running wild with all kinds of scenes for that evening. Picturing what Betsy's house would be like made him strangely homesick. Did she have posters on her bedroom walls and trinkets on her dresser? He considered his own bedroom's purple bedspread, hard to find Zeppelin posters, swim team ribbons, the Sony cassette player—it was like being uprooted from everything he knew as familiar. It was odd to feel sad on the brink of knowing things.

Ron produced the still unopened Damiana bottle from his backpack. They chawed and considered its squat, golden beauty. The night held much uncertainty and Jason was glad to have Ron as a sidekick.

"Hey dude, I got a stupid question for you." Jason tried hard to backseat his embarrassment. "Um, like what's the best way to put on a rubber?"

Ron stroked his whiskers and looked bothered. They'd never outright discussed Jason's virginity before and Ron didn't seem keen for it. Jason already felt robbed that Silly Bags had let him down and, seeing as he was going whole hog with Betsy in a few hours, Ron was his last hope.

"Look man, you want in on this party, then I'm going to need some tips."

"What the hell man?" Ron still wasn't having it.

Possibly Jason had assumed too much and sex wasn't on the table, but his experience with Betsy suggested otherwise—the girl moved fast. He'd considered sacrificing a condom and doing a trial run, but didn't think jacking off wearing a rubber would work. Was he supposed to tear it off and finish? At this stage of puberty, he couldn't just work up a boner and walk away from it, which felt akin to flying a kite and letting go of the string.

Ron laughed low. "The directions are on the box."

"Well I bought some fancy kind," Jason admitted. "They don't have instructions."

"The trick is to just unroll it onto your dick." Ron spoke quietly with his head low, as if reluctant to have given up hard-earned knowledge.

This made perfect sense to Jason. He stopped pressing for advice but seemed to have activated Ron's guide mode.

"If it starts feeling really good, that means you broke the rubber. I always carry backups in my fanny pack."

Jason frowned, "You mean it doesn't feel really good *with* a condom?"

"It does, just not as good as a live socket."

The chaw ran unusually thick in Jason's mouth and he felt drained of energy. He laid down on his bed and worried about bursting rubbers.

The boys flushed their chaw down the en suite toilet and picked their teeth clean. Ron went into full primping mode, smoothing his tie-dyed T-shirt over his potbelly and straightening his ropey hair while smiling at himself in the bathroom mirror. Jason figured he planned on flirting with Leah downstairs. This wasn't the first time a friend had had a crush on Jason's mom. It usually came with good-natured ribbing, but Ron never mentioned it. For a change, Jason saw the creepy side of Ron—which everyone else had seemingly already noticed.

* * *

Downstairs, Leah confronted Jason about the Spring Social. "I ran into Diane Black on her way to the Black Elk Hotel to help decorate. It sounds like everyone's dressing up."

Jason looked hurt. "I'm not even going."

The boys sat on stools around the granite island and Leah fixed them sandwiches: dill Havarti cheese with double lettuce and extra tomato on cracked sourdough.

"You'll regret skipping these types of things. The other stuff you'll forget. I remember my prom with Jake Green. I had the greatest time dancing, and I wasn't the dancing type. And afterwards we went cruising the Sunset Strip."

Ron was in total agreement. "At my old high school in Madison, I went to homecoming at the fancy downtown Hilton. The whole charade of dressing up lends gravitas to an evening. That cheese smells delicious, do you need some help?"

Leah set Ron up slicing bread on her new slate cutting board, a behemoth stone orb set upon stout peg-legs—her first mail order purchase in which the shipping costs had exceeded the purchase price.

Notching up the charm, Ron commented on the view out the southerly picture windows overlooking town, the Black Elk River and its namesake mountain range. "This kitchen is like something from *Sunset Magazine*. Kate started getting that when we moved out here."

Radiant snowfields remained on the treeless north-facing summit slopes. The lower flanks were a lush patchwork of greening aspens and maples among the purple sage, pinyon pine, and dark lava rock.

"How are your parents doing?" Leah checked her pager.

Ron politely cleared his throat. "Ray works all the time. I hardly see him. He's taking me back to Wisconsin for some work he's got there this summer. I'll hang out with my old friends and see some shows."

"Sounds like an adventure. Would you boys like some fruit? I buy all this fruit that Jason never eats."

Ron said he loved oranges, "They're the greatest food ever."

Half reading a *USA Today*, Leah approvingly watched Jason gobbling up the healthy snack. The big news today from the paper's *Life* section was Garth Brooks's sweep at the Academy of Country Music Awards, entertainer of the year, this on the heels of his Superbowl show and now North Helen was dedicating its Spring Social to his persona. Maybe Jason had been rejected asking someone to the social and here she was chafing him for not going. Motherly intuition told her that something had snuck up on him, the poor boy looked famished. It occurred to her that this was the twilight of her child-rearing years and she needed to soak up being a parent.

Leah's pager beeped and she frowned. It was the pulmonologist concerning a month-old baby with a serious lung infection. She needed to make the call pronto.

"I'm gonna be out late tonight." Jason blurted this through his sandwich as she headed for the library. "Gonna be late."

"What's this?" Leah stopped, wanted more details.

"Just going out."

Leah looked Ron directly in the eye and with the thinnest of smiles.

Ron immediately spilled the beans, "Jason has a big date tonight."

"It's not a date. I hardly know her." Jason's whole body shook in dismissal.

"What's her name? Why don't you take her to the social?"

"No way!" Jason blushed. "Her name's Betsy. She's just some girl I met through Isabel."

Leah's hopes faded. Isabel Perkins had been nothing but trouble since she'd been in diapers with Jason. "Is this Betsy in your class? What's her last name?"

Jason squirmed. "It's no big deal."

Ron gave up more dirt. "He doesn't know her last name. She's a junior at South Helen."

Leah held up a finger and forced a nod. "Let's talk about this later. I have to make a call." Her words came out on autopilot as she left the kitchen to make her call.

Leah was finishing her phone call in the library when a maroon 1968 Chevy Impala coupe chugged into Stone Bluff, trailing smoke and growling like a tractor. Bemused, she watched through the library window as the beastly coach parked at her curb. A young girl was driving, with another girl in the back and a man in the front seat. The passenger door swung out, barely cleared the curb and the man stood upon her lawn. He had a laborer's build and a mess of sand-colored hair that favored the back of his neck. A loose serape with indigo, ruby and golden stripes draped over his thick shoulders and chest hair poked through its V-neck opening. He had a lazy smile and appraised the Krabb home through squinty eyes.

The driver was a short, long-haired girl who was fit-looking. Her skimpy red tank top revealed tightly bound caramel skin and fist-like breasts, as if punching their way to freedom. The back seat passenger got out and was nearly identical to the driver; sisters, Leah thought, and they looked like trouble.

Chapter 12

The Impala's engine alerted the boys and they watched the arrival from the living room window.

"No way," Ron said. "It's Allen. Fucking sweet man!"

Jason was aghast to see Allen, Betsy, and Krissy walking up the path to his front door. What the hell? *DING DONG*, the fucking doorbell rang and his mom headed for the door. He heard the door open and froze as his mother called out, "Jason, your friends are here."

Ron told him, "Dude, be cool."

Jason nodded his readiness, had rubbers stuffed in his jeans pockets, an old pair of Vans on, and a raggedy button-down flannel with forty pilfered dollars in the breast pocket. He headed around the corner to the entryway where time and reality warped.

Allen spoke proudly, "There he is. You ready, buddy? Betsy's driving the spaceship tonight."

Jason ignored everyone but Betsy, who stood with her fingertips stuffed into the waistline of her drum-tight jeans, rocking back on her lug-soled black boots on the entryway throw rug. Her brown lipstick matched her eyes and a hair clip peeled back her bangs. Her lone braid, the color of crude oil, swung behind her like a tail. Effort had clearly been made on her part and she wasn't in the least nervous to be standing here alongside his mother, who frowned at him.

"Jason," Leah said. "Do you have anything nicer to wear?"

He stared her down, not now, Mom.

"Hey guys." Jason said, "You ready to go?"

Allen frowned. "Dang man. I was hoping for a tour."

Jason couldn't believe this, but he couldn't say no to Allen. They toured the downstairs and Allen acted as if he was in a fascinating museum, mouth agape, hands clasped behind his back. Betsy and

Krissy stayed close behind Jason, giggling at his unenthusiastic descriptions, "Here's the library where nobody reads and the living room where nobody, um, lives."

The kitchen, with all its gadgetry and soaring views, stunned the guests.

"Holy crap!" Betsy said. "Some view you got up here Dr. Krabb."

She knew his mom was a doctor? Jason didn't know if he liked this, and Leah didn't respond.

"Well there you go," Jason said. "The rest of the house is dirty." This was a lie. The weekly maid service had just cleaned and the house was in perfect order.

"The rest? How much more is there?" Betsy asked him.

She was so hot it was dumbfounding. Her face looked older and wiser than he remembered: eyes shining like varnish, haughty lips worthy of a George Michael video. Seeing Betsy in his bright kitchen like this brought back that jackpot feeling and turned it on like a hot shower.

"There's a whole downstairs and upstairs," Ron said.

"Bet your room's nice and big," Betsy said. "I can't wait to see it."

"It's a total mess." Jason was afraid to see his mom's reaction and keenly avoided looking at her. Suddenly feeling self-conscious, he was embarrassed about his house. His fancy pants and Toyota Camry had given him away from square one. Betsy had come here knowing he was a rich kid. This sucked, things had seemed so anonymous up at the bonfire.

Jason led them to the front door.

Allen complimented Leah on her house. "I could see myself in a place like this. Gonna have to lay some serious pipe though." Using his fingers like a dog's claw, he scratched at the golden stubble on his neck and glanced with astonishment up the main staircase to the sunlit atrium.

"Pipes?" Leah asked. "Are you a plumber?"

Betsy laughed and revealed her smoker's cough. Leah visibly shuddered.

"No Ma'am, er, I mean Doctor," Allen said politely. "I work on the transport system for Intermountain Energy. That's just fancy talk for a pipeliner. You probably seen our pipeline setting out in the desert?"

"I haven't." Leah half-smiled, half-frowned.

Jason stepped outside onto the front pathway, keenly aware of the ornate flagstone, daffodils, and low voltage lighting. He didn't like these complications and felt rather like a piece of meat, even though in the scheme of things he felt like filet mignon and not leftover chicken. What would he find at Betsy's house? Would he care if it were small with cracked plaster and a stained toilet? These things hadn't mattered before and suddenly they did.

The warm May evening carried the smells of Stone Bluff in spring: steak sizzling on grills, cedar-mulched garden beds, sagebrush, and asphalt tar cooling in the shade. Jason saw his mom appraising him from inside the open doorway. "Please don't stay out forever. And Jason..." It looked like she wanted to run out and hug him, but this wasn't an option anymore and he couldn't remember the last time it had been. "What?"

"Have a nice time."

* * *

Allen's Spaceship Impala enthralled the boys, especially Jason, who'd never been in a car older than he was. Seated in the center of the giant backseat, he had two feet between Ron and Krissy to either side. While the car smelled of old fabric and gasoline, it ran solid and the heavy engine vibration wavered the voices of its occupants in a hypnotizing way. Betsy drove down the long grade and Allen fed a disc into the slit of a new Alpine CD player, which sucked it up with a robotic zing. He turned to face Jason, obviously proud of his stuff.

"You like Blind Melon? These guys are blowing up!" Allen drummed the back of the front seat with hands nicked and swollen from the week's hard labor.

"Sweet!" Jason hoped he sounded cool enough.

Betsy bossed the big car around town, her dark braid sucked out the window and wafting in her exhaled smoke. She was showing off, letting the big wheel slide through her fingers while accelerating out of corners. Her face was viewed by Jason in the rear view mirror and the sight of it made his intestines jumprope his stomach.

Krissy hadn't said a word since leaving his house, just fidgeted and stared angrily out the window, making him uneasy.

"Think your mom liked me?" Allen cracked open a can of Busch.

"Who cares what she thinks?" Jason arrogantly flipped his hair.

Betsy looked him over in the mirror like he'd said the wrong thing.

"I know how it seems," Allen said. "Me long-haired and hanging out with high schoolers. But Betsy's like a little sister to me."

Betsy interrupted with, "Motherfucking cop's behind us!"

Jason saw the cruiser in the rear view mirror, black and white, a box of lights on top and following much closer than Silly Bags recommended. All things considered, he had bigger fears than the law tonight. He'd never had problems with the police and cops always smiled at him.

Allen flexed his jaw muscles in contempt. "Be cool. Be cool."

The cruiser abruptly veered away just as they hit South State Street; this was Betsy's side of town and here the Black Elk Mountains rose like a wall at the end of the road. Allen laughed in relief and chucked his empty beer can out the window into a lawn full of thistles, pebbles, and dirt. "Way to maintain there, Sissy."

"Pigs don't scare me." Betsy rambled the car down the broad street with her arm out the window. The engine resounded like a train between the shabby houses, with ugly dogs that tried to charge them, barking through chain-link fences.

Allen faced Jason again, sweat beading on his brow. "Tell you what Jason, you ever see a cop start messing with me, you just run for your life."

Jason saw that Ron quivered beside him, clutching his backpack and looking ready to bolt, always a step ahead of him in these matters.

Betsy turned into a neighborhood and brought them down a pleasant looking street with modest homes set back under the shade of established oak and poplar trees. Parked in every driveway were pickup trucks with campers and boats under carports or covered by tarps. Jason recognized the crew cab Ford from the bonfire parked in the wide driveway of a squat house with brown siding and black-shuttered, aluminum-framed windows. The Spaceship eased alongside the Ford and everyone climbed out. Krissy grabbed the garage door and yanked it open as if it were made of cardboard.

Inside the garage, white deck chairs ringed a plastic garbage can holding a keg plopped in ice. The floor was stained with grease and oil.

Wrenches, sockets, a mechanic's creeper, and drop lights hung from a peg board. A huge workbench overladed with chainsaws took up the back wall. There were shelves upon shelves packed with grass seed, tackle boxes, camping gear, oil cans, gas cans, paint cans, glue cans, and boxes boldly labeled XMAS and HALLOWEEN and KITCHEN MISC. This garage, for all its stuff, wasn't at all messy; rather it seemed like a feat of organization, as if lovingly maintained. Jason's garage was barren in comparison and was three times the size. He couldn't help from making these comparisons, since getting to know people had never been like this before.

Allen primed the keg. "You like Icehouse? It's pricier but gets you drunker."

The boys accepted foamy beers from Allen. Ron wiped grease from his long nose and stirred it into his beer, noticeably shrinking the foam—the guy knew things.

Betsy switched on the workbench radio, Queensryche on Z-93. She danced over and plopped down on Jason's lap like it was still warm from her last visit. Feeling the contours of her butt and legs, he was thankful to not have worn cargo shorts as his soon-to-be monumental boner wormed up against her Wrangler Jeans. She relaxed drinking beer and somehow sat in a way that favored it, like she knew exactly how to deal with a boner probing her butt.

Krissy burst in from the house, talking on a portable phone. "Yup. Whatever. Fucking hurry it up. Buh-bye." She lit a smoke, grabbed a chair but then stood again to pace and told Allen to roll a joint.

Allen pulled the Tupperware of weed from his fanny pack and broke up the green-orange plant with his fingers. Jason hadn't expected pot to be so colorful or to smell so peculiar.

"Dig that smell? Like a skunk fartin' lemons." Allen expertly twisted the joint and put a spacer on the drawing end.

Ron exploded with flattery, "That joint is like something from *High Times* magazine!"

"*Gracias.* I go down to Mexico every winter, set myself on the beach and pretty much roll joints all day long."

Krissy hugged herself, looking cold. "Damn it hon! I can't wait to go to Mexico. I might just quit college and go live down there, it's always so cold here."

"Daddy know you're quitting college and retiring to Mexico?" Betsy chided. Krissy flipped her the bird. The fact that Krissy was in college comforted Jason, as if it somehow meant their family had it together. Strange how these details mattered, like he was going to bed with the entire household.

"My brother Stewart spends time near Manzanillo, he's got a nice casita on *la playa*." Allen sounded like he was describing a timeshare deal, even though Stewart Heber was an archetypical hoodlum. Stewart hadn't been in school with Jason, but every kid in town knew the story. Like Allen, Stewart had been expelled from North Helen for being a fearsome ass kicker, and had then gone onto the state pen for beating a state trooper with a fence post during a traffic stop in the desert. Jason remembered the cop tailing them on the way here and the hardness in Allen's voice. There was clearly some ass kicker left in him and thank goodness it wasn't directed at him.

A motorcycle pulled up out front and Krissy tossed open the garage door. Jason recognized gloomy Joey from the bonfire, climbing off the back seat of a sporty bike with knobby tires and travel cases. The driver wore head to toe road leather, stood tall and squinted into the garage, scowling at the boys. "The fuck's this?"

Krissy seemed scared to answer.

The biker had a long, sad face, bushy brown hair and deep-set eyes that said, "back the fuck off." He made his way through the garage, going into the house. Jason thought he looked familiar, not like he knew him, actually, but it was like when his mom had pointed out famous actors in Santa Monica.

Krissy and Joey hustled in after the biker and slammed the door behind them. Betsy downed a full beer in two gulps and rearranged herself on Jason's boner, now at half mast.

Krissy returned alone, looking sneaky and holding a tiny baggie that made Jason's stomach lurch. He immediately identified the contents as cocaine, having seen so many photographs in all those "Just Say No" pamphlets, accompanied by First Lady Reagan's scolding finger. Krissy placed a STIHL chainsaw owner's manual on an empty chair and carefully poured the coke onto it. It was lumpy and granular and not very powdery. She looked up and smirked at Jason. "You ever do lines?"

Jason shook his head and looked at Ron, who didn't look so cool anymore.

Allen wasn't happy. "You really gonna do this out here and everything?"

"It's a party, ain't it?" Krissy scowled. "I'm so sick a listening to a bunch of pipeliners, sitting around and shit talking. I want people up and dancing."

Betsy's hand went up the back of Jason's shirt, tickling his spine with her fingertips. "Wanna try some with me?"

"Sure." This seemed to please her.

Krissy covered the drugs with a piece of notebook paper and scraped her driver's license roughly over it. Mesmerized by the whole process, Jason noticed the notebook paper was lined with copied-down glossary terms: "Crisis Communication" and "Press Kit"—college terms, from "Mass Comm. 101." With the drug broken up, she edged out two big lines and three smaller ones, and then dropped her license on the floor. Jason picked it up for her and read her full name on it: Krissy Aarsdrager. This was also Betsy's last name. What kind of name was Aarsdrager? It sounded rough and extra-white, not the name he'd expected from girls with bronze skin and black velvet hair.

Krissy pinched a nostril and snorted a big line while Allen held her hair. She came up with her eyes wide, wriggling her nose and blinking a lot. Allen bent over sniffing and then sat back with little change.

Z-93 played "Welcome to the Jungle" by Guns N' Roses. Jason owned this tape, knew all the words and couldn't believe the timing of the song. From watching MTV, he'd heard that Axl Rose had gotten messed up on cocaine and trashed his house for no reason. In high school, Allen had worn a frayed jean jacket with a giant GnR patch on the back, opposing revolvers entangled with red roses—and he'd slammed that kid's head into the cinderblock wall for no reason. Jason didn't like the signals he was getting; what if Allen went nuts on cocaine and reverted to his old self? He imagined being thrown headfirst into the garage wall, items raining down from the collapsing shelves. Bags of birdseed, grout, and KITCHEN MISC. crushing him on the stained cement.

Like a spider deciding which fly to eat, Krissy looked hungrily at Jason and Betsy. "Betsy, you don't get any unless Jason does some. I make the rules here. I'm the oldest. My house, my party. Who's next? Huh? Hurry up before that line gets blown away."

Allen shook his head at Krissy. "There's no rules for or against it." He seemed mad at her. "They don't call it the devil's dandruff for nothing. Think I see why now, the way you're acting."

Silence. Jason's mind and heart raced, hadn't seen this coming. He'd been nervous enough about having sex and then the world had thrust *this* upon him.

"I'm gonna pass." Ron casually sipped his beer. "I got bad hay fever. My sinuses are already plugged up." He avoided looking at Jason. It seemed like Ron had seen this situation coming, throwing out a cool excuse like that.

"Fine with me." Krissy sucked up the extra line. "Not bad at all. Beats your heart and numbs your throat. Not bad at all." She made a troubled effort to swallow, which popped her eyes out from their sockets.

Jason decided to just do it. It was a little like going head first off the country club high dive. Except rather than a broken neck, he might end up clerking at the Trail King and trashing things for no good reason. This was the "peer pressure" that First Lady Reagan had warned about. It was a real thing, though her pamphlets had never described it with Betsy squirming on his lap, waiting for a turn while Axl wailed from the radio.

Jason got down on his knees and sniffed a line from the chainsaw owner's manual. Then he held Betsy's hair while she did some. His thoughts flatlined and he somehow watched the entire garage at once with his mouth open. Betsy reared up, shaking her head to the riffing guitar—as if saying no to something—her long braid writhing behind her.

Allen lit the joint and the air smelled like food cooking. Jason passed on the joint, suddenly too high to make another decision.

"Worried about something? You got no worries *amigo*." Allen's look turned mean as he held up a finger. "But I do have one rule about it."

It didn't matter how tough Allen was, Jason would fight his way out of here, go directly through the walls and fly away like superman.

"Nobody talks about the coke. Got it? *Silencia!*"

The warning came just in time. Cars pulled up outside. Voices called from outside the garage and people came in through the side door. Now it was a party, but everybody was in the garage or in the backyard where aluminum patio furniture was set upon a concrete slab. The crowd was college-aged but they didn't look like college kids to Jason, not with their leather and boots, tattoos and goatees, halter tops and hoodies, and body piercings.

People seemed to write him off as a high schooler, and he was fine not pretending to be cooler or older than he was. There were apparently no South Helen kids there to vibe him, which got him thinking about Betsy. Where were all of her friends? The coke drained from his nose. It half-burned, half-numbed his throat and made swallowing weird. He considered hacking it out but didn't want to look foolish, so he drank the rest of his beer. Betsy suddenly made him uneasy; he was convinced she was a lone ranger and her only friends were the guys she screwed. He considered the other guys lurking at the party and saw the motorcycle guy leaned up against the workbench, running a hand through his helmet hair and watching Betsy with his tough guy Hollywood eyes.

Chapter 13

Jason devilishly asked Betsy for a tour of her house. Turning into his arms, she kissed him in the midst of everyone and his brain crackled like a pork rind. He smelled her shampoo, tasted her lipstick, and felt her makeup sticky against his face. Embarrassed, he stopped to see if anyone had noticed them, but they were background scenery—absorbed into the party's fabric like stage props.

She led him up the garage stairs into a cozy kitchen with varnished wooden cupboards and blue and white linoleum flooring in a flower petal pattern. On top of the cupboards were smiling wooden animals painted with silly outfits: chicken in a bathrobe, a bow-tied pig, lamb in a tux, and a flanneled cow. It was a barnyard parade of cuteness. A wood-burned sign above the fridge read "Donna's Cookin!" in a western font. The laminate countertop was stained but otherwise clean and tinfoil lined the electric stovetop burners. The kitchen opened up into a small dining room with a square table and a sliding door to the backyard. The dining room wall had a framed painting of wild mustangs stampeding through a Great Basin wonderland of purple sage and golden peaks.

The Aarsdrager's home was a calm retreat compared to the garage. Jason embraced the calmness and relished the homey scents, something like hot dogs and air fresheners. He was amazed that everyone stayed in the garage and backyard. His idea of parties was one of homes under siege, beer sloshed on the upholstery, holes punched in the drywall.

Betsy read his mind. "My parents don't want us partying inside. Allen only lets the girls come in to piss, but you're fine." She danced up and hugged his waist. "We like you."

In the living room were side-by-side rust colored recliners with a lamp table between them, facing a big screen TV that was wedged between wall mounted gun cases. Dramatic landscape paintings hung from the wood paneling, full of snowy peaks, dreamy lakes, and stony streams with elk, moose, and bear poised in the foregrounds. Then there were years of family portraits with Betsy and Krissy looking more alike the younger they'd been. Jason fixated on her parents, hoping their images would explain everything about the family at once.

The girls got their long black hair from the alluring Donna, whose expansive hair darkened every photo. She looked glamorous with an open face and eager smile. Her skin looked supermodel smooth and was darker than her girls. Jason thought Donna would probably adore him, something in her look reminded him of how Betsy looked at him, like a front-row groupie at a sold-out concert.

Their pale-faced father was a buzz-cut and mustachioed man who posed like a frozen side of beef. The sight of him unnerved Jason as if it might reveal something irreconcilable.

"Sit down and put your feet up honey." Betsy pushed him into a recliner and swiveled up the footrest, half-joking. "Lemme get you a beer."

Jason counted twenty gleaming shotguns and rifles in the living room cases, lined behind glass so clear it was like nothing was there. He grabbed a *Soldier of Fortune* magazine from the wicker basket beside his chair. The cover had a shot of a mustachioed man crouched behind a machine gun, aiming the barrel squarely at Jason's face. He read the subscription tag: Aaron Aarsdrager, 2122 Ferry Lane, Helen Springs, ID. "Aaron Aarsdrager," he said to himself and the sound of it made him shudder.

Betsy returned from the kitchen fridge with a cold Busch which tasted like water compared to the Ice House. He'd had more beers tonight than ever before but they seemed to have little effect.

"Wanna a foot rub?" Betsy pulled the Vans off his feet and massaged them.

Her hands were splendid, like powerful machines working through his sweaty white socks and reaching hidden nerves with unforgiving pressure. It was remarkable how much interaction he'd had with her hands. He'd never imagined hands playing such an important role in intimacy, had thought the road to sex was mostly paved with kissing and dry humping.

Betsy said the Aarsdragers were in Elko, Nevada. "Mom grew up near there on a huge ranch in the Dorado Peaks. Know where that is?"

"In the middle of nowhere?"

"Pretty much. But my best friend in the whole wide world lives down there."

"Oh yeah?" Jason was pleased to hear she had friends.

"Molly lives on my grandparents' ranch. Got a coat like a chocolate chip cookie."

"That's too bad." Jason wasn't sure what she meant, but it sounded bad.

"She's a mustang. I could go live there, but besides my horse there's zip going on down there. It's better going to South Helen, especially now." She gave him groupie eyes.

With hands that smelled like his socks, she reached up and mussed his hair. "What's it like at North Helen?"

"It sucks. I need to get the hell out of there."

"You should go to the I.L.C. That's where Krissy met Allen." Betsy made it sound like a fairy tale.

"I'm taking algebra there. I didn't know Allen went to the I.L.C."

"Yup. When he got kicked out of North Helen. Krissy did senior year there, waitressing full time at the Black Elk Hotel. She likes doing that better than going to college."

This reminded him of the dance tonight, all of his classmates "Ropin' the Wind" down at the Black Elk Hotel. He knew Valerie was going but in a big group without a date. He imagined her leading a line dance, everyone lined up behind her and was mesmerized. Odd that he wanted to be there right now, throwing the punch bowl against the wall and tearing down streamers for no good reason. He chugged the rest of his Busch and cracked his jaw, feeling like an old hand at the world and not at all like the boy who could've taken Valerie to the dance.

"Algebra." Betsy curled up in the adjacent recliner. "You must be smart. I'm horrible at math. Never figured out those damn fractions."

"I suck at it too. You need it for college, but I'm going to play guitar, out in Portland and Seattle."

"Which one?"

Jason answered right away, "Both."

"Wow dude." Betsy was amused. "Hope you're good."

"Yeah I'm not as good as I thought I was, but I'm getting better. As long as you're trying hard at something it's okay to brag about yourself." He especially liked the way his voice sounded tonight. "You can't be a badass at anything if you're too modest."

Betsy squinted across to him, "Modesty's like not showing off?"

"Yup. All the top guys toot their own horn. Modesty is for background people. I'm not a background person." This was fantastic, like sitting in the front row with all the answers.

"I like to show off..." Betsy climbed onto his lap and kissed him. "And you came here knowing that."

All that remained of the tour were the bedrooms. The Aarsdrager's bedroom had a four-poster bed and light blue carpet. Jason noticed it was tidy and he looked, unsuccessfully, for an en suite. He liked that Betsy was proud of her house; he would've been uncomfortable if she was embarrassed by it or compared it in any way to Stone Bluff. Krissy's room was messy with bras strewn about the dresser and denim tumbling from her closet. Music posters featuring long-haired and snug-trousered rockers were tacked to the pink wallpaper. A tape player sat on her unmade bed and uncased tapes were scattered across the sheets.

Betsy's room had a single bed pushed into the corner beneath a windowsill. The pillows were propped up and smoothed and the white bedspread was crisply made up. Jason sensed, again, that effort had been made on his behalf. Atop her dresser was a stereo, a cassette rack, pictures of her horse and a box of smokes. Jason rifled through the tape rack, which pleased Betsy. It was well stocked with the long-haired and snug-trousered, the likes of Poison and Nelson, but her selection also had a thrilling, truck stop randomness to it with Tori Amos, Billy Ray Cyrus, The Beatles, and The Bangles all lined up together. Jason knew whatever he picked had the power to exult or haunt him forevermore—he wasn't shopping at the Trail King anymore.

Betsy made the decision for him, pressing down play until a tape hissed loudly. She sat on her bed and slowly removed her black boots. An electric guitar picked slowly, "*bock a chick, a bock a chick*" and it sounded like some kind of derelict sixties music, the kind with constantly riffing guitar. He closed his eyes and watched a shower of candy-colored specks dance across his eyelids. He wanted to know everything about this song. "Who is this? Those are some dreamy licks."

Betsy killed the lights and danced over to him, the blue carpet sparking at her feet. "No more words."

He remembered what was about to happen, as she unbuttoned his shirt and pushed him onto her bed. She removed her tank top, undid her bra and showed him her cupcake breasts in the silver light coming through the window. When he reached up for these jewels, she pinned his wrists against the bed and straddled him, lowering her chest to his face. Instinctively, he slipped a dark nipple into his mouth and held this rubbery bead gently between his lips and tongue like a bug he didn't want to harm. She pulled it out and it glistened wet, her chest pocked with gooseflesh. She released his wrists and let his hands explore her breasts. It was dizzying to consider how she handled him and that she had a certain way of going about this. The hand job in the woods had been something else entirely, more of a concession, but now she was clearly aroused and wanted something from him. The world couldn't get more exciting.

With a serious face, she rose and unzipped her jeans. Jason glimpsed her red underwear before she pulled everything off, twisting her legs free and stripping off her socks by the toes. Her legs were muscle-toned like her arms, their wavy outlines sharply leading up to a patch of dark fur. Aside from her breasts, there wasn't any loose flesh on her, just muscle and bone stretching through. This unlikely build had to come from someone, and Aaron Aarsdrager was the likely source. Krissy had the same chiseled body, and he pictured Allen upon her in the room next door, their muscles entwined like beautiful sculptures. Jason hadn't expected taking the whole person to bed, family and friends included. If they'd reached this point at the bonfire, was there a basic, more anonymous form of sex they could've had without all this other stuff interfering?

The strange music now had vocals, lazy sounding lyrics that he couldn't understand, like listening to a conversation from another room. "Is this like a mixtape?"

Betsy climbed into bed, pressing her chest against his. "You need to focus. No more words."

Her body was warm and felt way softer than it looked. He wanted her to unzip him before his boner railroaded right through his fly. It was zero hour, as Grandpa Krabb liked to say, and he might as well undress himself. When he got his pants off, she kicked them on the floor and viewed his cock, rigid and shining like an eel. She briefly smiled, then looked him in the eyes and it wasn't at all like flirting in the back row.

Betsy rolled onto her back and adjusted her hair beneath her, twisting the lone braid in one hand. Jason needed a rubber right now and looked down at his jeans, crumpled on the floor. But she didn't seem to be waiting around for a rubber to appear.

"Something on your mind? You should keep your eyes on the prize."

"Um..." He needed to act and stop waiting for instructions. Going for a rubber, he reviewed Ron's advice—didn't want to blow this. Betsy saw the condom and snapped her fingers for it. "Here, lemme do it."

Jason smelled raspberry bubble-gum and gasped while she quickly unrolled it over his prick. It was moist, cool and tickled him, especially when she reached the bottom.

Mobilized, he kept his eyes on the prize. It was so amazing seeing a real vagina and no illustration, he realized, would ever rightly capture its magic. She grabbed him with her feet; they were dry and cool on his thighs compared to the heat coming from between her legs. Her right hand took his prick and her left steadied his stomach. She slowly worked him inside, pinching her face whenever progress was made. He couldn't smell raspberry anymore, but what was that other smell?

"Hang on." She readjusted the angle and gained another hard-won inch.

Then something gave and he slipped fully inside. His nose filled with that wonderful new smell, a cross between maple syrup and body odor. None of his fears mattered anymore, even abduction by aliens stopped being scary. He could die now and it wouldn't matter, as long as he could glide inside of her like this.

"Oh shit!" Betsy yelled. "Oh shit!"

Fearing a burst rubber, Jason stopped. "What's wrong?"

Betsy opened her eyes and looked at him, distracted and breathing hard. "Don't stop. Keep going!" She lifted her hips and they pulsed together once more. "Oh shit!" she yelled, "Shit! Shit! Oh shit!"

It was remarkable, how her slippery flume seemed to bear the entire weight of his body at once. The bed squeaked and knocked the wall. Someone had to be hearing this racket, but she didn't seem to care.

"Oh shit!" she screamed and breathed, "Shit! Shit! Oh shit!"

He was obviously giving it to her, but the amazingness had lessened to simply good. He rammed back and forth in time with each "Oh Shit!" and grew sweaty on her—apparently sex required stamina.

"Ah shit! Shit! Oh yes!" She lifted hard against him and trapped his ass with her legs, as if he might escape. Prevented from moving, he watched her go away somewhere and come back fairly limp. Though his ass twitched like a short-circuiting robot, his cock went numb and stubbornly refused to ejaculate. Dismayed, he gently exited her flume.

Chapter 14

Betsy lit a cigarette in bed. "Shouldn't be smoking in bed. Crack that window for me."

Jason got to his knees, reached around her and pried open the window. Cool air streamed in across his chest. Now wearing a condom for no good reason, his prick swung directly in front of her. The rubber had loosened and it felt like wearing a sandwich baggie.

Betsy sniffed the air. "Smells like Juicy Fruit or something?"

"Um, something's probably blooming outside."

He had to remove it. It pinched and tangled his pubic hair and smelled stronger now, as if having sex had triggered some kind of scent-release technology. This wouldn't be a problem if her room had an en suite toilet—just stroll over, close the door and rip that bugger off. But he couldn't brave the hallway wearing a rubber. There were few options that involved privacy, funny how he hadn't anticipated needing any. He hoped to grow limp enough and shed it like a snakeskin beneath the sheet. If not, he'd just wear it around under his pants.

Betsy read his mind and offered the empty Busch bottle that she was tapping her ashes into. "Stuff it in here. Nothing's worse than a rubber in the trash bin."

Awkwardly, Jason peeled it off and stuffed it into the bottle, his pinky growing dark with ashes. At least now he was thankful for steering clear of semen and wondered how many condoms she'd previously disposed of like this. He remembered all those other, older guys at the party and imagined they'd left Betsy with some real messes. They shared her cigarette and relaxed on her pillows, which felt intimate and very adult to Jason. Indeed the whole experience, thanks to Betsy, had been far sexier than what he'd imagined. He'd been prepared to anonymously mash body parts but had never considered that sex might actually be sexy.

Feeling like a new man, Jason was ravenous to experience the world as a non virgin and the garage kegger beckoned to him like a savory meal interrupted by a bathroom break. Ron sat by the keg and talked to Shelly Stewart who wore a jean skirt and a red blouse. Sitting cross-legged and chatting with her hands, Jason thought she looked cool and collegiate. Her acne was in full retreat as if in direct response to Ron. Ben Stone and Isabel stood nearby, holding beers and smoking Camels. Isabel wore a paisley sun dress that looked picked from a thrift store rack, with shiny riding boots. She'd cut the dyed ends from her hair and looked like a different person with a shorter hairdo. Ben seemed out of place with the high schoolers and looked like he wanted to be with the other pipeliners. Ross Early, Bruce Simpkins, and Sean Patt drunkenly shit talked in a far corner. Ross gave Jason a tiny salute, but stayed with his crew.

Isabel was in a foul mood and teased Jason. "You look like you hit the jackpot."

Jason blushed and Betsy answered for him. "Well, here you are again. You do realize this is my house?"

"Don't worry, we were about to leave." Isabel slid close to Ben, who looked away.

"Gotta smoke for me?" Betsy held out her hand.

Isabel laughed. "What?"

Betsy touched Isabel's dress. "I like your dress, especially with those boots."

"Yeah but they're stiff as rails. It's hard to break in boots, not riding anymore."

Betsy flashed groupie eyes at Isabel. "You ride horses?"

"Used to, lots." Isabel slid away from Ben and offered Betsy a smoke. Jason was glad to see Betsy making nice, maybe she wasn't only friends with dudes.

Krissy barged in from the house, flaring her elbows and clearing a path to the workbench radio. Gloomy Joey followed her, but she wasn't so gloomy tonight. She sidled up to the stubble-faced, floppy-eared biker, her purple lips flapping nonstop about something. The biker ignored her, hooked his thumbs into his front pockets and watched Jason and Betsy. When he came over to fill his beer, Betsy's eyes gazed at the floor and she fiddled with her long braid. He pointed at Ron, "You got that bottle?"

The biker snapped his fingers and Ron pulled the Damiana from his backpack. Jason noticed the import seal had already been broken. The biker tipped it back like water after a hot, dusty ride. He passed a noticeably less full bottle directly to Betsy, who took a swig and handed it to Jason.

Ron pursed his lips. "Jesus Christ, take it easy!"

Sweet, sugary fire burning down the hatch! Jason's throat seized and his nose tingled with vapors.

"Goddamn it! Let's fucking party." Krissy screamed from the workbench, worked into a frenzy by the Poison song "Talk Dirty to Me." She bounced around openmouthed, like a wrestler before a match, head thrashing and too-tight T-shirt lifting over her belly button. Betsy strutted over to Krissy, fingers snapping and shaking her butt around. These girls loved rock and roll, and Jason liked having that in common with them. The partygoers took notice and leered at the sisters, tapping their boots upon the oil-stained floor.

The biker also watched and looked like he was gonna have to kick some ass over this. Krissy and Betsy posed back to back, holding imagined microphones and screaming together, their voices high and pure in the way of frantic, concert-going girls.

The party erupted into wolf howls and laughter, while Ron muttered something sounding impolite under his breath.

The room swung around Jason's head. It was like his consciousness was out for a spin, doing donuts in a parking lot. He sat down and drank more beer. Betsy danced and then sat on his lap, then danced some more, and then was back on his lap. He had to pay attention or else his head spun. Pay attention to what? There was that awesome music Betsy had played in her room. He tried to remember it but it was gone. It was like how sometimes in his dreams he heard the most beautiful riffs, the kind that he imagined could never be replicated in the real world. If he could get his hands on Betsy's mixtape, he could borrow it and learn how to riff like they did in the dreamworld. Who in the hell were "they?" The room had stopped spinning, but his thoughts were in a total whirl. He was also ravenous and the perfect idea came to him: he'd have Doug deliver him some pizza, something he'd never done before. Then best buddy Doug could hang out too. He found Allen, guarding the door to the kitchen smiling.

"What's up *amigo*?" Allen gave him a fist bump.

"I need a phone. Gonna order a Meat Lovers' pizza."

"Mmm… pizza sounds good." Allen nodded toward the biker, who was filling up Betsy's cup from the keg. "You meet *mi hermano* yet?"

Of course Jason hadn't seen it coming but it made sense.

"Stewart's cool. Though I'll admit he ain't the most social guy. You got any brothers?"

Jason slowly held up a finger. "Robert's at Princeton. He's kinda weird."

Allen frowned and dog scratched his chin. "That's a shame. A brother's better than gold. Next chance you get, tell your bro that you got his back." He pounded his mallet fist against his heart. "Come here, *amigo*." He wrapped Jason in his serape for a tight hug and it was like an oak tree had reached out and grabbed him.

Releasing him, Allen pressed a cellophane wrapper filled with weed into his hand. "Ron said you guys wanted some. Enjoy."

Jason reached for the bills in his pocket but Allen laughed at him. "Dude, I ain't taking your mom's money. My treat."

"Thanks man." Jason stuffed it into his pockets and felt it alongside his rubbers.

Inside Donna's kitchen, Jason grabbed a wall phone and called Doug's pizza place. "Hi, I need Doug."

He waited, spinning again, and finally heard Doug's anxious voice come on the line, "This is Doug."

"Hey man I'm at Betsy's. I need you to bring over like four jumbo-sized Meat Lovers'."

"Is this Jason?"

Jason nodded.

"Hello? Jason? Are you drunk?"

"Yes."

"Well, I need an address."

Jason dropped the phone, fetched the *Soldier of Fortune* magazine and read the address to Doug. "I got forty bucks for some big Meat Lovers'." He cocked an imaginary pistol at the soldier on the cover and fired.

"Yeah buddy, be right over."

The pipeliners walked inside, led by a chuckling Ross. "We heard somebody ordered pizza." Ross wore his sweatshirt hood up and stuffed his hands into camo, cargo pants.

Jason greeted him like a long lost brother. "Shit, I figured you guys would've been camping."

"We're sick of camping," Bruce Simpkins informed. "We were hoping there'd be more girls here." He'd gel combed his hair and worn a button-down shirt.

Big Sean Patt walked over to the sink, floorboards creaking, and spat chaw juice down the drain.

Ben Stone stuck his head in the door. "Later guys. Isabel and I are clearing out."

But the pipeliners rudely left him hanging until he left.

Bruce looked concerned. "Too bad Isabel's in high school. I wouldn't be comfortable myself, breaching the age of consent."

"Whatever." Ross wiped beer from his face. "I'd go in whole hog for her. Most of them high school dudes look older'n me anyhow."

Stewart Heber stomped in and everyone shut up. Jason froze and looked at him.

"The fuck you staring at kid?"

Jason stammered, "Um, hey, I'm friends with Allen."

"That's why you're here? Thought you was here for something else." He walked away not waiting for a response.

Bruce was worried for Jason. "That didn't go well."

Jason was glad to be out of his skull drunk, didn't think he would've handled Stewart as well otherwise.

The party was down to the pipeliners (sans Ben), the Aarsdrager girls, the Heber brothers, Jason, and Joey. It seemed that Joey and Stewart had a thing going, where she cozied up to him only to be brushed off. Jason wondered why the hell anyone wanted Stewart around, the guy was a giant, scary dickhead, while he himself was the life of the party, cracking jokes and ordering pizzas. Ron and Shelly were missing and Ron's fishing analogy drunkenly popped into Jason's mind, with the ghastly image of her slurping up Ron's worm like a carp. Catching girls now seemed a foolish analogy for something so complicated; his fresh perspective on sex was that he'd been "caught" up in the act of it, as if something beyond just the two of them had an awareness of the experience. His thoughts whirled again and he needed food to stop it!

Doug rang the doorbell and Jason opened the door. "Welcome to the jungle! Come on in, I'll give you a tour." Everyone but Doug and Stewart laughed.

"I have to go close up." Doug looked overwhelmed.

"Come on," Jason whined. "We got the rock-and-roll sisters here, these girls are hot for Poison man."

Betsy danced over to Doug and wagged her butt at the pizza boxes. Doug swallowed and backed away, taking in the gun racks and the Heber brothers.

"I gotta go, Jason."

Allen got up, acting fatherly, pulling money from his fanny pack.

"I got it, I got it." Jason thrust forty bucks at Doug.

Doug started digging for change and Jason stopped him. "Keep it man, and stop acting so old."

Krissy ordered everyone around the table. "Anybody makes a mess gets a nut punch." After four slices of Meat Lovers', Jason put his face down on a paper plate and passed out. Allen carried him into Betsy's bedroom and put him in bed. "I'll get him a puke bucket from the garage. You keep an eye on him."

"Yup," Betsy said, going to work on Jason. "Gonna strip him down too."

* * *

Jason dreamt about the country club pool. He was on the high dive, the only one in town, and the water looked far away. Jumping off was easy, but diving was mental—nothing to it really, just lean forward and fall. He dove in and couldn't get back to the surface, kept swimming upwards, wanting for air. Sick of waiting, he opened his eyes to kill the dream and saw a bruiser in the doorway, someone tall and bushy-haired with big ears.

Betsy slept against him, soft, warm, and so smooth. Her presence kept his head from spinning. He sensed that leaving her side would be bad for the both of them.

"Said you were here for something else," Stewart said. "Now steer clear, boy."

"I'm not moving." Jason went to autopilot.

"Get up and get out."

"I can hardly look at you without puking."

"What the fuck?"

"I'm gonna puke Meat Lovers' everywhere if you don't go away."

Jason heard the bruiser's breathing go slow and heavy, but he turned and left without another word.

Chapter 15

Leah brewed her third pot of coffee at sunrise. Her view of the snowy Black Elks was like a classic landscape painting, a dramatic crest of shining pink summits below a purple sky. Instead of stately animals, the foreground contained orderly Helen Springs, where pickups and sedans slipped along straight courses beneath fading street lights. Jason was down there somewhere and she hoped he knew what he was doing. Being able to stay out all night was just a matter of pride to him. She remembered herself at seventeen, begging for more freedom, only to be home bored and tired at ten o'clock.

Curtis wandered into the kitchen, in a suit, ready for work at daybreak on a Sunday. "He didn't come home?"

Last night after Leah had filled him in on Jason's dramatic departure, they'd had equally dramatic sex. Curtis then rolled from her body and slept the entire night without moving, while she'd paced around entertaining dark thoughts and drinking coffee. Curtis looked ten years younger this morning; it wasn't fair to her that he got a pass from the worst night ever.

Leah flipped icily through the North Helen High School Directory on the counter. "I'm handling it."

"I'm sure you will, just don't..."

"Don't what, Curtis? Are you telling me what to do after I waited up all night so you could get some beauty rest? I'll handle it. Be assured of that but don't start pushing me," her voice tightened, "I'm not getting pushed around anymore. He pushes everybody around, thinks he's king of the jungle. No more, Curtis, no more king of the jungle!"

He came to her and she wept on his shoulder. She couldn't remember the last time she'd cried and they were both unprepared for it.

Curtis brushed a puff of wild hair from her ear and whispered into it. "I was only saying, try to get some rest today. You look horribly fatigued."

Leah sobbed. "Thanks."

"I'm sorry I have to leave, but the deputy director flew in last night with two generals."

Leah sniffed. "I'm sorry honey. Seeing him leave in that ridiculous car with those trashy-looking sisters, I don't know, it made me realize how little time we have left. He'll go away, probably not to college, and I get the sense he won't ever call. At least Robert calls me. I miss Robert." More weeping.

Curtis patted her back. "I'm sorry, I have to go. Keep your pager on so I can reach you."

Left alone with the directory, she dialed Ron's number. Surely Kate Devry would understand, maybe the boys were over there, asleep in front of the TV. She got the answering machine on the first ring. It wasn't even a real voice, but one of those spooky robots. She hung up and looked up Doug's number. Gary and Suzanne Stills were consummate do-gooders and calling them looking for her wayward son the morning after a big dance would be especially humiliating. She hated being on the flip side of parental desperation.

Gary picked up the phone.

"Hello Gary, it's Leah Krabb."

"Oh, Dr. Krabb." Gary sounded happy to hear from her. "Well, hello!"

"So, so sorry to bother you this early, but Jason didn't come home last night and I'm worried. I was hoping Doug might know something, is he around?"

"If he does then we'll get to the bottom of it."

After a minute Doug came on the line, "Hello Dr. Krabb. I understand you're looking for Jason."

He knew something. Leah heard it in his voice, clear as the day dawned.

"Yes Doug, I'm miserable over here." Leah knew he wouldn't lie for Jason. "Did you see him last night?"

"Yes. I saw him last night."

Leah felt bad, hearing him shrink over the phone. "You did?"

"He ordered pizza to a house on the south side."

"Do you remember the address?"

"I'm not sure…"

"Doug, if I come and get you, can you take me there? I need to find Jason."

She heard him breathing. "Doug?"

"Yes."

Leah poured too much sugar into her coffee and bombed down the grade from Stone Bluff, blaring NPR's *Weekend Edition*. The new administration threatened to limit China's trade status over human rights and analysts feared tension; then a piece about the proposed redevelopment of downtown L.A. A developer hoped to attract some major retailers that would sell Chinese-made goods.

Nobody back home voluntarily went downtown, the drug gangs were reportedly out of control these days. At least in Idaho she needn't worry about gangs. Jason could stay out all night defying her, but he wasn't in danger from one of those drive-by shootings her mother had been talking about. Her mother blamed everything on Mexico, "They have crack factories down in Tijuana, little children cooking huge vats of it, like a Chinese sweatshop for illegal drugs. That's NAFTA capitalism for you. We might have to move to Idaho, if Santa Monica has anymore problems. I won't go south of the 10 and forget about crossing the 405, it's Carjack City over there."

Leah thought her parents would blend in poorly in Idaho. Her dad had been an outspoken Democrat until Dukakis lost to Bush and ever since had refused to talk politics, though Leah knew he was dying to accuse the new president of being a closet Republican. Her mother had her groups: walking group, cards group, charity group, coffee group, salad group and book group, all with fifty-something Jewish women, something that Idaho had in short supply. The comparative lack of gossip in Helen Springs would likely do her in.

Pulling up to the Stills' house, Gary stood in the doorway waving at her. She examined the tiny bungalow that couldn't be more than a two-bedroom. It was on a weedy lot with a cracked driveway, and backed up to the train tracks. It was sad seeing such a blatant downgrade. She remembered their ranch north of town with a sprawling home at the end of a long drive and animals grazing behind orderly fences. What had happened? She'd assumed that Mormons were like the Jewish, and they banded together to bail out the less fortunate. To Leah, the point of religion was for it to be a safety net during life—hedging bets for the afterlife was secondary.

"Hello Gary. Again, I'm sorry to bother you." Leah swallowed hard. "This is so embarrassing."

Gary ushered Doug out the door. "Don't be silly. It's not a problem. He's had breakfast and is glad to help you."

Gary stepped outside and closed the front door. Poor Doug looked like the Sheriff had come to put him in jail. Leah half-smiled, half-frowned for him.

"Suzanne isn't feeling well this morning..." Gary paused as a freight train rocketed behind the house. He was barefoot, wore a robe over some sweats and his face had several days of stubble. "Now don't worry, I'm sure Jason is fine. Young boys are just forgetful."

Doug directed them south. He sat quietly with his hands on his knees, wearing a collared shirt and fresh jeans. Leah smelled toothpaste and cologne on him, effort had been made, and she sensed it had been forced upon him.

"Doug, what's with all this staying out all night?"

"I'm sorry."

"How well do you know this Betsy?" Leah turned off the stereo. The Lexus was superbly insulated and noise from the road was minimal.

"Uh, I don't really. I mean I've met her but she goes to South Helen."

"Uh-huh..." Leah waited.

"Well, I know she likes to dance." Doug frowned and twisted his hands together.

"Uh-huh..."

"I met her when we went camping. And I wasn't feeling well so I kept to myself most of the night."

"Oh? Why weren't you feeling well Doug?" Leah heard him squirm against the leather seat.

"Um, I..."

"Never mind. Probably one of those bugs going around. What else can you tell me about Betsy?"

"Oh jeepers, I don't know. Let me think."

Leah knew from the relief in his voice that he would reveal what he knew.

"Well, Betsy's like really athletic looking but I don't think she plays any sports." Doug let out a big breath. "She's bad news and so's her older sister Krissy, who dates this guy Allen, who got kicked out of North Helen. Jason thinks Allen's really cool, but he's bad news too."

Leah smiled. "You're being a good friend Doug. This sounds like a bad crowd for Jason."

"I'm taking you over to Betsy's house. When I delivered pizzas there last night, everyone was pretty messed up, especially Jason. I didn't see any parents, I don't think they're around. I was uncomfortable and couldn't get out of there fast enough. I'm honestly afraid for what you're going to find. Jason might be, um, sort of with Betsy."

Doug seemed to finally realize what was happening, where this was headed. "I feel horrible for doing this, but I'm worried about Jason. They say doing the right thing is always the hardest, so this feels about right."

"Doug, you're sweet. I'm sorry I had to involve you like this."

Pulling up in front of the Aarsdrager house, Leah took in every detail. The Impala, the old Ford crew cab, the trees, bushes, greening lawn, fresh paint job, the orderliness of everything. It was a tight little abode, just like Betsy was a tight little package. She'd expected something more like Doug's dilapidated rental. To Doug's great relief, she u-turned to take him home, no need to make the poor kid any more of an accomplice.

* * *

Jason opened his parched mouth and thought his tongue was swollen, possibly cracked. The sun blazed through the window and lit the baby blue wallpaper of Betsy's room. The floral pattern wouldn't stop jiggling, its tiny flowers pulsed at him and made him queasy. Betsy was snuggled against him in panties and a T-shirt, her toasty warm legs tangled softly among his. She shifted in her sleep, wiggling and stretching against him. It was amazing how her body seemed to float upon his skin. He'd never imagined cuddling would feel so good.

As last night's wild details flooded his memory, the room grew smaller and the jostling wallpaper flowers became discerning, godly eyes that laughed at him. These gods, acting on behalf of the world, had sent him on the mother of all flume rides, just to have him wake up in a tailspin. He caught a whiff of his own sour breath and even Betsy's sultry presence couldn't restrain the queasiness anymore. He sat up and his brain started swimming in his skull. Betsy rolled away from him, grumbling to sleep more. At least a week of sleep seemed to be in order for him, as soon as he drank some water, had a lengthy pee, and vomited. He threw off the covers to find a monolithic boner raging through the gap in his boxers and aching like a broken rib.

Someone pounded on the bedroom door. "Betsy! Wake up! You need to wake up right now!"

Krissy barged in, not the least self-conscious about wearing a T-shirt and panties. "You better get some clothes on boy!" She saw his boner and looked away, disgusted. "Betsy! Wake up and deal with this. Fucking *ain't* my problem."

She came and shook Betsy until she woke up. "Fuck off Krissy! Trying to sleep." Krissy dumped her sister on the floor and Betsy came up swinging, spittle dribbling from her lips. Krissy deflected some blows, took some, and then grabbed Betsy's hair, forcing her into a headlock. "Jason's mom is in the living room. You hear me? Don't think I'm not gonna kick both your asses for this later."

Krissy released her, dabbed at her swelling bottom lip and walked out, pulling her shirt down over her ass, as if suddenly uncomfortable to be in panties.

"Oh shit!" Betsy scrambled into clothes and tied her hair back.

Jason eyed the window. "*Run for your life,*" Allen's warning from last night popped into his head. This wasn't happening. No way she was really out there. She couldn't know where he was. He barely knew where he was. Anyway, he didn't want to find out, and saw that the window was open from last night. He got dressed and had one leg outside before Betsy stopped him. "What the hell are you doing?"

"I'm running."

"Hell no!" Betsy was aghast. "You can't run away from your mom. What, and leave me to face her alone?"

Jason just imagined what awaited him in the living room. Where was Ron? It was always better to have a friend along when in trouble.

Betsy shook her head, "We're in this shit together, for better or for worse."

Right. She was braver than he was—he had to stay with her. The gods' laughter roared down like thunder as he went to face his mother with Betsy.

Frowning and wearing yesterday's clothes, Leah stood pissed-off in the doorway, eyes narrowing at the sight of them. Stewart Heber sat shirtless in Aaron Aarsdrager's recliner, looking like he'd been involuntarily woken up. He flexed his muscles and seethed at Jason.

"You look like crap," Leah blurted, waving him toward her. "Let's go."

Jason didn't move. Nothing mattered anymore. Every pretense he could imagine taking in this situation went scattering across the universe.

"Betsy..." Leah's voice was eerily calm.

Having overheard her phone calls his whole life, Jason recognized the tone of her voice—like when she recommended a child should see a specialist.

"I want you to stay away from my son."

"You gonna take that shit Betsy?" Stewart sat up, looking entertained.

Betsy nodded and looked afraid.

Jason's knees shook with anger. "Don't talk to her like that! You don't even know her."

"Just shut up and get in the car. I'm too tired for this Jason."

"Fuck you mom! What are you even doing here? Have you been spying on me?"

His mom visibly withered, but there was nothing to be afraid of anymore. He was going to run away and become a pipeliner, run with the Heber clan, and marry an Aarsdrager girl. By next year, he'd be smiling from a new portrait on the wall.

"Jason, your mom's right. Obviously, I'm a horrible influence. I don't want you to fight here, just go."

Betsy wiped a tear from her cheek and stared sorrowfully at her feet, wiggling her toes into the carpet. Jason thought it was an act, but his mom sure squirmed back towards the door. Things would work out, he knew, had that winning the jackpot feeling again. Betsy was beyond awesome, always knowing what to do. They locked eyes and she seemed aware of her awesomeness to him. Dreamily barefoot on shag carpet in a faded T-shirt and torn jeans, Betsy's beauty astounded him. He wanted to see her in a dress, a skirt, even cargo shorts and a sports bra, it didn't matter. It only mattered that he saw her again.

Jason followed his mom out to her Lexus.

"*Sayonara*, punk!" Stewart slammed the door shut.

This should've stung more than it did, but Jason had turned to cold steel in that living room—a heavy plate of armor was essential for surviving in this world.

* * *

Leah didn't dare speak, in case she started crying again. The king of the jungle sulked in the front seat, pale green and fuming with alcoholic vapors, but he would certainly seize upon any emotional weakness. She second-guessed her decision to roust him, which hadn't gone smoothly like she'd hoped. It had seemed the obvious thing to do. As a physician, she was accustomed to nipping things in the bud before they got out of control—a good doctor never lets anything fester. But what kind of mother rips her son from his tender love nest? The way they'd come out together to face her, she knew right away that they were in love, but by then she couldn't just back away from her plan. What had she ever done to wind up in this ridiculous position?

At home, Jason went straight to the downstairs toilet and peed for a minute straight.

"Close the door. Where are your manners?" Leah scolded on autopilot, wasn't capable of anything else right now.

Jason chugged cold water directly from the kitchen faucet. A moment later, a horrified Leah watched him puke into her stainless sink.

"Oh please! Really? At least run the disposal."

"Oh shit…" Jason spat and wiped his face on a dish rag. "I'm going to bed."

Leah watched him sleep from the bedroom doorway, snoring and stinking like a frat house bathroom. She remembered the little boy everyone had loved, the squeaky-voiced Jason who smiled and carried his toys everywhere, acting silly and always treating her sweetly. She grabbed his clothes from the floor and took them into the laundry room, was going to wash away the smell of that house, like cheeseburgers and Lysol.

Despite spending hundreds of dollars on new jeans, Jason had worn an older pair that was too small and stained. Leah pulled the strip of condoms from the pocket and time went into slow motion. Especially alarming was the empty wrapper, and she tried not imagining what had become of its contents. Something else was in the pocket and she wanted Curtis home—right now—so she could have a time out. Her fingers dug in and found the pot. She'd gone to Berkeley in the sixties and had smoked weed a few times before medical school—though never with Curtis. From the citrus smell and by the look of it, she could tell this was high grade stuff.

* * *

Leah frantically called the lab and insisted Curtis come home and confront Jason. Leaving without bewildering or upsetting the bigwigs who'd jetted in to see him wasn't possible, he told her. He blew her off until that evening and came home to find Jason was still asleep. Curtis sat irate and red-faced through her briefing, arms tightly folded across his chest. Certainly this was serious, but not enough to pester him at work on such a momentous day.

"I'm a zombie," Leah said. "I need you to take over. I can't face him again."

"What am I supposed to do?" Curtis stared at the empty condom wrapper and the marijuana laid out on the kitchen island. He longed to be back at work, surrounded by the familiar pressures of need-to-know information and heavyweights breathing down his neck. Pot and condoms were such an about-face that he was totally thrown.

"Be his father. Explain the dangers of having sex and doing drugs."

"Isn't that obvious?" Curtis frowned. "What's the punishment?"

Leah shrugged. "I don't care. You're in charge of this mess. I'm going to bed."

He waited downstairs alone, thinking about the day at the lab. The generals had given him the third degree but seemed pleased, as did the contractor. The director hardly said a word all day. Curtis was a master at reading the director's body language and anymore it was like he could read his mind. The situation in the Sheepeater Desert was an all around murky situation. The only clear things about it were that Curtis's career was on the line and the contractor must be protected at all costs.

Previously, big brass had always arrived at the lab's airstrip on Energy Department or military aircraft. So Curtis found it unusual last night when two generals and the deputy director were flown in on an unmarked and exceedingly quiet jet owned by the contractor. His take-home message was that the contractor had big medicine and the natives better get in line. Jason stumbled into the kitchen, looking to raid the fridge and Curtis spooked him, "Jason, come and see this."

Seeing the contraband, Jason blanched.

Curtis held up the empty condom wrapper. "You didn't even bother hiding this stuff?"

"I was ambushed. Whatever. Now you know."

The blatant stupidity of it all—an empty condom wrapper!—really bothered Curtis. The world didn't reward carelessness. "Acting like you don't give a damn is a one-way ticket to nowhere. With that kind of attitude you'll never be entrusted with anything."

Jason shrugged.

"How long have you been taking this junk?" Curtis pointed at the pot like it was a dog turd on the counter.

"A few times."

"You could go to jail for it. Or go crazy. It's illegal for a good reason."

Jason still didn't seem to give a damn.

"Does this girl get your pot for you?"

"Shut up! Don't even talk about her."

Miss Betsy was clearly the way to shake him up. "What am I supposed to do about this? I have every law enforcement agency within a thousand miles on speed dial at the office."

"Leave her alone. She didn't do anything wrong. I got it from some homeless guy."

"We don't have any homeless people!"

"He was down at the truck stop, just passing through."

"Jason, it's obvious you're lying."

Curtis wanted to slap the indignant look from Jason's face and make him understand that nobody with a track record like this ever makes the cut. "You act like the king of the jungle, but you haven't earned it, buddy. Just wait until the real world gets hold of you."

"Whatever." Jason gestured at his present situation. "It's already got me by the balls."

Curtis sneered. "Oh yeah? Wait until you're swirling down the pipes with all the world's shitheads."

"That's fine if it gets me far away from your world." Jason sounded even more smug. "Why are you so demanding anyway? Is there something you're not telling me about the world? Some fake list I gotta make, or something?"

Anxiety crashed Curtis's nervous system, drying his mouth and speeding his heartbeat. He only wanted to help his son but clearly didn't know how. There was nothing he could say that wouldn't escalate things. All that confidence from a successful day swirled down a black hole of depression. He couldn't shake feeling doomed, like being involuntarily swept up by an evil force. Jason backed slowly away from him, as if he'd seen a ghost.

Chapter 16

A creaky dining room table served as headquarters for Mr. Chakrabarti's brisk tutoring enterprise. Hello Kitty coloring books, *TV Guides*, and food crumbs had been pushed aside so Mr. Chakrabarti could steer Jason through his final lesson of quadratic equations. The math tutor wore a stained polyester shirt and frequently rubbed his brown hands together. The nearby kitchen reeked strongly of curried tomatoes and fish sticks, that distinct Chakrabarti odor that Jason could smell way out at the curb.

The problems were difficult and Jason couldn't remember seeing anything like them before. He waited for Mr. Chakrabarti to work his magic.

"Umdokay, let's see about this one." Mr. Chakrabarti's pencil happily scratched across the paper. "We first put the equation into standard form. See? Then we find the roots."

Presto! The man made sense of problems simply by solving them and it was fascinating. After this nudging, Jason rooted out two more quadratics on his own and worked down the lesson page, solving the most convoluted problems at the bottom, the ones presented ass-backwards just to make them trickier. Mr. Chakrabarti laughed and dished out praise, "That's the ticket. Good for you!"

The accomplishment pleased Jason, but it also felt hollow not knowing exactly how he'd done the work or for what purpose. He thought about writing songs on his guitar, which he'd been doing a lot since getting placed on house arrest. It was intimidating thinking that someone had figured out quadratic equations all on their own, just sat down and came up with it. Who discovered this stuff and how did they do this? It didn't seem as groovy—or as easy—as writing songs. A song pleased the ear and lifted spirits, whereas math existed to demonstrate rules. It seemed that music, the kind he played, didn't have many rules but he thought rules, to some extent, might benefit his playing. Since the fateful morning at Betsy's, Jason had experienced a surge of creativity that was obviously fueled by heartbreak and embarrassment. He thought something similar must inspire math wizards, but imagining his brother Robert or Mr. Chakrabarti pouring out their souls and grooving through equations didn't seem to relate.

"Umdokay Jason. One last test tomorrow and you're free. Any summer plans?"

"Maybe California to see my grandparents. But everyone's so busy it probably won't happen. I want to get a job pipelining this summer, but I need to get my car back first."

Jason kicked back his chair and filled Mr. Chakrabarti in. "See I lost my car and then I got big-time grounded, just for seeing my girlfriend."

"Oh sure." Mr. Chakrabarti winked and smiled out the right side of his mouth, like he was happily confused.

"I think she's mad at me. I haven't talked to her in three weeks, not since my mom banished me from seeing her. It's killing me, you know? I need to know if there's something there or if I should just start being sad."

It felt good chatting with Mr. Chakrabarti about Betsy, as his socializing had been harshly limited. Though Leah had taken the phone from his room, he'd twice called the listed number for Aaron Aarsdrager from the library and nobody answered. He wanted to try again but didn't even know what to say.

"Whoa! You sure got some girlfriend trouble." Mr. Chakrabarti looked politely embarrassed and wiggled his oversized eyebrows.

"I never thought having a girlfriend would be this hard." Calling Betsy his girlfriend still made his stomach feel warm, even if it wasn't the case.

Mr. Chakrabarti chuckled. "Shucks Jason, I wish there was a formula for fixing things with your girlfriend. But acing this test might get you back on easier terms at home. We'll do a refresher tomorrow beforehand, just to be sure."

It was good to know that Mr. Chakrabarti had his back. The math tutor winked again and attempted to dry his sweaty forehead with a napkin as he walked Jason to the door.

The living room was over-cushioned and gray with a dominating portrait of the Mormon Jesus hanging over the couch: the son of God atop a summit, gazing over the Intermountain West like a superhero. There were nature paintings too, teeming with majestic species and mountains rising high above unruly rivers. The Aarsdragers' wild America decor came to mind and the smells of Betsy's house flogged his memory: stale cigarettes, hints of raspberry and meaty residues. He swelled with affection for all things Betsy.

Mr. Chakrabarti waved to Leah waiting in the Lexus and nearly skipped off the front porch to go chat with her.

Leah whirred down the passenger window, chewing and wiping chocolate from her face with a tissue. "Do you need a check?" She shouted to be heard over the blaring public radio.

"Gosh, no, Dr. Krabb!" Mr. Chakrabarti looked ashamed. "We're all taken care of there. Just wanted to say it's been a pleasure working with Jason. He's all set for tomorrow. And if you need any assistance come next year, well I'd sure be glad to help."

"Curtis still wants your job, but he doesn't have the magic touch."

"Well jeepers, it's not his fault." Mr. Chakrabarti waved his hands as if shooing away flies. "My son Frank won't have anything to do with me when it comes to math."

Frank was in Jason's class and would sometimes raid the fridge during lessons, glaring gnome-like at Jason before disappearing into his basement lair. Out of sympathy, Jason avoided him at school, thinking it must suck having random classmates pop into your home, seeing how you lived and smelling your smells.

"See now," Mr. Chakrabarti chuckled, "the universe has rules prohibiting fathers teaching their sons math."

Leah laughed.

Jason realized he wasn't likely to come back if he got on Allen's pipeline crew. He heartily shook Mr. Chakrabarti's greasy hand and looked him in the eye.

"Umdokay Jason." Mr. Chakrabarti patted him on the back. "Take it easy on your parents this summer." He winked at Leah in the car.

Inside the Lexus, his mom reverted to being severe, her new standard ever since that horrible morning at Betsy's. Jason refrained from switching the radio to Z-93 IDAHO ROCKS. Pulling away from the shaded curb, sunshine blasted the windows and it felt every bit like summer. Summer meant freedom, or it used to anyway. Jason daydreamed about swimming at the river flume on a hot day with Betsy, the two of them drying their bodies on a smooth slab of desert bedrock.

All Things Considered reported on a federal study estimating that marijuana had surpassed grapes and almonds as California's leading cash crop, with much of it distributed to nearby states.

Leah nearly punched off the stereo. "Do you have homework to do? Finals are coming and I haven't seen you do anything in ages but play guitar."

Jason dropped his ace card. "Remember? Doug's picking me up. We're going to jam over at Marty Bachmann's house. You already said I could go."

"Does his mother approve of this?"

"Why would she care? They built a music studio in their house."

Leah diverted course from Stone Bluff to Sunset Range, the Bachmann's more recently planned community and Jason shrugged. His story would check out. Jamming at Marty's was at least a start at freedom. Hopefully Betsy would wait for him and hadn't been giving Stewart hot earfuls of dirty talk. That guy was bad news. No wonder she didn't seem to have any friends—not with him creeping in the shadows.

Sunset Range was a sprawling complex of massive neocolonial homes with circular drives and transplanted greenery. The development on the town's northern fringes had formerly been rolling pastureland along the Black Elk River. It had a clubhouse, golf course, a pool, and a restaurant that everyone called "the grill."

In the Bachmann's driveway Leah warned him, "I'm coming back in two hours."

Marty opened the front door, greeting Jason with a laugh.

"What's so funny?"

Leah tapped the horn, waved and smiled at Marty.

"Nothing. How are you Jason?"

"I'm okay."

Marty considered Jason with his typical off-putting, brainy confidence. The boys had learned to hate each other in grade school, undergoing forced playtime while their moms lunched in a country club gazebo. Jason had tried to show off, fearlessly climbing the high dive for another plunge, while Marty heckled him from the shade, stealing all the attention.

Marty's basement studio was the real deal, equipped with a multi-track recorder, microphones, and a gleaming array of high-end instruments, it was like walking onto the set of a VH1 video and Jason giddily picked up a Gibson Les Paul. "I played one of these at Musicland."

"No you didn't." Marty snorted. "Musicland sells knockoffs. That's an original."

Jason guessed this meant expensive. The Bachmanns were noted wealthy people in Helen Springs. The family had been raising chickens in the heart of cattle country for decades. They owned swaths of poultry farms and had just built a monstrous nugget factory west of town.

Jason plugged into a stage amp and ran through a blues scale. Marty frowned and handed him an electric tuner.

Jason ignored the device. "I usually tune by ear."

Marty waved for the Les Paul, quickly tuned it and gave it back. He then grabbed a bass guitar and walked all over the blues scale that Jason had played, never repeating a riff twice. Jason jumped in and soloed for two minutes straight while Marty, acting bored, held the jam together with complex-looking bass chords.

"Okay. Okay." Marty stopped and studied Jason as if he were deciding something. "We gonna play twelve-bar blues all day?"

Jason had come over expecting the third degree. "Relax. I'm just warming up."

"I'm not looking to just jam." Marty shook his curly red hair. "This Z-93 Band Battle is legit. We need to play real songs. I've never heard you play a full song before."

"Dude, I know songs."

"No, you know parts of songs and only if they don't have more than three chords."

Marty set his bass down and picked his front teeth.

Being lazy and self-taught from cassette tapes obviously hadn't done Jason any good. But while Marty was fiercely competitive and played amazingly well, he didn't know things that Jason did. Jason had played hot coals, bedded an Aarsdrager, faced down a Heber, and spun out his consciousness while Marty had played it safe in his studio lair, practicing scales and memorizing chords. Striking a wayward course had to count for something, and it was time to finally get a leg up on Marty Bachmann.

In the midst of this silver-spooned standoff, Doug arrived, worried and wondering how Jason had gotten here.

"His mommy dropped him off," Marty snorted.

Not inclined to joke, Doug checked over the drum set like a pilot doing a pre-flight inspection. At Doug's insistence, they jammed another twelve-bar blues and Jason, not inclined to count, missed a few changes.

"Okay. Jesus." Marty stopped them. "It's a *twelve* bar blues."

"I play without counting." Of course Marty would use numbers.

"Christ. Shut up. Let me show you. It's basic theory. And another thing," Marty lectured, "you drift out of key when you riff. You need to learn more chords and know what scales they work with. Then you can mix chords and bars into your leads and it grounds them out."

Marty plugged in a Stratocaster and demonstrated clean chord bursts and staccato picking with his hands contorted across the frets. It looked difficult, sounded awesome, and made Jason want to pout.

"You're a one-man band." Jason flipped his hair. "You don't even need me."

Marty exchanged a somber look with Doug.

Doug spoke calmly, "Let's mix it up with something else. Jason, I know you've got something up your sleeve."

"I'm not feeling it anymore."

Doug slid into a sturdy eight beat and dressed it up with double bass kicks and tom-tom taps. Doug's improvement floored Jason—music was supposed to be his thing, not Doug's. Doug had trig and AP stardom. Jason wanted to drop his guitar and storm out of there. This whole band thing was like a kick to the nuts, but then a pipeliner certainly wouldn't stand around taking nut shots. Might as well strum a little of that new song he'd written, the one with the F6 and the Csus2, and see what happens.

What happened was the trio formed a circuit and a current rose up among them. Switching on a microphone, Jason was excited to sing his home-spun lyrics. The timing seemed right, having snuck up on him like Betsy had at the bonfire.

Singing 'bout our scene, those American liquid dreams
Long hair and sneakers, blues riffin' on the speakers
Moby Dick met Mary Jane and we were on our way
Gettin' messed up on the range

Marty scrambled to adjust the PA system, which legitimized the experiment for Jason. It was thrilling to be accompanied by a band. Like the high dive, singing was a huge rush, and he climbed up for another headfirst leap.

Isn't it grand when you can hardly stand?
Soaking it up till it feels just right
Keeping one on through the burning night
Drinking down your perfect potion
Whatever suits your best emotion

The verses weren't set in any hard order and so Jason signaled the changes with massive hair flips. Doug's steady *tick-tock-a-boom-boom* and Marty's bass rumble were perfect, like parts that had always been there deep in his mind's ear.

Singing in the choir at the shitkicker bonfire
Rock on Black Boots Woman, dancin' in my dreams
Breaking the rules and beating the fools ain't easy like it seems
What you do or don't you do
It's only up to me and you

Jason bellowed and screeched into the mic like it was an atmospheric teen line that could reach Betsy across town:

Shiver and shake
Like a lemon squeezing earthquake!
Ahhh-aaa-AA-AA-A LEMON SQUEEZING EARTHQUAKE!

Marty unplugged, set his bass down and gave Doug a less somber look. "Okay. Jesus. Was that last part the chorus? It had three bars and so did the first verse, then the middle ones all had five verses. Your voice sounded good though, really good."

Jason quivered and needed a cool-down. It was hard getting to know Marty again. Seemed like he had to get to know everybody all over again these days.

Doug sweated on his stool. "It's good Jason. I like it, it's cheesy."

Jason sneered. "What?" Even best buddy Doug was like somebody new, dealing with people was easier before they started growing up.

"I mean, we love cheese. Nine times out of ten I'd rather hear cheese than anything cool."

Marty spoke up. "It sounded like a love song."

"It's not a love song." Jason didn't like the sound of this either. "It's a drinking song!"

"MARTY?" Marty's mom boomed over the intercom, scaring the boys. "LEAH IS HERE FOR JASON."

Shit. He wanted to keep playing, this was loads more fun even than any high dive.

Chapter 17

Test time at the I.L.C. With enough whispering and discreet scribbling, Mr. Chakrabarti had Jason on track, solving and minimizing problems on his own. Algebra was like digestion, breaking stuff down until there was nothing useful left. Jason's final products glared at him from the paper like turds.

Other kids waited in line for Mr. Chakrabarti, but he shooed them aside when Jason walked up to hand in his very last test. The math tutor smiled from the corner of his mouth and waved Jason over to his side of the desk for an inside view of the grading process.

"Umdokay, let's see here. Good. Good." Mr. Chakrabarti pulled Jason down for a huddle conference and lowered his voice. "Here we forgot to cancel these guys out, which would leave us this." He corrected it with his own pencil. "See how that works?"

Jason nodded. Having other kids watch this process always embarrassed him and today he felt especially guilty for shirking.

"Congratulations Jason! That's it for algebra. Maybe we'll see you next year for trig?"

"Wouldn't count on it."

Mr. Chakrabarti walked Jason out into the hallway. "You know, Jason, this algebra stuff… Well it's like those brain teasers in the back of the newspaper. Good to give the brain a little exercise."

Jason realized that he'd soon be finished with his formal education and it wasn't half bad having a teacher get personal with him.

"Some teachers like putting their students on the spot, but trial by fire never made sense for me. Why start someone out by handicapping them? My guess is no one's ever going to put you on the spot for algebra." Mr. Chakrabarti shrugged. "Truth is everyone gets an A from me and I don't lose a wink of sleep over it. Don't tell your mom that. I just wanted you to know."

"Don't sweat it."

"Umdokay then." Mr. Chakrabarti shuffled in place and smiled. "Got a mess of tests to fix up before lunch. So long Jason."

The I.L.C. classrooms were on open tiers surrounding a large gymnasium and the block concrete structure amplified sound from every corner. Jason amused himself by hissing and grunting at the gym floor thirty feet down. It seemed dangerous letting high school kids run around next to thin air. Back in the day, Allen could have easily tossed a kid over the railing for no good reason. Allen and Krissy had met here. He pictured them in jean jackets, groping each other in a dark corner.

Hitting the downtown streets a free man before his mom picked him up, he walked in the sunshine past banks, stationary shops, clothiers, and delis. Save for the banks, everything looked empty and outdated. A summer wind swirled around the street corners and made him think about getting his car back. That was the dream: moonroof open, cheese on the tape deck, cruising over to Betsy's for another garage kegger.

The Black Elk Hotel was the oldest building in town. It was a hundred-year-old, six-story rectangle of red bricks with narrow, white windows. A farming corporation had renovated it in the 1980s, modernizing the rooms and converting the ornate rooftop garden into a handball court. The lobby retained its original wood paneling, golden lighting and a metal letterbox behind the front desk. The Sheepeater Steakhouse had also been spared and kept its white tile floor and cross-hatched columns from when it'd opened in 1893.

Jason walked through the lobby towards the restaurant, wondering if Krissy was waiting tables. A sign by the empty hostess stand advertised the nightly potato bar had more fixings than any place in Idaho. Krissy burst from the kitchen one-handedly carrying a plate-laden tray. Her black tights, black skirt, and swishing hair matched the lengthy window drapes and her white blouse looked one size too small on purpose, a family trait it seemed. Setting down steak sandwich platters, her arms popped through the sleeves and her resemblance to Betsy made his nuts itch.

Krissy saw him staring and marched over with cutthroat intent. His best defense was always his hair, which he flipped across his eyes like a shield.

"Mommy know you're here?"

"I don't care." Jason blew the hair from his face with a haughty breath. Never let a bully see you sweat.

Sighing, she tucked the tray under her arm and combed the hair from his eyes with fingers that smelled like a delicious, sizzling steak. Up close she was red-eyed and exhausted. Jason feared she might cry.

"Goddamn kid. I'm due for a smoke."

She led him through the kitchen where a grumpy, bearded man washed potatoes in a T-shirt and a skinny boy scrubbed pots with snot dripping from his nose. A portable radio was tuned to Z-93, playing Thin Lizzy.

Krissy faced down the teenaged dishwasher. "I'm going on break. Clean yourself up and get out there." He quickly removed his apron and wiped his nose with it.

In the back alley was a folding chair next to a SYSCO bucket full of water and cigarette butts. Krissy pulled off her shoes, rubbed her feet through her tights and stared at something far away. Jason stood clear of the smoke, his mom smelling smoke on him would make it hard to leverage his aced algebra test.

"Thought we'd scared you off for good."

"Huh?"

"We're bad news. Your mom's got sense."

"I'm not scared of anything. Well maybe Stewart, but that's different."

Krissy snapped back into the nearsighted world. "Stewart? You seen him?"

"Huh? No. Not since the party."

"Oh." She spaced out again.

"I tried calling, but no one answered."

"You ain't talked to Betsy? Better get on that. She's leaving for Nevada when school's out."

The bad news made his guts squirm like worms. It surprised him that Krissy wasn't up on things, had figured they talked about everything. He wanted to ask if Betsy had said anything about him, but this seemed a sappy move.

Krissy looked at him and sighed. "She took your cherry. Knew it when you showed up here like a lost puppy."

Jason nodded.

"I've known my share of north side boys, always angling for the you-know-what. That's why I've been a bitch to you, but I'm sorry you got yourself steamrolled. She's beautiful, ain't she? Gets prettier every day."

Jason nodded.

"She got the looks and I got the brains." Krissy laughed out smoke and heaved to catch her breath. "Then why are all my professors scared of me? It's not because I'm smart."

"Sounds like college isn't all its cracked up to be."

"You're sweet. She's a fool to leave you hanging."

She stood and hugged him in a needy fashion—just as Allen's big red Impala swung into the alley. Jason jerked away. Fuck! It was Friday afternoon and after a brutal week on the pipeline, here came Allen to find his girlfriend embracing him. Krissy wasn't fazed, stepping back into her shoes and lighting another smoke. Allen pulled up, lurched into park, and looked heavy at Jason, like he wanted to toss him headfirst into the alley wall.

"Remember this guy?" Krissy mussed Jason's hair until recognition swept across Allen's face. He killed the engine and leaned through the window for a fist bump. "*Mi hermano!*" He motioned Jason inside the car. "Grab a seat!"

A week's worth of body odor wafted from Allen's tattered serape and a joint smoldered in the ashtray. Krissy bent inside Allen's window and gave him a weak, needy kiss. He picked up the joint and offered it to her with a grease-grimed hand.

She shook her head. "You know what I want. Hear anything?"

"Nope." Allen frowned and shook his head.

Without hesitation Jason accepted the joint and pulled deeply. He coughed and coughed until it *was* good. Allen opened a zipper case of CDs and carefully inserted one into the disc slit. Blue and green dashes chased each other through a pattern on the digital readout.

"Sublime." Allen smiled with eyes like disc slits. "These guys are dope!"

They sat stoned in the alleyway while Allen vented about work. Jason loved hearing pipeliner gossip. Ben Stone was slacking off and had Allen in a bind.

"He's not in it for the money, more like he's trying to prove something. I'm like shit motherfucker, this here's a job, nothing more to it." Allen threw his hands up in confusion. "Hey babe, got any grub in that kitchen?"

Krissy left and Allen turned to Jason. "She don't look so hot *amigo. Es no bueno.*"

Jason thought he knew what was going on. "Devil's dandruff?"

Allen nodded and threw his hands up again. "Don't know what I'm gonna do about her."

Jason regretted doing cocaine at the party. He blamed it for his inability to have an orgasm. He wished First Lady Reagan had put *that* in her pamphlets. Would've steered clear of it for sure.

Krissy returned with a pan of hamburger patties. Allen fingered one out and chomped on it, his chin dribbling with grease. The smell of beef fat overwhelmed Jason and he gobbled down two patties.

Krissy shivered in the alley. "Your mom's coming for you?"

Jason nodded, should be more nervous than he felt. His cheeks tingled and his brain slinked down his spine. The music reminded him of summertime and going to the pool and sunshine blasting the world brighter than ever.

Krissy placed gum in his mouth. "Chew this."

He chewed. Warmth spread around his mouth, down his spine and raised the fuzz on his balls. His spine seemed fused to his nuts, like a stem to roots.

"Spit it out before you see her. Else she'll know something's up."

The moment seemed too final for Jason, couldn't imagine leaving and going on without any contact from them. "I'm going to call Betsy! Tell her I want to talk to her."

Krissy nodded with eyes far away. Allen lit a cigarette and bumped fists goodbye with Jason. The river flume came to mind, they could roll in the bubbles like stoned trout and it would carry them from reality. "You guys ever go fluming? The one over the Black Elk Gorge out past Stone Bluff?"

Allen mimicked swimming with his arms and looked sad. "*No gusto agua*. I can't swim worth a shit."

"You don't have to swim." Jason was excited. "It's like four feet deep and you slide across the flume moss."

On the pavement he assumed a sideways flume stance, arms poised like Zeus unleashing a thunderbolt. "See. And you go whoosh!"

This proved a saving move. Krissy broke into laughter and stopped looking like a zombie. This worked wonders for convincing Allen. "All right then. Getting wet doesn't sound so bad."

Thrilled to have hatched a plan, Jason walked back to the I.L.C. His feet had a mind of their own though, like they wanted to moonwalk or dance a jig—do anything but walk normally.

* * *

Managing Jason's house arrest had crimped Leah's schedule and forced her to use the hospital's staff pediatrician to cover some call shifts. This resulted in an astonishing amount of paperwork—would've been far easier just stashing him in the physician's lounge while she made rounds. After an hour of signing and dating (and too much sampling of the mail order chocolate in her bottom drawer) Leah walked over to the hospital to personally thank Dr. Mokri.

Dr. Mokri's third floor office had no antiques, sculptures, or artwork serving as distractions, and her degrees were framed in cheap aluminum. Leah thought medicine was far too stuffy and therefore remodeled her own office every two years. Nothing warded off burnout and fatigue like a properly refurbished office.

Afareen Mokri brushed off Leah's thank you and looked concerned. "I hope you weren't ill?" Her Farsi accent was heavy but understandable.

Leah half-frowned, half-smiled in the doorway. "No. We're having difficulties with Jason."

"I see. That's unfortunate." Afareen scooted up to her laminate desk and clasped her hands.

Leah hated feeling like a patient, but she didn't have anyone to talk to these days. Curtis worked all the time and had more or less absolved himself from parenting.

"I raised Robert on autopilot, and he's happy at Princeton. Maybe I'm too involved with Jason?"

"A simple handwashing can be very effective. It depends." Afareen's silken hair spilled over her white lab coat like an arctic oil spill. She tilted her head, wanting the dirt on Jason.

"Parenting Jason the last few months has been a string of concessions..." Leah laid out the sordid details of Jason's debauchery and felt like a failure, especially knowing what the Mokris had overcome in life. As the hospital board's pediatric advisor, Leah had interviewed Afareen years ago, fresh out of a UCLA residency and newly married to Arash, who was a neurologist in town. During the recruitment visit, over Bud Lights and white wines in Leah's Stone Bluff living room, the Mokris had discussed fleeing Iran during the Islamic Revolution. Afareen's son, Farhang, was Jason's age and was currently rewriting the book on overachieving at North Helen—the one Robert had written. Leah'd always had every advantage of a civilized democracy and yet here she was on her knees.

Afareen frowned. "This is a sad phenomenon, kids pretending to be adults and adults wishing to be kids. Has Robert settled on a major yet?"

Afareen was a sharp detective and Leah had plenty to confide.

"He's taken an interest in legal philosophy. Curtis is coming to terms with this."

Afareen raised her severe brown eyes and Leah decided to go off whole hog about Robert. "He's coming home this summer to work at Herman Smith's law firm. That's his Mormon girlfriend's father. Yes, Robert, who won back-to-back National Honor Society awards in math, chemistry, and physics and who had his pick of Ivy League universities is coming home to be a paralegal. We're thrilled. It will be nice to have him home."

"Thank you for considering me your friend Leah. I don't have many peers willing to be candid."

Leah understood. They were both outsiders here, professionally and otherwise, and outsiders banded together. "Time to wash my hands of what I can't control."

Turning over a new leaf was exciting. She was going hands-off with Jason and taking her life back—no more binging on coffee and chocolate for energy. The chocolate was a problem. She'd placed a small order and by the next week chocolatier's catalogues were piling up, all of which she'd ordered from. They were as bad as the drug pushers. Back at her office, she distributed her bottom drawer stash with the staff, after hiding a smidgen of extra dark in her purse. It was textbook addiction, she knew, but admitting it was the first step.

In the Lexus, Idaho Public Radio advertised next Sunday's "A Prairie Home Companion." Indeed her life would make quite the show, but the starring role had lost its appeal:

Leah's peaceful home on the range is gone. Her idyllic western hamlet isn't what it seemed to be, not with her son tramping around and doing drugs. He must confront these evils on his own and learn to swim above the trash that's sinking him. She tears up and wishes there were another way, but her shackling him only adds weight to his struggle while raising her risk factors. Early-onset diabetes, depression, and hypertension are the calling cards of stress. Her shattered ideals rain down like autoglass in Carjack City.

Basking on the front steps of the I.L.C., Jason didn't recognize her car at first. He climbed inside, humming a tune and smelling like a Burger King. Staying true to her new zen outlook, she didn't interrogate him. Symbolically, she switched the radio to Z-93, playing Nirvana's "Smells Like Teen Spirit."

"Whoa! Turn that off, like I can't hear music right now. I've got this song worked out in my head."

"How'd the test go?"

"Huh?"

"Algebra?"

"Yeah, I got an A. Seriously I can't talk right now. A melody is a fleeting thing. Ugh, see what you did? It's slipping away!"

"Jason listen to me."

"Shhh Mom…"

"No you shush. Look, you are officially ungrounded. So you can stop this silly act."

"Huh?"

"I said stop acting like you've been getting high in some back alley."

"Oh. Okay."

Chapter 18

Trying to follow Marty's advice had Jason stumped. Figuring out which chords worked in a given scale was painstakingly slow. It seemed that scales were intertwined with key and his concept of playing in key was mixing up chords from songs he knew. He needed a good glossary to spell it out for him.

In the piano bench he found a music theory book that had come with the grand piano, which nobody ever played. The book's glossary wasn't very helpful, but the index steered him to a diagram called "Chords In Key Formula." The "formula" word momentarily stunned his brain but he focused and saw it was just a pattern to follow, alternating major and minor chords through the seven degrees of an octave's twelve. There was an easier looking diagram for a scale formula. At this point it seemed necessary to learn some notes on his guitar. The book had a piano note chart so he sat down at the piano with his Catalina guitar and ear-matched keyboard notes to guitar notes. With notes as reference points, he could now follow the scale patterns on any given string. Jumping scales between strings was harder but seemed doable with some practice, which was how he occupied the waning days of his junior year.

His mother mostly left him alone, Doug and Marty were entrenched in AP finals and Ron spent all his time with Shelly, was even planning a Milwaukee rendezvous with her that summer. Calling Betsy hadn't worked out either, nobody ever answered the phone. What kind of family constantly ignored a ringing phone? She was gone and he was wrecked. So obvious was his heartbreak that Valerie Smith and Becca Black had stopped flirting with him and offered plenty of sisterly sympathy. They gave him pouty faces and back pats, but never played with his hair anymore. The raging boners of yore didn't seem as bad when compared to the emptiness of being ditched by the greatest love he'd ever know. After a few weeks of melancholy isolation with the guitar chord diagrams in his Zeppelin anthology and the theory book, he could play chord progressions in any scale he wanted. Strumming the chords of a scale was awesome, like using the grand staircase instead of the back stairs. Following rules actually sounded good for a change and this bugged him, but at least he'd gotten here by working backwards.

The melody he'd worked up waiting for his mom at the I.L.C. had turned into a shrine-to-getting-high song, though he'd mostly composed it while being cold sober and more focused than at any time in his short life. As such, "Mighty High," while being more than a tad sing-songy, benefited from his newly acquired music theory:

Did what I had to do
Wanted to do what I had to do
But when I had to
And I didn't want to
I got high, so high
Mighty high

Backup Vocals:
We come to play
Ever-y-day
Sunshine or Moon
Midnight or Noon
Gotta plan to fly
So mighty high

When I was done
With what I wanted to do
I didn't think
It'd matter to you
I got high, so high
Mighty high

Backup Vocals:
We come to play
Ever-y-day
Sunshine or Moon
Midnight or Noon
Gonna stay so mighty high

Now I'm done
With what I did
I'm getting high
So high
Mighty high

Backup Vocals:
We come to play
Ever-y-day
Sunshine or Moon
Midnight or Noon
Gotta plan to fly
So Mighty High

Hopefully Marty or Doug were keen on singing backup vocals, as they were integral to the song. Jason desperately wanted finals to be over so the band could get back to work. As for his final exams, he was all set to skim over the glossaries and roll the dice. Not that it mattered, since he wasn't planning on returning to North Helen for his senior year. It was zero hour for his music and by next year he'd be in Portland and Seattle, making the whole world rock out.

* * *

Finally, Betsy or Krissy answered the phone.

"Um, it's Jason. Betsy?"

"Yup."

Not what he'd expected. It was a mistake to call. "What are you doing?"

"What are *you* doing?"

"Playing guitar."

"That's right. You're gonna be a big deal."

"Trying anyways."

A curt voice echoed in the background. Who was that? Maybe a parent or maybe Stewart hanging out in her room?

"I saw your sister. And Allen."

"Yup."

She wasn't into him anymore. This was like Margo Mullen dumping him all over again. His tongue went dry. He knew nothing about girls, kept stumbling and making them mad.

"I'm sorry about my mom. I don't know why she did that."

"I do."

"Are you going to Nevada this summer?"

"I miss my horse."

"Wanna hang out this weekend?"

"Maybe."

"I wanna go to the flume. It's north of town, out past my house."

"I heard about it. You don't want to be alone with me?"

This stumped him. Was he supposed to ask her on a date or something? That seemed too cheesy for Betsy.

"I'm kidding Jason."

"Ha-ha."

"No way in hell I'm coming to your place. Because things are different now. I was all yours, but your mom fucked that up."

"So we're just friends?"

"Were we ever not just friends?"

Right, he was just another dude in a long line of buckaroos.

"Come over to my place Saturday morning. I want you looking sharp, for meeting my parents."

Stumped again.

"I'm kidding."

"Ha-ha."

"Kidding about you looking sharp."

Chapter 19

Friday morning's health class covered summertime heat safety. Summers around Helen Springs were no joke, despite being near the lofty Black Elks it was primetime desert down at four thousand feet where there was enough elevation for wicked sunburns while lacking the chilliness of higher terrain. Recent summers had seen some heat stroke deaths and Silly Bags seemed to have taken these personally. Jason read the heading on the overhead projector, "Staying Cool Out of School," which was followed by a diagram of sun rays blasting the mountains.

Coach scribbled lines curling down from the mountains to the valley and held up his hand. "Also working to dehydrate you is the wind. Around here, it dries you up head to toe and soon you've flaked off a pound of flesh and have scabs up your nose."

Always a sucker for health class humor, Valerie put her head down to chuckle. Her curly blond hair was pulled back into an enormous ponytail and she wore a sleeveless tank top with an almost-too-high pair of red shorts. Of course everyone had worn shorts for the last day of school and the weather was quite hot which made this final day feel all the more celebratory.

Coach continued, "Chapstick is okay but I prefer vaseline. On a hot summer day I'll smear some in my nose and over my lips, and lemme tell you it makes all the difference."

Becca, Ron and Valerie all snickered but Jason wasn't in a joking mood. With the world again in his favor, he wanted it running smoothly while he cemented his love with Betsy. Whatever problems the world faced, people like Silly Bags would be up at the crack of dawn solving them. Indeed, Saturday's forecast called for record heat and he envisioned Betsy in a swimsuit at the flume, basking on a slab of river rock with her long braid dripping down her back.

As with driving and sex, Silly Bags had a mantra for hydration, which was written on the projector sheet: "Drink a Lot when it's Hot and Never Fret when you Sweat!" Coach wore a poly-blended pair of thigh-clenching shorts that showcased his massive legs and Jason noticed they were unusually blond and hairy.

"The worst thing you can do on a hot day, besides not drinking water or not wearing sun protection, is to go swimming in an irrigation ditch. They're freezing cold, swift-flowing and impossible to exit. They're extremely deadly."

Last summer, a kid's drowning at the flume had made big news. But then another kid had drowned in the country club pool under a lifeguard's supervision. Water was dangerous, just like the world was full of puddle-strewn forks, hot coals, and devil's dandruff. Jason had never been afraid of the flume. It wasn't any more dangerous than the high dive but was way more awesome.

Valerie bumped him in the hallway after class. "Hey knucklehead, heat stroke is no joke!" Her giant doll eyes were flirty for a change and Jason was flummoxed. During his whole dreary house arrest, she'd ignored their minivan kiss and treated him like a stepped-on puppy. Now that he was back on track with Betsy, he got the George Michael treatment.

Becca flanked them and flashed Jason a flirty smile. "Heard you're gonna party at the flume. Can your new friends buy me beer? I want one of those MGD party balls."

"Who have you been talking to?"

Becca wore the highest shorts of anyone and her tanned legs pulled in student eyeballs like wayward planets. "I dunno. Also heard you're hooking up with a Mexican hottie."

Jason shrugged as Betsy's ethnicity was still up in the air. The Aarsdrager family portrait suggested that Aaron was from a long line of white people while Donna clearly wasn't. Complicating matters was that Jason had only been with Betsy while drunk and high. According to his memory, she'd looked bronze-skinned dancing around the shitkicker bonfire and then snow white dancing to Poison in her garage. Meeting her parents tomorrow might clarify things. But he wasn't looking to forward to this, in fact was dreading it.

In the oncoming chaos of classmates, Shelly Stewart swaggered by in running shorts and a ribbed tube top. Jason watched a flat strip of creamy stomach pulse above her waistline just as the lunchroom smell of loose-meat and pickles hit him. Maybe high school wasn't such a bad place; leaving North Helen forever was suddenly a stark reality. Of course this had crept up on him—just like everything else he hadn't seen coming.

Behind him, Ron greeted Shelly in his lowest voice. Jason spun around and saw them high-five like two dudes at a concert. Isabel came along, watching Ron and Shelly with disgust. She'd totally ignored the world's rules about wearing shorts on the last day of school and had on baggy jeans, a thrift-store men's shirt, and black velcro shoes. "It's like they're in on some joke together. Drives me nuts. Like I'm glad her skin's cleared up and she's got a boyfriend, just don't stick it in my face."

"You think Ron's her boyfriend?" Jason was still amazed that Ron had swooped in and snatched Shelly. Flirting with her at the Trail King before the bonfire seemed like only yesterday, strange how much things had changed.

Isabel twisted up her hair, which hadn't been dyed but still didn't look natural. "Totally. It's the creepy guy act. The right kind of creepy in a guy can be totally hot."

"You'd know. How's Ben?"

"He got fired from the pipeline. Moves around town in his camper, hiding from the repo man."

"Really?" Jason wasn't fond of Ben but disliked hearing about his downfall. Isabel would likely ditch him for a guy in a different role; that was her cycle.

"I'm still coming to the flume on Saturday."

"You're the one telling people? Did you call Betsy a Mexican?"

"Isn't she?"

"I don't know."

"Does it matter?"

"Um, I don't think so."

In the lunch line, Jason counted out two dollars and change, enough for a double lunch. Might even get a third loose-meat if he traded someone for his cookies. His mom had stopped getting him up in time for breakfast, just called his teen line from downstairs and said he had ten minutes to get ready for school. Her going hands-off was mostly good except for totally ignoring his food requests. Last night's unsatisfying dinner of chick pea lettuce-wraps had seemed to vaporize before making it to his stomach, much like the summer rain never reached the desert floor.

Sitting down alone, he nearly came undone tearing into his sandwich. Brown grease stained his fingers, which he'd sniff throughout the day in order to relish that beefy smell. Valerie and Becca sat one table over among some loud-mouthed boys in sports jerseys, high tops, and cargo shorts. Becca reigned supreme here, nibbling vending machine pretzels and casually ignoring the full court press of attention from her lunchroom boys. Jason was pleased to see Valerie happily joking and stealing fries from the jocks. It was a good thing that Betsy had intervened before Valerie got all mobbed up with him.

Ron, Shelly, and Isabel sat down with Jason. Ron had taken to carrying around a large sketchbook that he opened now, wowing Shelly with his colored pencil concert scenes. Dancing hippies jumped from the pages with distant eyes and gone-away smiles, this guy doing a barefoot stomp boogie and that girl fluidly twirling. Jason could see the full arc of their dances but most impressive were their detailed fanny packs and artisanal tie-dyes. The characters were all perfectly costumed, as if dressing like a hippie required some great effort.

Doug and Marty also joined the table which gave Jason a boost of power—it seemed everyone wanted a piece of him. He glanced at Becca as if to say he understood her powers and had them too, but her flinty look back conceded nothing.

Marty handed over his entire loose-meat sandwich to Jason. His attitude had changed since hearing Jason's drinking song and, with band practice on hold for finals, he liked to placate Jason with food. Unlike Leah, Marty understood that fatty foods were essential to Jason's happiness and he needed his new "frontman" in good spirits to record a demo tape for Z-93's Fourth of July Band Battle Blowout.

Doug worked on trig problems from the back appendixes, the extremely difficult ones that were harder than anything expected to be on the final. "I'm desensitizing myself."

In pointing out number four of the B appendix as a real doozy, Doug knocked Jason's milk carton off the table. Shelly one-handedly saved the milk, stunning everyone with her lightning-quick reflex. Jason realized she was more athletic than a whole table-full of jocks and he was proud to be surrounded by talented and smart people. It was sad leaving high school, now that his classmates were fully behind him and taking part in his very own lunchroom scene. As if reading his mind, Isabel pushed across her own uneaten loose meat.

A warm breeze blew in the open windows of Mr. Ebbett's seventh period literature class, carrying whiffs of motor oil and asphalt up from student parking, that sea of hand-me-down sedans and pickups baking in the sun. The breeze ruffled the tassels on Mr. Ebbett's western shirt and he looked tired, hopefully not in the mood for throwing anyone into the fire. Despite this, Jason purposefully honed his "takeaway" essay in order to rattle his teacher's cage.

Mr. Ebbett asked for a volunteer to read their semester takeaway essay aloud. Isabel selected herself, proudly stood and read her title: "New Femininity in the Age of New Malaise."

"You may read it sitting down, Miss Perkins."

"I'd prefer to stand, Mr. Ebbett!" Isabel's face reddened as she got down to business, "This essay will define modern femininity in this new age of golf-course misogyny and corporate crime waves. Since cave-dwelling times, women have..."

Mr. Ebbett waved and she stopped. "I'm unfamiliar with this 'femininity' term. Where did you come up with it?" He opened his dictionary. "I don't see it in here. Did you make it up?"

"Not!" Isabel looked disgusted. "I read authors who are actually alive today. Stories written by real live women instead of dead white guys who went to war."

Jason heard the twang rising in her voice and figured Mr. Ebbett had it coming to him.

Mr. Ebbett spread his chalky hands, "So what is femininity then?"

"Well I was defining it before you interrupted me."

"Did my interrupting define it for you? Ha!" Mr. Ebbett usually didn't joke around, especially not with Isabel. Something strange was up with him.

Isabel's thrift store men's shirt was similar to Mr. Ebbett's and ditto for her jeans and velcro sneakers. Jason had seen her wear many outfits over the years, but had never imagined her dressing like Mr. Ebbett. It was weird seeing her stand there, clothes matching her adversary.

"Yup, men don't care what women have to say." Isabel's twang sounded downright professorial. "Femininity means shuttin' up and sittin' pretty. Just give me a charge card and I'll shut up."

Mr. Ebbett slowly clapped. "Now, now, Miss Perkins. Lemme tell you something…" He seemed to forget what he was going to say.

"No, I'll tell you something." Isabel suddenly lost her twang, "How about including some women authors in your lit classes and I won't rat you out for being drunk in class today?"

The class murmured with surprise. Mr. Ebbett made no effort to deny it and didn't seem to care. "Well okay, but you'll have to recommend some. I'm not aware of any."

Isabel and Mr. Ebbett shared a good laugh which further shocked the class.

"Krabb!" Mr. Ebbett walked to the back row and grabbed Jason's essay. He read the title, "Something the Devil May Care For," and the smell of booze floated down with his breath.

Jason shrugged and flipped his hair while Mr. Ebbett read his short essay, "When the devil rears his head, I will play guitar. Something the devil may care for."

"Please, Mr. Krabb, the devil isn't lazy." Mr. Ebbett strolled back up front, taking his time in order to not sway. "What if he burns your guitar? Do you fight him or let evil have its day?"

Jason's little pun now seemed in poor taste since Mr. Ebbett had been outed for drinking in class. He struggled to explain himself. "Playing cool music will keep him from, you know, like starting wars and stuff."

Mr. Ebbett leaned back against the chalkboard, erasing old algebra problems with his shirt's back. "Sounds like one helluva gig, one that lasts an eternity."

It occurred to Jason that he didn't know much about the devil, it was just an expression he used. His parents never talked in terms of good and evil. "Well not all the time, just a song every now and then."

"I see, give him your soul one piece at a time. That's like mortgaging off your house, the bank's eventually going to own it and kick you out."

Jason didn't want to be on the spot anymore. "Umm, well those delta blues players went down to the crossroads and it really charged up their aesthetic."

"Now wait a minute, don't you mean *aesthetics*?"

"Umm, I mean, sometimes you need a different perspective. The best view is from the cliff's edge."

"Making deals with the devil..." Mr. Ebbett's eyes glazed over with sadness, "that's a helluva cost for a worldly perspective."

Jason felt pathetic and his thoughts turned to the world pulling his strings lately. Had something been angling for his soul? Other than having a good time, it still didn't seem like he'd done anything wrong. If he'd steered clear of Betsy, taken Valerie to the dance, and buckled down in school would his soul still be up for grabs? Souls seemed strange; did they float through the air like pipeline gas or something?

"Discipline," Mr. Ebbett said, "more than anything else, discipline saw me through the war."

With Mr. Ebbett back to his usual business of discussing war, the class relaxed and settled in for one last war metaphor before summer.

"But then I came home and it seemed my tour hadn't ended. I spent lots of time in the desert, by myself, just marching around and acting tough. It helped me a great deal and I fell in love with the desert."

This didn't sound like teaching anymore and Jason sensed that Mr. Ebbett, like himself, wouldn't be returning to North Helen next fall.

"I'm talking about the Sheepeater Desert. That's on other side of the Black Elk Mountains in the Great Basin where the rivers die in the dirt. Nothing out there but crumbling canyons, sagebrush, and elk, and of course the cattle are everywhere now. It's the most desolate and difficult place I know of, a true no-man's land. It's a place where an old man like me can never let his guard down. It requires constant vigilance and discipline, much like Vietnam, but without all the evil and suffering. Now I visit the Sheepeater every chance I get because, more than ever, I crave constant vigilance and discipline. Unfortunately for you, my dear students, those traits seem to be slipping away from me."

Massive, milky tears poured from Mr. Ebbett's eyes and it was like watching a zombie cry. Jason was riveted and wanted to hear more about the Sheepeater Desert, where he anxiously pictured himself laying pipe with Allen and keeping the lights on in Portland and Seattle.

"Anyway," Mr. Ebbett controlled his blubbering, "these days I depend on an ATV to get around the Sheepeater because my knees are putty. I got the fanciest one I could afford that's loaded with lovely gadgets like a bun-warmer for the seat and halogen spotlights. It's perfect for getting out where the elk live, though to be honest I haven't shot one in years. Just like watching them through my scope.

"I apologize for being mind-boggled today. While it's no excuse for my poor behavior, I might clarify the situation by adding that today's paper said the BLM has fast-tracked the Sheepeater Desert for federal wilderness protection, all hunting and vehicle traffic prohibited forever! Come fall, the only way for me to get where I want is to walk for fifty miles. Us old guys don't like change and, well, I'd just planned on growing old out there on my ATV."

Chapter 20

After school Jason watched his beloved peach Camry pull slowly to the curb with his brother Robert uneasily gripping the wheel, hands firmly at ten and two. Robert's return was a welcome surprise as Stone Bluff had been rather lonely with his mom going hands-off—it'd be nice to have someone around. Robert crept away from the curb in the now empty lot while triple checking over his shoulder. "I wish mom would let you drive. I haven't driven in nine months. It's terrifying."

Jason punched the radio to Z-93. "I won't tell if you won't."

Driving wasn't one of Robert's strengths—Mindy had driven him in high school. He jerked back to the curb and wiped his sweaty forehead. "Thank you."

Jason cruised while they listened to the Scorpions, Steve Miller, and Nirvana. What a gift on his last day of school. He couldn't imagine ever taking driving for granted again. He zig-zagged across the town's flush grid, taking all the time he could, hanging his arm out the window and enjoying the warm breeze.

Robert talked softly and seemed jet-lagged. "Dad's coming home for dinner. We should get some more onions from the store, since Mom and I are spearing veggie kabobs. I need a glass of water. It's so dry here."

Jason hoped to impress Robert by relating the news about the Sheepeater. "No more four wheelers and hunting. What's the big deal anyway? It's the middle of nowhere."

"That's what everyone's asking. It's a desert wasteland the size of Connecticut. Our congressmen won't take Herman's calls, which is unusual. He fears it has wide congressional support. It's likely part of some murky deal and we'll never know the details. It certainly made my first day at the firm seem disastrous. I read case law on federal energy leases all semester when I should've been reading up on wilderness protections."

"That sucks bro." Jason remembered Allen saying, "A brother's better than gold" and it felt good being chummy with Robert.

"We'll likely drop the case for now. Herman's other work is mainly agricultural partnerships. I'm not thrilled to be doing business law."

On State Street's industrial strip, Jason pulled into Grandpa Krabb's storage units. Robert acted like it was odd dropping in on Grandpa, but Jason was curious, having glimpsed Grandpa from the road, speeding on a tractor with a man riding in the front lift bucket. In the back lot was a skeletal forest of upright I-Beams bolted to smooth concrete slabs—the bones of Grandpa's new storage unit. The lot abutted the brushy bank of the Black Elk River, which ran gin-clear with dam-fed snowmelt. In the tractor's bucket rode an unkempt, barefoot blond man in nothing but coveralls, holding a steel rafter. Bill Krabb lifted him into position where he climbed onto the frame, slid the rafter into place and bolted it down. Grandpa Krabb was all business, driving fast and working the lift smoothly.

Robert was bemused. "That doesn't look safe. Do you think he sees us?"

"It looks fun. Bet that's Storage Unit Ted riding up there. Sure looks crazy, doesn't he?"

Jason got out of the car and waved. Grandpa Krabb killed the tractor, lowered the bucket and the man scurried down to the river. Grandpa climbed down and walked across the heat-blasted asphalt at a fast clip, annoyed until he recognized his grandsons.

Jason shook hands with his smiling grandfather. "That your guy Ted?"

Bill Krabb laughed and slapped Jason on the back. "He keeps fishing gear in that thicket, catches buckets of trout right here in town."

With the tractor off, Jason heard the river splash and gurgle below. It smelled like a fresh breeze of earthworms and flowers. The water was obscured by thick tamarisks and willow jungles, a hidden oasis for Storage Unit Ted.

Grandpa seemed to read his mind. "Doesn't like company though."

Jason nodded knowingly and thought about Mr. Ebbett ATV-ing about the Sheepeater. It was nice having a place to hide when the world lined up against you.

Robert exited the car, shielded his eyes, and squinted through the sun at his grandfather.

"That Robert back in town?" Grandpa Krabb startled Robert by shaking his hand too hard. "All dressed up for something?"

Robert smoothed his pleated slacks, explained his position at Herman Smith's firm and repeated the details of the Sheepeater deal.

"Is that right?" Grandpa Krabb didn't seem fazed by the big news of the Sheepeater Desert. "Let's go have some Sanka and get out of the sun."

In the front office he served Sanka in styrofoam cups. Robert sniffed his and set it on the desk as if it were tainted. Jason sucked his down and seared his mouth. Grandpa Krabb sat on a folding chair behind an empty desk and winked at Jason. "Robert, you're a college man now. Would you like a beer instead?"

Robert was intimidated and declined. Jason remembered that Robert had always been slightly afraid of their grandfather. Grandpa Krabb wore a snap-button shirt and dirty khakis with greasy channel lock pliers poking out of the front pocket. His forearms weren't that large, but they were tense and lined with muscles. Jason considered his grandfather and saw a buff old man who was spring-loaded with gumption, which was cool since most of the old men he encountered were frail and soft—even the old cowboys hanging out at McDonald's had nothing on Grandpa Krabb.

Grandpa Krabb asked about their educations. Robert was still an undeclared major at Princeton, but pointed out that this was common for freshman. Jason said he was skipping senior year to build pipelines.

This concerned Robert. "Do Mom and Dad know about this?"

Jason shrugged. "What're they gonna do? Pipeliners make thirty bucks an hour. I'm gonna buy a camper to live in."

Grandpa Krabb smiled. "Is that right?"

"Yeah, I'm hoping my friend Allen can get me on his crew."

"Good for you, Jason, a man with a plan. What are you, seventeen?"

"I'm eighteen in August. Mom held me back so I'd be the oldest kid in my grade."

"You'll put some hair on your chest."

"Um, yeah. You went to war at seventeen?"

Robert glared at Jason as if the war was a taboo subject not to be discussed. Jason shrugged and looked at him as if to say, well it happened didn't it?

Bill Krabb nodded. "My older brother was seventeen when he died fighting in the Solomon Islands. I wanted to go fight in the Pacific but I ended up in Europe on the other side of the world. Always thought that was kind of funny."

"You flew in bombers?" Robert wanted into the conversation now, even sipped his Sanka.

"That's right Robert. I was a ball turret gunner." He got up and left the room to rummage for something in a back room, confusing the boys.

Jason imagined a ball turret as a glass ball of death. Grandpa talking about the war was exciting and it hadn't happened before as far as anyone knew. Bill Krabb emerged from the back office holding a vintage, reel-to-reel tape player. He placed it on the desk and handed Jason a tape canister labeled "MOTHERLODE - BERKELEY, CALIF. 5-20-68."

"Consider this your graduation present." Grandpa Krabb chuckled. "Your uncle Stevie was the guitar man for this band. Don't ask me how I got this, but I thought you should have it."

"Wow, thanks!" Jason was thrilled. "It's like a bootleg?"

"It wasn't authorized by the band, if that's what you mean." Grandpa Krabb chucked his cup, coffee break was over. "Good to see you boys. Stop by anytime."

Robert treated the reel-to-reel player like an Egyptian artifact, making Jason wedge it carefully in the back seat between the seat rest and a coat. "Always keep the tape in its canister, a stray EMF could damage it. I'm already suspect of the emulsion, especially if it was recorded with sixties-era surveillance equipment."

The questionable origins of the tape made it all the more exciting to Jason. He hoped Uncle Stevie had played some badass, derelict hippie music.

At the Fred Meyer grocery, instrumental Little River Band played on ceiling speakers. Robert was nearly run into the deli case by the

Mormon mothers pushing overladen carts with their wholesome-looking, well-behaved children in tow. He was perplexed by all the children and seemed to be in culture shock. Jason, fluidly in step with the Mormon-belt supermarket scene, whistled along to "Lonesome Loser" and dashed in for a package of hot dogs like an old pro.

In the checkout aisle, Robert admitted he hadn't been shopping in nine months. "Princeton's such a bubble, it's actually been wonderful."

"If only Mindy was out there, then you'd be all set."

Robert frowned and Jason felt bad for him. "I like Mindy. You know Mom doesn't like the idea of you converting?"

"It's none of her business." Robert looked around and loosened his collar. "How often does she mention it?"

"I dunno. We don't speak much anymore."

Driving up the Stone Bluff grade, Robert suggested not mentioning the Motherlode tape. "Dad especially will make a big deal out of it."

"Huh?" Jason had planned to waltz up and stick it in his dad's face for no good reason other than to make him jealous.

"Things are tricky between Dad and Grandpa. Anyway I need to sort out the equipment before we can listen to it."

"What are you talking about? It's my tape!"

"Just trust me."

Well, it had just fallen into his lap, and Jason was growing wary of things coming easy. Might as well let Robert take charge, he was a Silly Bags type of guy who knew the best way of doing everything—typically the hardest way.

* * *

Hi-fi speakers rumbled out Idaho Public Radio and jingled the fridge contents. Leah switched on the sink disposal and Curtis watched the fridge lights dim. When upgrading the kitchen circuits two years prior, he hadn't foreseen an onslaught of load-pulling gizmos arriving by mail every week. The coffee maker gurgled, the rice-cooker steamed, and wait a minute, was that a new bread maker plugged into the island receptacle? Holding the fridge door open looking for a Bud Light also strained the circuitry, but all day he'd been focused on getting home, putting on sweats and having a cold one. In one week his job had gone from berserk to benign. The signals he got from the director, which came from the contractor, suggested Curtis could write his own ticket. For now, at least, he could focus on science. Today he'd assembled a team to install cutting edge optical sensors inside a test reactor. This contractor, the one who made the sensors, had promised stunning results that Curtis hoped would shed light on some confusing things.

Smiling at his own joke, he found a lonely Bud Light in the back of the fridge near Leah's month-old white wine. "Honey, have a drink with me?"

"I'm making coffee."

"I came home early."

"And you put on sweat clothes. Are you planning to exercise?"

"If you drink enough wine."

Sweats made a man horny, lots of breathing room down there and they were so easily stripped off—he could take her right there on the island counter like a rogue PE teacher.

Busy making dinner, Leah ignored him, but it was understood that she got the memo. Curtis drank his cold beer and read *USA Today*. CERN in Switzerland had released software allowing anyone to build a server to access the World Wide Web. Good for them, but what about particle physics? Must be pretty lax over there in Europe. Sounded like a bunch of longhairs, wearing sneakers at work and taking too many vacations.

The boys entered the kitchen with groceries, and Curtis honed in on Jason, stubble-faced and lean with blond hair down to his shoulders. He looked capable, as if someone had entrusted him with something. Curtis recognized the look of power. After all it was the universal body language in a top-down hierarchy like the Energy Department. More likely though, Jason was still a clueless, know-it-all teenager.

Robert washed veggies and Leah skewered them. Curtis drank his beer and bashed CERN, hoping to incite Robert into some kind of discussion, anything to get him to open up about this undeclared major business. "We've been on the Web for years now. Wanna know what the guys use it for?"

Robert turned off the sink to hear better.

"Fun and games." Curtis sneered. "They send out riddles and banter like kids, making little pictures with the symbol characters. I suppose it's a nice job perk."

Curtis never talked specifics about work but doing so had clearly piqued Robert's attention.

"What kind of riddles?"

"Number games, brain-teaser kinds of stuff."

In the dining room, Leah drizzled beet-juice remoulade over a platter of skewered cucumbers, onions and mushrooms. Curtis realized the only other fixings were a steamed artichoke, a small bowl of white rice and a questionable looking olive loaf from the new bread maker. He hadn't been home for dinner in ages and this is what she made? At least she'd poured herself wine and he'd fill up with another Bud Light after dinner.

The eating part of the meal was over quickly. The food was tasty enough but everyone was ravenous and there hadn't been much. The bread was too firm and only Jason ate it.

Curtis stretched back like a honcho and clasped his hands behind his head. "Robert, have you ever used a Web browser?"

Robert shook his head.

"I could give you a demonstration. If you wanted to drop by the lab."

Robert's smile reminded Curtis of Robert the younger boy, curious and enterprising beyond his years. "I will admit, Dad, I like the idea of using it for fun. I'd imagined it was only for nuclear physicists. You know, conspiring to blow up the world."

"Nah, it's just fun and games. It's not like I let the guys come in and tinker with the reactors after hours." Curtis laughed, but caught himself as if joking about such a thing might be a security breach.

Jason returned from the kitchen, complaining to Leah. "I swear I bought some hot dogs. Did you see them?"

"I put them in the freezer." Leah sounded righteous. "I can steam another artichoke."

"There are hot dogs?" Curtis was still hungry.

"They are frozen honey. And you don't need meat every night."

After dinner, the family gathered on the back patio. The landscaping bloomed and buzzed with bees and the comfortable outdoor furniture was clean, having spent the winter in the spacious basement. The Krabb family watched as the sun hit a river bend, casting a golden shimmer across Helen Springs. The Black Elk Range loomed above mammoth-like, the snow cornices of the high ridges had collapsed and looked ruddy in the sunset lighting.

Curtis had Jason fetch two Bud Lights from the garage fridge and offered one to Robert, who awkwardly cupped it from below. At twenty years old it was his first beer and it turned out he disliked it, "Think I'll stick to flat state liquids."

Leah prodded Robert about his college social life.

"I never leave campus. It has everything I need."

Jason blurted, "It doesn't have Mindy."

Leah asked what Princeton girls were like. Robert set his beer on the patio and acted like this was a stupid question. "They're smart."

"Come on, man, what it's like living in a dorm with a bunch of guys?" Jason picked up Robert's beer and took a drink. "Don't you have a roommate?"

"I have a suitemate and he's become a good friend. He even builds guitars."

"Really? That's cool. Can he play?"

"No, the funny part is he doesn't actually play. Just decided one night to turn his half of the room into a luthier's shop!"

"Maybe he can build me one." Jason got up and went inside.

This was the most Robert had ever talked about college. Curtis was irked it was Jason who'd finally got him talking, but then Curtis hadn't thought to ask about life outside of academics.

"This guy a humanities major or something?"

"No, Dad, he's undeclared."

"Should've guessed. What's the big idea with all this undeclared major funny business?"

"Not now Curtis," Leah chided. "They're just freshmen. What's his name?"

"Barnaby Brody." Robert made a sly grin and laughed. "The third."

Robert rarely laughed, let alone chuckled, and his parents noticed.

Leah snickered along with him, "That's quite the name. Does *he* have a girlfriend?"

"Several, I think." Robert frowned. "I'm not having a *college* girlfriend, Mom. I'm with Mindy."

Two beers on a stomach of cucumbers and mushrooms and Curtis was getting to the bottom of Mister Undeclared Major here. "What's your plan Robert? Another year of indecision will get you cut out of some programs."

Robert answered, "Relax dad. It's a different mindset these days. I do think the recent influx of powerful and affordable processor chips in the computer industry is a far more pertinent subject than my undeclared major."

"What's this?" Curtis didn't like seeming out of touch with things. "Do you mean software code engineering, or we talkin' bout hardware?" Hopefully that'd sounded knowingly.

Robert stood up and rolled his eyes at Leah. "I need to find some Chapstick."

Left alone on the patio, Curtis considered that he didn't know computers as well as he should. Modern circuitry had undergone transformations that took precious time to fully understand and anyways he got the gist of what was happening to the world. In fact he knew more than he wanted to!

Jason came out with a plate of hot dogs. "I thawed some hot dogs. You want one?"

Curtis drooled with pleasure. They ate and watched the town's lights sparkle upward into the quiet dusk. It seemed busier than normal down there, even for a Friday night. He thought about jokingly congratulating Jason on his I.L.C. algebra A but decided it was a moot point. "Pretty good hot dog, huh?"

"Duh. Hot dogs are never bad." Jason took a huge bite and finished Robert's beer.

* * *

Upstairs in the master bed, Curtis rolled over and kissed Leah. She said he smelled like hot dogs and feigned pushing him away, which only intensified his arousal. He kissed her again but she playfully twisted her lips away. If he couldn't be useful upstairs might as well go downstairs. He stripped off her panties and dove in tongue first. She yelped and struggled to remove her reading glasses. His dick grew harder and larger than ever, and it kept growing, it seemed, once it was inside of her. Sex had never been so thrilling and Curtis came for what seemed like a decade of seconds.

Sweaty and panting, Leah opened the picture window and cool air streamed in from the range, smelling of sage, juniper, and minerals. Curtis reflected how her body had changed since their Berkeley days and thought he liked it better now. She'd been a trim, Southern California blonde with a kitten-cute face and the tightest buns ever. Now she was stately and leonine, with a drooping ass and long tits that aroused him enough for another hump, though this time they did it silently and with much eye contact. In the cozy aftermath, they relaxed in bed and stared at the starlit snowfields up on the Black Elks.

Curtis mentioned Jason being a clueless know-it-all and Leah groaned, "I thought we'd moved beyond this?"

If that was true, well, then Curtis didn't know what to think about it.

Chapter 21

Jason woke up on Saturday morning with a bad case of nerves over meeting the Aarsdragers. He felt like a kennel-bound puppy that couldn't wait to scurry out the door. The day was warm and cloudless and promised to be perfect for the flume, which was going to be his own awesome party, if he made it past Aaron and Donna. Was he supposed to shake Aaron's hand and then bow to Donna or something? Already being on thin ice with Betsy, he couldn't afford messing this up and it sucked having no idea what was expected. There wasn't anyone to ask advice, at least not around this house.

His parents were shut inside their bedroom and he heard his father talking through the door. What was he still doing in the bedroom? Hadn't ever beaten that guy out of bed. Robert was awake and unpacking tube socks and Izods into his dresser. The CD player on his dresser was accompanied by his lone U2 *Joshua Tree* disc. Robert had never been one for music, but Jason remembered him tinkering at his desk in high school, playing this album on repeat with the volume hushed. The reel-to-reel was hidden in Robert's closet but Jason had a full plate today and wasn't in the mood to listen to it.

"I'm going to the flume today. Remember that place?"

Robert grimaced. "A kid drowned in the hydraulic jump there."

"I saw a girl's swimsuit ripped off in there." Jason had glimpsed her own flume moss and then gone back for another ride without a second thought. "She was in high school and I was in middle school. I'll never forget it."

Robert frowned at him.

Jason shrugged. "People drown in the country club pool too."

"I'm sure you'll be fine Jason. You were always king of the high dive."

Curtis emerged wearing Eddie Bauer slacks and a Tommy Bahama shirt, ready for a weekend office day, had even gone without socks in his loafers. He strutted into Robert's room acting like one of the guys. Seeing his dad so chipper and dressed in patio wear, Jason pounced on the opportunity. "Dad, can I have my car today? Some friends are going swimming at the river flume."

"No." Curtis turned to Robert, "Let's have some breakfast and get to work. I'm hungry as a hostage."

His father's disinterest in Jason's plans pinged a little. He used to be an important problem, but today not so much. Then his inner voice chimed in with reason, telling him to split and enjoy the sunny day with his hoped-for girlfriend.

His Trek bicycle exceeded the speed limit down the long grade to the interstate. The gas pumps at the Trail King were crowded with suburbans, station wagons, and pickups—people were headed out for summer, just like Betsy was urgently headed to Nevada. The tape racks beckoned to him but his business here was with the men's room condom machine, though its selection was as confusing as the smut counter's. Did a regular condom even exist? He bought two French ticklers and was pleased to not smell any fruitiness on them.

Headed south on State Street, Grandpa Krabb's storage units looked shiny and sleek among the body shops and fenced-in warehouses. He didn't see the tractor running and wondered what Storage Unit Ted was up to. Downtown was shady, cool, and empty and his squeaking pedals echoed around the quiet streets. Crossing the river into the south side of town, the sun blasted down and his cargo shorts grew swampy. At a convenience store, he swerved around a scrawny man in frayed jean shorts who crossed in front of him drinking milk directly from a carton. Every dog in the neighborhood saw him and rushed their fences, snarling. A stout black dog that resembled a wild boar scrambled over its chain link and gave chase. Its angry owner screamed after it and Jason pedaled for his life, spinning his tires and nearly crashing.

The pig-dog pulled back and Jason poured sweat, cursing the slippery roadway that was littered with wind-driven pebbles. It was more range than town down here. The road stretched ahead like a runway into the foot of the Black Elks. He fairly expected a tumbleweed to blow by. Not remembering exactly how to find the Aarsdragers, he took the first right and spent fifteen minutes searching the grid until he found Ferry Lane and stopped at the corner. He saw Betsy's big crew cab Ford poking out of her driveway. Sweat soaked his T-shirt and tube socks. Dehydrated and it was hardly noon—Silly Bags wouldn't approve. Valerie would find this funny and he considered there was still a chance to turn the corner and steer clear of Betsy. He imagined sticking around for senior year, wooing Valerie with George Michael songs on his guitar and trying to get into college. This made him sad though, poor Betsy didn't seem to have any friends, save for a horse and a strung-out sister. At the start of all this, he'd sought an "easy" girl and now Betsy was anything but easy.

Betsy answered the door in jean shorts and an extra snug tank top. She nodded at Jason and then averted her eyes, licking her brown lipstick. Striding barefoot across the living room shag, he noticed her lone braid's diminishing V pattern looked especially tight, as if a special effort had been taken. Jason was astonished by her and couldn't understand how he kept forgetting how beautiful she was. He zoned out and followed her into the kitchen as if she were a light at the end of a dark tunnel. He didn't dare glance elsewhere, fearing he might come face to face with Aaron Aarsdrager. Betsy stopped and stuffed her hands into her back pockets and Jason sensed a motherly presence.

Donna Aarsdrager was short like her girls and had long, flowing hair the color of worn-out asphalt. Her flat nose lacked the cute upwards hook of Betsy's and there was nothing sharp-edged about her, she was all curves. It was strange how curious he was about this woman and now, being under her appraisal, he realized she felt the same way about him. The two of them studied each other as Betsy introduced them. "Jason, this is Donatella."

"Hi Jason. Call me Donna."

Her syrupy voice relaxed him, and he thought she liked him. Bowing seemed inappropriate and he tried flipping the hair from his eyes but it was stuck with dried sweat.

"Jason rode his bike here from Stone Bluff." Betsy didn't sound impressed.

Donna made him an ice water, which he thanked her for and gratefully drank. The kitchen was free of dirty dishes and the counters were wiped clean. Donna seemed posted up there, with a newspaper tabloid and a coffee, as if some country cookin' might soon start. Betsy sat down at the table, crossed her muscled legs and said that Krissy and Allen were on a beer run for their flume outing. Jason squirmed, not wanting to discuss alcohol in front of her mom, but Donna was unfazed. Obviously things were different here.

"Are you hungry, Jason? Betsy's dad will be up soon and we'll have some lunch."

Jason politely thanked her and Donna started making lunch. She appeared stiff and took breaks to blatantly stretch in a way that suggested she'd just woken up. Her jeans were awfully tight for a mom and her black blouse dipped low to reveal a pink bra with red roses and freckled boobs that were much larger than Betsy's. He hadn't anticipated a peep show from Betsy's mother and couldn't stop from making comparisons.

"Jason plays guitar. He's gonna start a band in Portland *and* Seattle." It seemed Betsy enjoyed making him squirm today.

Donna dumped two dozen hot dogs into some boiling water and squeezed the juice from each bag. "Sounds like a real guitar man."

He liked being called a guitar man—unless she was being sarcastic.

Donna opened Tupperware containers of what looked like salsa and placed them on the table. Betsy explained, "Green's hot, red's not. You ever had real chile Jason?" She pronounced it chill-ay and said it was Donna's authentic family recipe.

"Is it like salsa?" It smelled citrusy to Jason and was thin as juice.

"No, hon, it's chile." Donna smiled thinly at him, just like Betsy had been doing.

"We eat it on everything," Betsy said. "My Nevada grandma makes green chile butter. It's awesome on pancakes. I can't wait to get back down there, this place is so boring."

Jason's heart punched his stomach. "I thought you said it was in the middle of nowhere?"

Betsy twisted her braid in her fingers and he noticed her painted nails were the same brown as her lipstick. "It is. But I got the run of the place. Wake up and have my pick of toys."

Jason thought she'd said "boys" and panicked. She was so awesome, there simply had to be others pining for her—even in the middle of nowhere.

"It's the perfect place for me. Trucks, ATVs, and my horse. My grandparents gave Molly to me for my *Quinceañera*."

Jason didn't know this word. Betsy said it with a flourish that sounded second nature, unlike when Allen used Spanish. It probably meant something like aesthetics, because everything was aesthetics or could be.

"Do you know what *Quinceañera* means?" Donna pronounced it even more wistfully than her daughter.

"Is it like beauty or something?"

Betsy blushed and Donna smiled not-so-thinly anymore. Must've been the right answer.

Donna plucked hot dogs from the pot with tongs. "A *Quinceañera* is a traditional event for young girls. In the old days it meant you were ready for marriage. Anymore, it's just a party, where my family comes from anyway."

"Oh," Jason said. "Is that like Mexico?"

Betsy laughed like he'd said something stupid.

"No," Donna said cooly, "we're from Nevada." She pronounced it Nay-vahda.

Entering from the garage, Allen came to hand-slap-fist-bump Jason. He wore man-sized cargo shorts, flip flops and his colorful serape. "What's up *amigo*?" His thick face and beefy arms were deeply tanned and his bushy brown hair was gold-tinged, likely from pipelining through the recent heat spell.

Something completely the opposite had happened to Krissy, who looked like she'd spent the past week in a coffin. Acne pocked her gray face and ribs poked through her tank top. She complained about Jason's sweat-pasted hair, "The hell happened to you?"

Betsy reached over and straightened his bangs, lifting his sunken heart. "He rode his bike here. Now get Daddy up for lunch."

The house suddenly felt very small and Jason desperately wanted to skip this part. Jason heard a man's throat clearing, heavy footsteps in the hallway, a sink running, and what sounded like muttered cursing. Donna set a platter of foil-wrapped hot dogs on the table and quietly said "*¡Pobrecito!*" to no one in particular.

Betsy kept messing with his hair, like she was purposefully trying to act smitten with him when Aaron Aarsdrager marched into the dining room. Jason had tunnel vision again and became horribly stuck on staring at Aaron. Their eyes locked for a split second in which Aaron seemed to size him up and paint a target on his forehead. Jason forlornly realized he didn't add up to much in Aaron's world. Shit. Why did Betsy's dad have to be like this and, furthermore, why was the world so full of hard-assed men?

Making a big show of his daughters, Aaron walked up to Krissy and rubbed her shoulders. "How we doing Sissy? Feeling any better?" She ignored him and sneered at the table. Donna again said "*¡Pobrecito!*" Betsy he called "baby girl" and Jason was forced to scoot his chair away to let the big man in to hug her. He smelled like mustache wax and mouthwash and his steely arms left no doubt in Jason's mind as to where Betsy'd acquired her unique build. Aaron's arms popped with veiny definition, as did his red neck, red face, and most likely everything else on him.

"Daddy, this is Jason." Betsy smirked like the whole charade was a setup.

"I can see that." Aaron spoke without looking at Jason, hitched up his blue jeans and sat down at the table's head. He looked at nothing and idly picked a greasy thumbnail, biceps bunching through a plaid, snap-button shirt, the kind they sold at the tractor supply store. Donna piled hot dogs on Jason's plate and asked him, "Red or green chile hon?"

"Green's hot, red's not," Betsy reminded him.

Not wanting to show weakness, he asked for green. Donna winked and spooned some off to the side of his hot dogs. It was soupy, full of white seeds and nearly glowed green. Allen and Aaron passed on the green and took the red. Jason rolled a hot dog into the green chile and learned that a little goes a long way. Sweating again, he drank water and melted ice cubes on his tongue for relief. Even his teeth burned from the spice. Betsy scooted closer and slipped a spoonful of red chile into his mouth, "This has lemon juice in it, helps to bring down the heat."

The red was briny, soothing, and delicious. He couldn't understand why anyone would make something too hot to eat, but then Donna and her girls lapped up green chile like it was truck stop gravy. Betsy tickled him with her toes under the table and he felt Aaron seething at him. The man had a freakish bearing with a plagued expression on his face as if much effort was required to simply hold up all those muscles. Even his gunslinger mustache seemed powerful, probably swatted flies with that thing. Jason daydreamed of a small bomb going off, one just big enough to distract everyone from his awkward presence as the new boyfriend.

Aaron talked shop with Allen and Jason paid close attention. Aaron worked at the propane plant but used to pipeline with Ferdig, Allen's foreman, and it sounded like they were still drinking buddies.

Allen talked with hot dog filled cheeks, "Ferdig says by this time next year, it's *sayonara* Idaho. They're moving us to Oregon for the next phase. I wanted to get on a drilling crew around here, but they're not gonna open up the Sheepeater Desert. Would've doubled my pay, but that's all fucked now."

"That Sheepeater Desert is a goddamned No Man's Land." Aaron raised a fence-post arm and wielded his fork above the table like a torch. Jason noticed his fingers gripped the fork with his thumb jagged and protruding. It looked like a hand that didn't work easily anymore.

Allen shrugged. "Everyone I know's shaking their head about it."

"No Man's Land!" Aaron quivered his mustache in anger. "Got the man keeping us from No Man's Land." He relaxed a touch and Jason picked up traces of his Aunt Judy's associate professor of something or other tone. "Yep," Aaron said, "I like the sound a that, would make a good bumper sticker."

It took Jason a few red-chile laden hot dogs to put out the fire in his mouth. He complimented Donna on the chile and then turned to Aaron, "Thank you, Mr. Aarsdrager, for having me."

Aaron kept not looking at him and Donna began clearing dishes. Jason went to help her, as if doing the dishes would make him up to snuff.

* * *

Jason scrubbed at the sink while Donna asked him questions. He got the sense that she was already on board with him. When he mentioned his family was from California, Donna said her ancestors were the "Californios" who'd settled northern Nevada. "They put the place on the map, wrangling horses and selling them to the army."

"Do you ride horses?"

"Every chance I get." Donna sounded heartbroken. "Krissy never cared for it. Aaron grew up cowboying, but now with his arthritis so bad," she quieted her voice and leaned close, "he can barely sling a wrench at the gas plant. He's lucky to be working at all."

"Betsy sure seems proud of her horse." Jason handed over dripping dishes and Donna dried them.

"Betsy loves to ride, considers it a family tradition. Does your family have any traditions?"

"Maybe working all the time. My mom likes force-feeding us health food."

He wondered if Donna knew about Leah barging into her house.

"That cabinet above the fridge," Donna smiled at him. "That's where I keep the snacks. Slimjims, candy bars, and chips. Take whatever you want, hon, whenever you get hungry. My girls don't eat enough, but I grew up with brothers and I know how boys eat."

Jason sensed that Donna had wanted a son, but he was thankful she didn't have one as Aaron supplied more than enough testosterone already. He imagined the bruiser that Aaron's male spawn would be, a high school hulk with a mustache and Popeye arms who loved nothing better than kicking preppy, north side ass.

Everyone took to the garage after lunch. As if retiring to some plush parlor, they sat in plastic chairs and smoked with the garage door open. Donna sipped a bottle of Busch and asked Jason about the flume.

"A boy drowned there last year?"

Aaron answered, "A rancher found the body tangled in a head-gate way out in the desert. It was a big deal in the paper."

"Jason knows what he's doing," Donna said. "Betsy said he was on the high school swim team."

"What swim team?" Aaron was confused.

"They had a swim team at North Helen hon. They drained that pool though, turned it into a weight room I heard. The girls haven't done much swimming Jason. Of course, we don't have any pools on this side of town. The north side's got the public pools, even though they already got their country club pool."

Krissy perked up to rib him, "Betcha Jason learned to swim there."

Denying or being embarrassed over his background was futile as these people were obviously aware of it. “Yeah I grew up swimming there. There’s an awesome high dive.”

“That’s rad.” Allen was impressed. “Always wanted to try one of those.”

“I’ll take you anytime. The country club’s been empty. Everyone goes to the new club out at Sunset Range.”

Aaron harrumphed at all this. He stood and slowly walked, bowlegged, out to pop the Ford’s hood. “All right, Mr. Country Club. Come start this truck for me.” He waved Jason over with his curled hand. Betsy was all smiles.

Hopping in the driver’s seat, Jason saw the angry steer on Aaron’s belt buckle glaring at him through the hood’s opening. He recalled driving a stick shift under the watchful gaze of Silly Bags and was grateful that, in this case, his favorite teacher hadn’t let him down. Pushing in the clutch took some effort and he wondered how Betsy managed it. The engine turned, Aaron listened for a second and then shouted to kill it. He went for a wrench on his pegboard, came back and tightened something while Jason watched through the crack in the hood. Aaron’s frozen-up hand gripped the tool like a monkey did a vine and his hand seemed to have been molded by wrenches. He slammed down the hood and pointed at Jason’s Trek leaning on the fence. “That your bike?”

Jason nodded and shrugged. Even though it wasn’t his prized Camry, he still took pride in his bike. Aaron’s mustache flickered, perhaps the beginning of a smile?

Allen loaded beer and ham sandwiches into an ice-filled cooler and fetched his fanny pack from the Impala docked at the curb. The girls emerged from the house carrying towels, a boom box, and cigarettes. Betsy wore black boots, cut-off wranglers, a red bikini top and dark oval shades that looked straight off a rack at the Trail King. She looked album-cover worthy and Jason gaped at her, astonished to have wound up with a girl like this. Krissy was barefoot, carried an open beer and wore only black bikini bottoms and a heat-stamped Tesla T-shirt.

Aaron called out from his chair, “Betsy, let Jason drive.”

Happy to hear this, Betsy patted the driver’s seat for him and then fused herself to his hip. Donna walked over and poked her head in Jason’s window, and he was sandwiched between them. Donna’s hair fell across his left arm, carrying kitchen fumes—that beefy lunchroom smell he liked—but also a mild, sultry body odor that was intoxicating.

"Jason, I'd hate for the summer to start on a sour note." Donna clenched her jaw. "You watch my girls for me, they haven't done much swimming."

Donna wasn't being nitpicky about the world's dangers, but she was clearly putting him in charge. "I got it. We'll be careful."

Jason started the truck, popped the brake and the big Ford rumbled down the driveway. It was gigantic and had a momentum unlike anything he'd ever driven. Back on State Street, he slipped an arm around Betsy but she coolly slid away and lit a smoke. She'd showered him with affection in front of her father, but now she was hard to get again, all because his mom had pissed her off. What strange game was this? Parents had never factored into his girlfriend fantasies.

Chapter 22

The upper Black Elk River Valley started north of the entrance to Stone Bluff, where Allen picked out the Krabb home high above them. The big Ford owned the two-lane up the wide valley. Ranchers and farmers nodded and finger-waved greetings to Jason as he barreled through the stunning oasis of sunshine, rich gumbo soil, and federally-subsidized water flowing in unlimited quantities from a larger than necessary reservoir. They passed the road to Grandpa Krabb's place and then came Doug Stills's former ranch. Jason noticed it was unchanged, the new owners must've found things to their liking.

The flume was only a couple miles up from Stone Bluff where the otherwise languid Black Elk River cut through a basalt gorge on its way to the Snake River, a hundred lonely miles to the north. Surrounding this gorge, the valley narrowed and the rocky range resumed its grasp on the land. There was little buildup to this change, the placid waterway weaving through bucolic pastures suddenly gave way to a frothing, narrow gash that cleaved into the earth.

Jason found the unmarked access road and followed it through rock outcroppings to the canyon's edge where a parking area had been cut into the cliff. The place was deserted and the goat path of a road leading upstream to the flume was barricaded with a tall chain link gate that was topped with coils of razor wire. A large sign read, "CLOSED TO PUBLIC USE. DANGEROUS WATERWORKS AHEAD."

Betsy exited the truck, looking unimpressed. "Looks like the man shut it down."

The sound of rushing water echoed everywhere and the sight upriver took Jason's breath away. Immediately upstream of the flume crossing, the river cascaded over a thirty-foot diversion dam, spitting out misty rainbows before flowing under the arch supports of the flume. The flume seemed higher above the river than Jason remembered, dripping, sagging, algae-stained, and humming with a deep unnerving tone. He examined the gate and smiled at Allen when he found a section of chain link that had been unwound enough to crawl under. "It doesn't say no trespassing anywhere."

"If you say so *amigo*."

The foursome worked up a sweat getting everything under the fence, down the path and up a steel ladder to where the flume emerged like a waterslide tube from a dark hole bored through the canyon wall. A narrow inspection walkway with rusty rails ran atop the flume's struts and made a convenient footbridge across the river gorge to where the flume plummeted over a ramp and vanished into the rocky horizon. Jason climbed up and stood on the walkway. He reached down for Allen to pass up the cooler and caught some vertigo from the water pulsing out the mountainside perpendicular to the churning river a hundred feet farther down.

Allen reached the walkway and gripped the rail with both hands. His bushy hair and serape were soaked with sweat. Jason hooted and extended his fist for a bump. Allen carefully obliged him. Krissy climbed just high enough to see the water rushing by in the flume. "No fucking way Jose."

"It's only four feet deep," Jason yelled down.

"And I'm five feet deep. Ain't much leeway." The flume had jolted Krissy from her trance. Her eyes came alive and her face flushed red.

Jason shrugged and walked across with the cooler in his arms. Cooling drafts came off the water, smelling of wet rock and moss. The water was going to feel great and yet everyone was all worried. Didn't they realize that kids in Wisconsin didn't get to do cool shit like this?

The ladder down the far side had come partially unbolted from the structure. Jason tested it and found it passable. When a wide-eyed Allen caught up, Jason pointed down to the solid-stone ledges above the flume's turbulent plunge into an irrigation canal. This inviting, pink-hued playground received mist and spray from the dam and a heartier fauna than otherwise possible thrived here: oak and chokecherry trees sprouted from the crags, while rusty-red Indian Paintbrush and wild white lilies grew in the tiniest of cracks.

"No way." Allen was clearly blown away. "It's like something outta the Flintstones."

With no sign of the girls, they passed down the cooler and stashed it in the shade. After a proper fist bumping, they stripped down to shorts and headed back to find the girls on the ground where they'd left them. With an encouraging, "This place is so rad!" from Allen, they were coaxed up and started over the flume with the remaining gear. Betsy quietly put one black boot in front of the other while Krissy cursed him the whole time, "Fucking great idea, Mr. Swim Team. Get us all killed here!"

The sisters shrieked upon seeing the rocky ledges. Krissy was most enthused, "Now we're talking."

Thrilled to see Krissy emerging from her fear, Allen embraced her and they made out loud enough to be heard over the falling water.

Seizing the moment, Jason surprise-kissed Betsy, their first time while sober. Her mouth was slippery-hot and traced with tobacco and green chile. She kissed back for a moment before stopping him with a moan, "Mmm. Stop showing off." But he sensed a breach in her coolness, like maybe she was embarrassed or flattered—anything besides pissed off about his mom.

They lowered the last of the gear and walked back across to take a ride. Jason lowered himself into the flume's stream by hanging from a strut where it exited the tunnel in the canyon wall. The current lifted his feet up and flapped them on the water's surface, creating a small wake. He threw his head back and watched the water's reflection twinkle and dance across the blasted surface of the tunnel's roof. The tunnel disappeared into the stark blackness of the earth and emitted a spooky mix of bubbling, burping and swishing that sometimes mimicked the cadence of speech. If he tried really hard and paid close attention, he might discern a word or two of this language, but where would that get him? It would be foolish to take meaning from such an ethereal source and he let go of the strut.

The cold water swept him away, seized his breathing, but then it was awesome. He stood up to skid over the slick carpet of flume moss and the vibration from this spongy resistance was as full-bodied and pleasant as anything he'd ever known. Allen shouted something excitedly in Spanish and Jason spun into a moonwalk which had been his signature move here, back in middle school. His Vans worked well for this maneuver. He knew they'd stink badly afterwards but didn't care.

Reaching up to grab another strut, his body again became an obstacle. The water frothed around his legs and tried to peel him away, but a quick pull up and a leg-hook had him back on the footbridge. Exiting the flume midstream like this seemed harder than when he'd been eighty-pounds and twelve-years-old. Also, it seemed the flume hadn't run as full back then.

Seeing Jason in action had charged up Allen. He dipped a toe in from the ladder and expressed shock.

Jason felt great, dripping dry on the warm footbridge. "Get it over with, man, it feels awesome!" Why was this such a hard sell?

Allen puffed a few big breaths and looked fearfully down at the water. It was off-putting, seeing tough guy Allen so afraid, and it occurred to Jason that his idol was totally out of his element. Allen awkwardly lowered himself from the strut and immediately fought the water. His upper body spasmed and bulged, revealing muscles that Jason hadn't known even existed on a person. With a defeated scream, Allen splashed down and Jason watched him thrash underwater. He surfaced in a full-blown panic, slapped the water, lost his footing and went down with a gasp.

Krissy was horrified to see Allen wash away, drowning. Just as she opened her mouth to lose her shit, the tunnel hissed loudly, silencing her and shaking Jason into action. He didn't understand a word of this ghostly whisper, just knew it was the most hideous thing he'd ever heard.

"Stay out of the water. Okay?" The sisters nodded and he jumped in.

Sidestroking like a frogman, Jason reached a floundering, sputtering Allen within a few seconds and tried to help him stand.

"Relax man, you got it." Jason spun backwards and faced him moonwalking. Allen grasped forearms with Jason and finally got to his feet.

"Don't let go Jason!" Allen laughed. "Holy shit this is rad!"

The two of them slid over the Black Elk River in this ridiculous fashion, as if locked in a doubles skate at a roller rink. Allen grew confident, let go and promptly fell, but Jason pulled him up. Nearing the plunge, Jason grew tense. It looked different from down here in the water and not the way he remembered it—what was up with things doing this? The water accelerated toward the brink and everything went quiet going over the edge. Jason couldn't believe how far down the pool looked and anxiously wondered if the chute had fallen apart, exposing rebar and other jaggedness that would shred him like pulled pork.

Shooting deep underwater through the rapid at the bottom was like melting into a new world. Jason's eyelids blasted open and water filled his sinuses through his eye sockets. He saw clearly down here and was spellbound by the countless tiny bubbles scattering the light into a Milky Way of prisms. Allen drifted past, aimlessly spinning in the turbulence and not fighting anymore. Jason hooked him by the armpit and kicked up toward the light. They surfaced near the wall of the cement canal but this was an eddy that sucked upstream into the rapid. Jason found a handhold in a crack and held them along the wall, fighting the current. Allen not struggling made him easier to handle but his eyes were waxy and cloudy, not at all the way they ordinarily looked. He couldn't believe how badly Allen was losing it—losing all of it.

The cement handhold was sharply broken and it shredded Jason's left hand. Blood stained the concrete, though he didn't feel any pain. Allen's head felt like holding a giant bowling ball in the crook of his shoulder, and another swirl might finish him. He remembered now that there'd always been a rope to exit the canal but where was it? He cursed himself for forgetting such a huge detail. What an idiot he was! It'd been so awesome having everyone lined up behind him but it turned out he wasn't up to snuff and didn't know things. Fucking hated not knowing things. He screamed at the world for being the world and pulled them farther up the wall, where his feet found a foothold. Allen gurgled and made a desperate attempt to cough, which further adrenalized Jason's upward surge. He knew from health class CPR that Allen's breathing was a good sign. Doing CPR wasn't possible here anyways, as every inch he raised Allen from the water only made him heavier to handle. Jason yanked and twisted but the only way to pull Allen upwards was by hooking his neck, which choked him.

No problem, he'd just hang tight until Allen got better. "Allen! I screwed up." At the sound of Jason's tired voice Allen blinked. "I spaced on the rope man, should've looked for it." The death fog half-lifted from Allen's eyes. "I need your help getting out of here." Allen gulped air and looked around as if regaining awareness was the scariest thing possible.

Then came the lifeline of Betsy up on the slab, lowering tied-together towels with Krissy hugging her legs as an anchor. Jason let go of his handhold to grab the towel and briefly lost Allen to the swirls before clenching a fistful of his hair and holding onto him. In a jolt of strength, Allen grabbed Jason's wrist and together they clung to the towel and clawed up the wall. Jason was astonished how firmly Betsy held the towels. Reaching the top, he saw that she'd smartly notched them into the crack, which held all the force.

"Oh shit baby, your eyes!" Krissy went crazy on Allen. "What's wrong with your eyes?"

Allen vomited flume water and coughed violently. He burped, heaved, rolled over and threw up again. Then he came up laughing like a crazy man.

* * *

Trying to make sense of what had just happened made Jason dizzy. He noticed delicate flowers growing in rock fissures around him and thought they provided a good explanation: survival was everything. But survival had a stomach-tightening somberness to it and he didn't care for it as a state of mind. He thought about poor Mr. Ebbett's eyes boiling with confusion while stuck on war tangents—it seemed that what he couldn't get over about the war was surviving it. Allen certainly wasn't hung up on the issue. He cracked a cold Busch and sat down with his fanny pack to roll a joint. While shocking, it was after all the natural thing for Allen to do and a sign to Jason that he was normal again. The world was confusing in clever ways like this, as if always forcing him to grasp knowledge out of thin air.

Walking perfectly plumb atop the flume came Shelly Stewart, who paused at the loose ladder and waved at them. Silhouetted by spray and sun beams she looked like Wonder Woman in a one-piece orange Speedo. Her legs flared with muscle and her breasts exploded from her chest like cannonballs. In contrast to her striking presence was Ron, cautiously following, clutching the rails and tentatively stepping forward. His outfit was a rainbow tie dye shirt and red swim trunks that looked to be from his middle school days. Seeing Ron in swim wear revealed that he was predominately made of flab and goatee.

The walkway filled up behind them with Isabel and the pipeliners, now down to three since having dropped Ben Stone. They passed down more supplies: six packs, towels, boom-box batteries, and several to-go bags of fried chicken from the Fred Meyer, which greatly improved Jason's mood—fried food always made the world less confusing. Having grown up on a ranch in the valley, Bruce Simpkins knew the flume and had made everyone stop at the family spread to grab life jackets from their speedboat. He sat down on a baking rock high above everyone else and put on a neon life vest, double checking each buckle and over tightening the straps. He cracked a beer and nodded with his typical concern, "Seen some close calls here."

"You got no idea bud," called out Krissy from Allen's lap. "It sucked Allen under till he came up fish-eyed!"

Shelly, Isabel, and Ron were alarmed as Krissy described the event, but the pipeliners listened passively as if it was just another story to be shared around a shitkicker bonfire.

Jason hoped Allen was really okay. "Maybe Allen should go and get his lungs checked or something. They could run some tests." He stared down at his soggy sneakers, ashamed for causing such a ruckus.

Ross Early chuckled at this. "Allen Heber's a goddamn Rambo. Bleeding guts out his asshole, a quick field dressing and it's back to work." The pipeliners laughed. "Anything to avoid doctors."

Allen didn't laugh. "No disrespect to your mom *amigo*. But doctors got so many gadgets anymore, you can't tell what they got in mind for you." He placed the joint in his mouth, lit it and watched the smoke rise into the misty air.

Betsy edged her warm body against Jason and massaged his neck. "You saved him Jason, your mom'd be proud. I'd tell her myself if she didn't hate my guts."

After a good hit, Allen blew up coughing. He doubled over, one hand clutching his chest and the other held up high, fingers wiggling as if signaling for help. Jason sprung back into rescue mode and approached him, but Allen pushed him away and spat a milky loogey onto the rocks. Jason thought it had a pink nucleus and hoped this was just the granite showing from beneath. Allen recovered and then gathered Jason in a brotherly embrace. "You still don't think I'm gonna survive? Well shit, *amigo*, you got to believe in living."

Jason took a small hit but didn't inhale. He didn't want to get high right now, a shame since getting high at the flume had been a primary goal of his summer.

Sean Patt was a poor swimmer and none of the life vests were big enough for him. Bruce instructed him to clip another jacket around his thighs to double up on flotation. Sean seemed appalled to have been talked into such a ridiculous idea. Wearing the vest like a diaper, his swim shorts bunched upwards and revealed his massive thighs white as marshmallows. After much laughing at his expense, he raised a middle finger to the group and headed off towards the ladder.

Remembering that he was in charge, Jason warned that the rope was missing. Betsy had it covered, "I got tow straps in my toolbox."

Back at the truck, Betsy pulled out the yellow tow straps she'd used to free his Camry from the puddle-strewn forks. She passed them down to Jason and casually mentioned her dislike of swimming, which she'd mainly done at the Black Elk Reservoir on family camping trips. "Daddy has a good spot when the lake is low. Backs down above this muddy little beach. I never liked putting my head under. I hate those creepy sounds you hear underwater, like something's coming for me."

Jason explained the voice-like echoes he'd heard coming from the flume tunnel. She smiled and shook her head. "Better ease up on Allen's weed there. It's too strong sometimes."

"Does he get that stuff from Stewart? Stewart's a drug dealer, isn't he?" Putting her on the spot about Stewart was risky and her squinting eyes confirmed it. She didn't answer but Jason was getting to the bottom of this. "Stewart reminds me of Allen when he was at North Helen, like he's gonna beat my ass for no good reason."

"Stewart ain't like that." Betsy answered right away. "He only kicks ass when he's got reason to."

She wasn't joking and there was an eery desperation in her eyes. The various ways that she'd appeared to him all flashed through his mind right then: dancing alluringly in the bonfire light, shining with hotness in his Stone Bluff kitchen, singing to Poison with top tier confidence, cursing and panting beneath him on her twin bed, professionally pouting through the whole episode with his mother. It was like his memory updated their entire relationship right there on the spot, standing on the gravel path to the flume. With all this new perspective to work with, it was obvious that discussing Stewart had robbed the moment of any magic and left her clenched-up and anxious. Not able to stand the sight of this, he pulled her in for a slow and sweaty kiss. She seemed unaccustomed to this level of tenderness which made it all the more special. They headed back to the flume holding hands, with Jason trying to figure out what had just happened.

Chapter 23

The pipeliners were huddled around Allen and having a deep discussion on the stone slab. Bruce broke rank, showed Jason how to hitch the tow straps together, and then asked his opinion about which tree to hang it from. Jason chose a sturdy oak above where the concrete had buckled into the canal like a wing to form a slack spot. Bruce seemed pleased and helped Jason tie off the strap with a bowline knot.

Ross offered Jason a cold can of Busch. "We're all gonna shotgun a beer together."

Betsy, Krissy, and the high schoolers watched but weren't included as the pipeliners circled around Jason with unopened beers. Sean Patt tipped his can over, punched a hole in it and passed his pocket knife around the group. When everyone held a pierced can, they opened the tabs together and sucked down cold beer through knife slits. Jason was by far the slowest and spilled most of it down his chest. Despite that, it seemed like he was up to snuff and he led his friends back over the flume like ducklings, though Ron and the Aarsdrager girls still wanted nothing to do with the flume and waited below.

Jason didn't think the flume was any more dangerous than before, not to him, and the final plunge into the canal went just fine without a lifejacket. Shelly also didn't wear a lifejacket but turned out to be a superb flumist and challenged Jason to a race down their second lap. He lead across, but she swam below him in the plunge pool and beat him to the straps. Krissy and Betsy were laid out on towels under a large shade tree where a rock ledge made a handy bench. The boom box sat nearby, playing Rush's "Freewill" on Z-93, and they'd made a spread of fried chicken and ham sandwiches on paper towels with bags of chips, creamy dips and a huge watermelon someone had carried in. Jason ate half a chicken, a bag of Funyons, and washed them down with several beers that he drank quickly before they warmed up.

Between the adrenaline, the frigid water and the gut-flipping encounter with Betsy back at the truck, the beers seemed to have little effect on him. Betsy finished a watermelon slice and said she wanted to flume, but only if he went with her. She peeled off her jean shorts and he gaped at her red bikini while securing the life vest. Where the harsh sunlight spotlighted Shelly's shoulder acne and Isabel's mole clusters, Betsy's skin was absolutely flawless in the brazen daylight. Her skin glowed like sunshine hitting pine sap and he couldn't recall it ever being so lustrous.

"Oh shit! Oh shit! It's cold!" Betsy rode his back across the flume, laughing and cursing. Taking the plunge, she constricted around him like a snake and he swam her over to the safety of the straps. She climbed up and wrung her wet braid out across Krissy, who said it was her turn to "ride Jason," which elicited a sneaky snicker from Ross.

Krissy was quiet on her flume ride and Jason thought she was scared. She wrapped herself around him and he became overly conscious of her body which was a touch larger than Betsy's. More so, it seemed Krissy was aware of him making comparisons and was pleased about it, like she'd also decided he was up to snuff. Approaching the plunge, she started to panic, "Jason! Fuck! I can't do it! I'm closing my eyes!" He guided them smoothly down the ramp but they separated in the turbulent pool. She came up sputtering and Jason pulled her to the straps where she climbed out like a fleeing spider, unaware of her twisted bikini bottoms. Everybody caught a glimpse of *her* flume moss.

Krissy climbed on top of Allen, who delighted in the cool soaking. "Hey there Sissy, wasn't planning on a peep show." She stood and pushed him onto his back, letting her hair drip on his chest while immodestly fixing her swimsuit bottoms. Allen removed her lifejacket and pulled her down for some loud kissing.

"They keep that up, I might need some privacy." Ross pointed up at the cliffs. "Ain't above rubbin' one out in a cave."

Ron muttered a lowly "Jesus Christ" under his breath. He'd been cowering in the shade all day, smoking Isabel's Camels and paying close attention to things. Jason offered him a Busch from the cooler. "Sweet place, huh?"

Ron did his little high laugh and drank without acknowledging the majesty of the flume. Jason had long bragged to him about how the flume was the coolest thing to do in the summer. But here they were with cold beer, girls, and ganja and Ron still wouldn't acknowledge that it was epic. Jason's role as Idaho tour guide was over. What else could compare to this?

Leaving for Wisconsin was all Ron could talk about. "Got tickets to see the Dead at Soldier Field. Chicago shows are the trippiest." Now he laughed like a diesel starting on a cold day and rehashed to Jason his network of privileged friends that were all supercool and mostly now in college and who would cart him around the finest midwestern concert venues. Jason had started to doubt that Wisconsin was the exotic rock-and-roll paradise that Ron claimed it was, but nonetheless he was glad for him. "Sounds like a great adventure."

Ron laughed high again as the pipeliners geared up for another round of shotgunned beers. "This what you got in store all summer?"

"I dunno. Betsy's going to Nevada to see her grandparents." Jason frowned and his intestines went into trapeze mode. "Maybe I'll hang out with Allen, if he's around. And try to get into the Z-93 Band Battle."

Ron nodded, "Allen's cool."

Shelly came and bugged Ron about not fluming, poking him in the shin with a wet, painted-red toe. "Are you going or what?" Water trickled down her Speedo-clad body as she stretched up to redo her ponytail. She had a "make way for the queen" attitude and Jason got the sense she was gloating.

"I don't know about that." Ron adjusted his glasses twice, tucked a sweaty glob of hair behind an ear and laughed right between high and low.

"How about a piggyback ride, like how Betsy went with Jason?" Shelly smiled at him.

Ron dismissed her with, "Fuck that."

Jason left them alone, pleased to not care what they had going on. He got that jackpot feeling again, seeing Betsy sitting cross-legged behind Isabel and braiding her hair. Through a cigarette parked in her lips, Betsy mumbled about her horse, "Running her on the playa is faster than rolling down the four-lane."

Jason studied the braid in Isabel's hair and thought it was an upside down version of Betsy's. The diamond pattern was still there but in a different format, and he couldn't distinguish exactly what was different. Perhaps it was just Isabel's strange hair color that brought out some complexity. Even in its natural state, her hair had suffered one too many chemical baths and now resembled crispy-fried egg whites.

Betsy finished and held up the braid for Jason to inspect, presenting it like a zookeeper would an exotic animal.

Jason was pleased to see the life had returned to Betsy's eyes. "It's very aesthetic."

"The hell's that mean?"

"Whatever you want it to," Isabel said.

Isabel told Jason she was going to visit Betsy in Nevada. "You should come with me. We can ride horses on that playa."

Betsy's reaction to this plan was to go pee behind a bush. Jason felt embarrassed; he'd only just met her parents and so visiting out-of-state grandparents seemed a big step. Isabel nodded mock sadly at Jason. "She took your cherry?"

He blushed, hadn't ever imagined being embarrassed about losing his virginity—especially not around Isabel.

The sun dipped and shade spread into the canyon. A joint came around and Jason inhaled. He coughed and his thoughts soared upward, tingling with wildly running thoughts of saving Allen. He didn't want to contemplate survival so directly, though, and his stomach knotted. He wished he wasn't king of the flume—couldn't handle his duties, and whatever they were he'd forgotten them.

Z-93 had strayed from classic rock to VH1 type stuff, which still seemed odd to Jason even though it'd been happening more and more. Tomorrow, he'd ride down to the Trail King and go whole hog on the tape rack, couldn't stand the thought of quality cheese evading him and getting lost in the past. The challenge of finding the perfect cheesy song was like trying to hammer down some grand perspective that kept popping into his head.

Allen made sure everyone had a fresh Busch and then set a single unopened can on a flat rock. Everyone circled around it like it was a bonfire. Krissy was loaded, humming and slowly spinning her head to a K.d. lang song.

Bruce Simpkins had known the kid who'd drowned here. "Guy

named Toby. Nice guy. His father owns a furniture store on State Street. Toby came here with his girlfriend and she watched him take the plunge with a big smile on his face. But he never popped up and she never saw him again. His body went through a hundred miles of canal before snagging."

Everyone went silent and Jason tried to imagine a hundred miles of canal.

"Poor guy," Allen said. "I know exactly how helpless he felt." He raised his hands to give a speech and thick muscles danced across his chest like waves in a waterbed. His thick hair had dried twisted and his eyes were wide as moons. "I gotta say, Ben's been on my mind all day."

Allen faced the high schoolers and described Ben Stone's being fired, "Two weeks ago they pressure-tested and found leaks on every section that Ben inspected. Ferdig told me to watch his ass and I caught him napping. Far as I could tell, his inspection duty consisted of sleeping in the truck."

The pipeliners looked sad. Jason couldn't tell if they were being sad for Ben or about him, though Isabel clearly looked sad for Ben.

"I started out maintaining active lines. Safety's a big deal to me." Allen picked up the Busch at the center of their circle. "We had an explosion one time. A guy named Joe burned up real quick and I had to, I had to…" Allen trailed off, confused. "um… had to use the fire extinguisher on his remains."

Everyone looked up to Allen like he was preaching from a pulpit. Jason saw Sean Patt's chaw-filled lip start to quiver. Bruce and Ross stared right through Allen with wet eyes.

Allen cracked open the lone Busch and poured it slowly out on the rocks.

Sean Patt, who'd never said a word, ruptured at this, snorting and blubbering uncontrollably. Ross and Bruce slapped him on the back and took deep breaths. Allen finished pouring out his beer and raised his own can to drink and everyone followed. Jason didn't quite know how to act, hadn't mourned anyone before, let alone strangers, and drinking for the dead stirred his blood.

Now Krissy crooned badly along to K.d. lang's "Constant Craving."

The pipeliners welcomed the distraction and poked fun at her.

"So what?" Krissy shot out, drunk and feisty. "Been likin' this one. They play it all the time now." She sang louder, and over the hiss and roar of falling water, boldly hit the right notes for the chorus.

Her voice stunned everyone, especially Isabel. "Wow, you were like jumping lines."

"The fuck's that mean?" Krissy didn't wait for an answer, just scowled and danced around in the poured out beer like a witch.

Allen dumped the rest of his beer out over Krissy's head and she didn't even seem to notice. "And that's for Toby. Long may he flume."

Isabel pointed out two red-tailed hawks, circling in the sunlight above the cliffs and said they were obviously Toby and Joe's spirit animals.

Allen drunkenly donned a lifejacket. "Gonna finish this off right." Then he threw a vest at Ron, who flinched but caught it. "Time to get baptized *amigo*."

Jason knew this was the stiffest peer pressure Ron had ever faced, even during his hedonistic, Wisconsin upbringing. He tried high-laughing it off, and when that didn't work he turned to Shelly, High Queen of Flumers, but she shook her head. Jason thought to step in on Ron's behalf but now it seemed he lacked the authority. Knowing things inevitably led to proving yourself up to snuff.

"Excuses don't mean shit around here," Allen told Ron. "And I bet you're full of them."

Ron said, "Fuck this shit!" To everyone's surprise he removed his glasses, stripped off his tie-dye and tried fastening the lifejacket around his pasty torso. "This one doesn't even fit me," he whined.

"I said no excuses!" Allen climbed the rickety ladder to the walk-way.

Jason offered to ride down with Ron, who snapped back, "Jesus Christ dude! Don't hold my hand."

The tunnel opening was in the shade now, looking darker and colder than Jason could ever recall. Allen hopped right in, shouting, "*Muchos frios amigos!*" He floated off on his back, not fighting the current and mostly in control.

Jason jumped in, swam down and grabbed a strut to wait for Ron, who cursed at Jason while jumping in.

The cold water cleared Jason's stoned head and he savored the ride, laughing and trying to calm Ron down. Ron kept his head high above the surge, trying to see what was coming for him through squinty eyes and then he shrieked like a stepped-on cat going down the plunge.

Down below, Shelly towed Allen across the pool by his vest. He floated lazily behind her, splashing and kicking the water like a toddler at bath time. Ron got stuck tumbling in the hydraulic. One moment he was there and the next he wasn't, as if caught between worlds. This went on for some time until he magically popped up near Jason and activated his country club skills, stroking quickly to the straps and scaling them in a flash.

The flumers packed up while continuing to party. Heading over the walkway, the setting sun hit the canyon rim and droplet-filled gusts from the diversion dam diffracted the orange light and flickered like wildfire. The flume beamed fat and golden in this light, especially when compared to the depleted Black Elk River, dribbling by in the stony darkness far below.

The pipeliners all passed out in their respective camper shells, save for Allen who stumbled up to Betsy's truck looking more faded than a rack of stonewashed jeans. Jason again felt ashamed for nearly drowning him earlier. "Sorry I got you into that mess."

"No sweat *amigo*, I knew what I was getting into. Probably why I jumped in. Kinda like things scary."

Feeling sorry for Allen seemed impossible, but that's how Jason felt—probably should've felt bad for him back in high school when he was throwing kids into walls.

Isabel wasn't up for driving home and headed to the Ford along with Ron and Shelly. Allen got in the backseat next to Ron. "Bring it in here for one *amigo*."

With everybody watching, Ron submitted to a massive hug from Allen. Jason knew first hand how stifling and powerful an Allen hug was. On an impulse Jason perfectly mocked Ron's low foghorn laugh, which made everybody laugh.

Still in her Speedo and full of energy, Shelly tried pushing Betsy from behind the wheel. "You're trashed, lemme drive."

Betsy glowered at her, pushed in the clutch and started the engine. But then she slid over with instructions, "Start in second. First gear's for creeping." She kicked off her boots and pulled her slender, tan feet under her butt and watched Shelly closely.

Shelly puffed her cheeks and pulled the heavy shifter into gear. She nodded excitedly as the one-ton truck lurched up the path, putting her hands at ten and two as if modeling for Silly Bags. Shelly didn't mess around and watching her operate all day had been eye-opening for Jason. He remembered liking that she was an athlete back in algebra, but only because it was something other than high school—not because he'd ever seen her in action. He admired her immense confidence and wondered how to accomplish something similar as a guitar man.

Suddenly he was wide awake and tuned in Z-93, expecting Little River Band or Nirvana but getting Led Zeppelin's "Ten Years Gone."

He listened as the world went right again. When the truck reached the pavement, Shelly shifted gears, turned up the song, and Robert Plant's crooning filled the truck: that a river's changed course always finds the ocean.

Chapter 24

Back at the Aarsdragers, Donna didn't want to talk about where Aaron was and Betsy frowned as if she'd seen this before. Donna sat in her recliner with a box of tissues, watching recorded soaps on the VCR player. The lamp table beside her overflowed with Busch bottles and a maxed-out ashtray. Even though he wanted to believe he'd made inroads with Aaron earlier, Jason didn't mind his absence in the least. Without being asked, Betsy cleaned up Donna's mess, more out of care it seemed than because she was embarrassed about it.

"Betsy, mix me a gin would ya?" Donna looked pleased to see the kids back and wanted to ramp up the party a notch.

Betsy fetched Donna's drink and then sat down with a moan in Aaron's chair. Allen laid down flat on the living room floor and went immediately to sleep. Jason suddenly felt like a stranger and wished they hadn't dropped Shelly, Isabel, and Ron at the Trail King. He sat by himself in the love seat and Betsy made no effort to join him, a shame as she looked sexier than ever, exhausted and sunburned in blue-jean bottoms and a red bikini top. He imagined that Ron and Shelly were cuddled up by now, watching VH1 in Shelly's dark basement.

Krissy had the portable phone to her ear, kept hanging up and redialing with no luck. All day at the flume, she'd seemed content, at least by her standards. Now she was lip biting, fidgeting and looking unwell, as if she might throw up on the shag carpet.

"Get off the phone." Betsy was angry. "It's bugging me."

"Want your fuckin' face punched in?" Krissy couldn't stop hanging up and redialing.

"I know who you're calling. Sick of this bullshit every time you need a snort."

The phone exploded against the wood paneling above Betsy,

narrowly missing the largest family portrait. Krissy shouted "Fuck!" and scrambled on her knees to put the phone back together. Allen snored and Donna put her head down, burying her eyes in a tissue.

Betsy led Jason to her room, shutting and locking the door. Her eyes were moist and narrow and her nose flared with every breath. She grabbed a smoke from the pack on her dresser, opened her window and smoked, staring at the twilight over the Black Elk Mountains. Jason tried rubbing her shoulders, but she tensed and he diverted himself to her tape rack. He looked unsuccessfully for the mix tape with the derelict '60s music she'd played while taking his virginity and settled instead for Cheap Trick. Studying her horse pictures, and now with some background on Molly the Mustang, he thought the animal was indeed a good-looking creature.

"This is a good picture. Is this Molly?" Jason showed her a picture of Molly, knee-deep in sagebrush with steep, craggy mountains in the background that reminded him of the strange picture in his Grandpa Krabb's basement office, the one that looked like an ad for something.

"Well she's a fine-looking animal." Jason spoke with his utmost gumption.

Betsy sadly agreed. "Pretty aesthetic huh?"

Jason laughed and sat down on her bed. She flicked her smoke out the window and sat with him. "I don't wanna do it with you tonight."

This was unexpected and it hurt. He hadn't even been thinking about sex, had genuinely been thinking about Molly the Mustang.

"You can sleep over if you want."

"Doesn't sound like you want me to?"

"Kind of. I mean, I do, but Stewart's probably coming over."

He wished this conversation was like a cassette tape, so he could rewind and record over that last bit. But this was real and it sucked worse than anything. "Is he your boyfriend or something?"

Betsy frowned and bit her lip. She looked old to him, and not college-girl old, but old like an adult facing serious business. The lovely features of her face, the softly upturned nose, piercing lips, and high cheek bones turned hostile. "I'm not talking about it."

"Whatever. That guy's a creep. He already told me to steer clear and I didn't."

She took his hand and squeezed it too hard, like she was scared.

"You should leave Jason. He told me he's gonna do something about you."

"When? Have you been seeing him this whole time?" Jason's mouth dried out and his jaw shook. He should've taken Valerie to the Spring Social back when he'd had the chance. Smooching and dry humping never floored a guy like this. But he'd made his choice back at the shitkicker bonfire and the world had been tossing him around like a hot coal.

Betsy wiped her eyes and shook her head. "I'm not talking about it."

"Okay. Goodbye. Say hi to Molly for me. Nice knowing you."

Betsy carelessly unraveled her artful braid and faced him with eyes like wet varnish. Jason knew a confession of sorts was coming.

"Yeah, I've seen him. The night after the party he came in here and pinned me down again. Like he's been doing since I was fourteen."

The braid was gone and her black hair formed a curtain for her to cry behind. She sobbed for awhile and then parted her hair to face him. He'd never seen her without the braid and she didn't look nearly as tough without it. "I never told anybody that before. But I thought you should know why he's gunning for you."

Betsy sighed like a forty-year-old. "Still want to spend the night?"

Jason waited to land before speaking. "Sure."

A switch closed and questions flowed through Jason's mind like current. What the hell was going on in this south side family? Did her parents know and not care? Did Allen know and not care? Everything Jason had imagined about the Aarsdrager family was uprooted and it was depressing. He wanted to believe that they were good people and couldn't stand thinking otherwise. Betsy was a good person, this he didn't question, and he was astonished she'd kept it together so well.

Betsy was always a step ahead of him. "I'm sure you got questions. It's not that bad. It's my own fault. I could've stopped it, if I wanted too. Pretty sure my mom knows everything, that's partly why we're going to my grandparents."

"I don't want you to go to Nevada."

She massaged his neck and it turned to butter. "I don't think we're coming back to Helen Springs. Things are going south with my parents. I'm gonna stay in Nevada with my mom, Jason."

Of course he wanted her to stay but realized Stewart would still be in the whole twisted picture. The guy was evil and he needed to take his devil's dandruff and movie star hair and get the hell out of the Aarsdrager family portrait.

A high-pitched engine raced down Ferry Lane and a motorcycle sputtered to a stop out front. Betsy jumped up and motioned Jason out the open window. "You gotta split. I'll call you later."

She was dead serious and very adult about this. Jason realized that she hadn't been allowed the chance to be a flighty teenager, having been forced into adulthood right here on her tiny twin bed. Jason studied the Black Elks towering into the night and remembered the strong sense of freedom he'd experienced on his way up to the shitkicker bonfire. Every bone in his body wanted to stay, and despite his great fear of an ass kicking, the last thing *he* wanted to do was leave. He'd already faced his mom with her, no point in turning coward now. "I'm not leaving you."

Betsy hugged him with relief and fear. He planned to deal Stewart a potent stream of bullshit followed by a disabling sucker move. That would be his only chance. Jason had never fought anyone before—let alone a Heber! Going to war was the scariest thing ever and he looked around the room, unsuccessfully, for a weapon to use.

This war took its time in starting, though, as Stewart, Krissy, and what sounded like Donna had their share of devil's dandruff. Jason couldn't stop trembling and was embarrassed to be doing it in Betsy's strong arms. "What about Allen? Think he'd talk to Stewart for me?"

"Wouldn't do you any good. Allen's an idiot."

Jason looked hurt and Betsy explained. "Look, Allen's a good guy but he won't push his brother around. I know for a fact that Stewart's the only guy to ever kick Allen's ass."

Jason again wished Betsy had an en suite toilet, this time for throwing up in. "Let's both leave, I'll sneak you into my house."

Betsy wasn't having it. "No way. I'm not running out on my family."

They passed the time holding each other and Jason zoned out with adrenaline, playing out various scenarios in his head. His favorite was Stewart collapsing from a bloody nose, like something from one of the Just Say No pamphlets.

The door knob twisted. "The fuck's this?" It jiggled harder and they waited glacier-like for Stewart to bust open the door.

Jason went over and opened the door on autopilot. Hands raised in surrender, he small-talked Stewart. "Hey man, what's up? Remember me, I'm Allen's little buddy? Anyways, um…"

"Steer clear." Stewart spoke through his teeth and flexed his neck muscles.

Jason noticed that Stewart was sharply dressed. His dark jeans were tapered unlike any Levi's found at the Desert Crossroads Mall, his purple shirt had ceramic buttons and dense fabric that shined in the hallway light. His helmet-tousled hair was thick and a lighter shade of brown than the plentiful stubble on his muscular jawline. Jason felt outclassed, not only could Stewart whoop his ass, but he was better looking and had a sort of primordial male attractiveness that Jason, at seventeen, doubted he would ever acquire.

Stewart flared his arms at Jason, making him jump. "I said steer clear."

Jason couldn't stand being intimidated anymore. "No dude, you steer clear!" A sliver of doubt flickered in Stewart's stone-age eyes. "She's a high school girl and you're coming to her room dressed for cruising the Sunset Strip."

Jason boldly rubbed Stewart's sleeve between his fingers. "You can't even buy threads like this in Helen Springs. You must do your shopping out of state, that's what all the snobby girls at my high school do. They make a big deal out of it, always talking about the best malls down in Salt Lake. I bet you know where all the good malls are."

Stewart stared at the sleeve where Jason had stroked it, taking giant horse breaths that shook the floorboards. Jason was in free fall, knowing he'd crossed a line by mentioning Stewart's duds—probably should've just called him a rapist and got punched out.

Stewart flashed a hand up and choked Jason. The immense pressure was so steady that he was obviously going to kill him. Betsy screamed and came to beat helplessly on Stewart's arm. There was no struggling out of Stewart's grip but Jason fought back anyways because, at that moment, survival was the strongest force in all the universe.

In a final surge of strength, Jason landed a sideways punch to Stewart's ribs and the iron grip released. Jason collapsed but couldn't suck any air in. He struggled and waited for a chance to breathe while darkness filled his vision.

Then god's voice boomed down the hallway, "Get outta my house scumbag!" It was Aaron Aarsdrager, twitching his King Kong arms at Stewart. "I ain't warning you again."

Stewart pulled up his shirt with a huff. "Chill out old man." He had a pistol tucked into his fancy pants.

"Go ahead and pull on me, won't do you any good." Aaron was confident, as if bullets didn't affect him.

Jason looked past Aaron at the gleaming gun cases, curious as to why he'd faced Stewart unarmed.

"Chill out then!" Stewart's voice went higher as he grew nervous. "I said chill out, okay?"

"I'm counting to three. One…" Aaron held up a curled, arthritic finger and sneered until Stewart walked down the hallway and scooted past him. "Two…"

"Jesus man, chill out!"

Seconds later, Stewart's motorcycle raced off down the street and Jason finally caught his breath.

Betsy followed her father into the kitchen and returned a minute later wiping tears from her eyes, but these were teenage tears and not adult ones. "I dunno what's going on Jason. You'd better leave."

"Okay." Jason wanted to go home anyways, had never missed Stone Bluff as badly.

"I'll call you from Nevada."

"Call my teen line, okay?"

She hugged him and he was afraid it meant too many things. It was a mixed-up war hug, full of love, friendship, and *sayonara.*

The bike ride home was surreal. The guard dogs on South State Street ran at their fences and whimpered at him. He didn't see a single person the whole way home and had no idea what time it was. The house was dark and Leah hadn't waited up for him. It seemed that having the ultimate hall pass was the loneliest thing ever.

Chapter 25

June was a hard month for Jason. He'd woken the day after the flume to a severely abraded left hand from clinging to the canal wall with Allen, along with a sore and contused neck from Stewart's choke hold. To Leah, he'd admitted to being in a "scuffle" but didn't elaborate. He told her to butt out of his business, which she'd done.

The boys had made a demo tape and gained acceptance into Z-93's Fourth of July Band Battle Blowout. Marty was even more demanding of Jason, despite his injured hand. That first week had been the most painful, with his hand crumpled up and oozing pus. But at least staying busy with the band had eased the heartbreak of Betsy not calling the teen line.

By month's end his hand had healed and his playing was more solid than before. His fingers felt newly trained as he rearranged his lead for "Black Boots Woman" for the umpteenth time. He practiced downstairs at the grand piano, plotting out riffs on the keys and transferring them to the guitar. This was difficult backwards work, but juxtaposing the two instruments provided him with valuable perspective and made it easy to work hard.

Robert stumbled through the front door, struggling with a large computer tower. Together they moved several more towers into Robert's room, which was uncharacteristically messy with monitors, cables, and complex-looking components of which Jason could only guess their purpose.

Robert explained the mess. "I upgraded the law firm to a network platform in exchange for all the old equipment."

On his desk, a computer tower sat gutted of its circuit boards. Each board was aligned with a piece of notepaper where Robert had drawn schematics with notes. One piece of paper that particularly appalled Jason contained only formulas. These weren't just any formulas, they were multistory behemoths subset with tiny numbers, fractions, and unidentifiable punctuations.

"I thought you were studying religion. Where'd you come up with this stuff?"

"It's just circuit theory. I need to tweak Herman's old equipment before I can run the new Web server software on it. A guy at dad's lab burned me his copy with modifications he made on the lab's time." Robert chuckled like he'd pulled one over on Curtis.

"What's software?" Jason had a vague idea of what that word meant.

Robert answered immediately, "Instructions for a computer to store and release information in a certain way."

Jason thought this was like how Betsy's full persona had been slowly revealed to him, with each bit of new information changing his behavior. Had he known the whole story from the get go, he might have steered clear up at the shitkicker bonfire. He nodded at Robert, "Yeah, perspective is everything."

Robert looked pleased with this answer. "Some circuits lead to more perspective and others hit a one-way diode." He chuckled again, "And wham! The electrons lose exactly half of their perspective! If you accept electron theory that is."

"I dunno about that stuff." Jason shrugged. "The more I know things, the more I see what I didn't know."

"Interesting Jason. Knowledge flowing through time like a feedback loop. I should write that down, my humanities professors would adore something so painfully analogous."

But Robert had that Aunt Judy tone again and lost interest in the conversation. He booted up an intact tower, went and turned on his sole *Joshua Tree* CD to a nearly undetectable volume and watched the monitor come to life. A screen displayed numbered lines of tricky equations with few words. Robert added to these, typing fluidly with one hand.

Jason peered over his shoulder. "Hey, that looks like a smiley face."

"It is." Robert smiled. "It's for Regnor. He lives in Norway and has solved every problem I've put on the Web. This is my math pun chat room, anyone on the Web can watch and participate, if they want."

"Whoa! How'd you connect the computer to Norway?"

Robert provided Jason with the least technical answer possible, "The teen line."

"This computer stuff ties up the teen line?" This was both good and bad.

"Yes."

"For how long?"

"About a month."

"Like all the time?"

Robert explained that the teen line was now a "dedicated modem circuit" and that he'd connected the phone jack in Jason's room to the main line, which Jason had been using without a clue.

"Switch it back Robert. Please! I can't believe this."

Robert frowned. "That's impossible right now."

Jason brainstormed the situation. He had to reach Betsy in Nevada, to apologize and explain that big brother Robert had commandeered the teen line for the purpose of math. It was also possible that she hadn't called, but he wouldn't know until he reached her.

"I'm sorry Jason. Is this about a girl?"

Jason nodded. It felt good admitting his love woes and he was glad to see Robert genuinely sorry. He remembered Allen telling him that a brother's better than gold. Strangely this wasn't true in Allen's case with Stewart, at least not from Jason's perspective, but it seemed like good advice, nonetheless. He missed everybody so bad; the whole crew had been lined up behind him and then they just dissolved for the summer, possibly forever. Allen hadn't contacted him after the incident with Stewart—not that Jason expected him to—and ditto for the other pipeliners. Meanwhile, Ron and Shelly were having a teenage honeymoon in Wisconsin and Isabel had taken to chain-smoking in a Trail King booth, reading women authors and flirting with dirtbags.

Robert fetched the reel-to-reel player from his closet. "Want to have a listen? It's quite good. First let me explain this equipment..."

Coming from a background of truck stop cassettes, the reel-to-reel seemed an ultra-fine machine and Jason was again thrilled with his graduation present. He paid close attention to Robert's thorough instructions for the care and handling of thirty-year-old surveillance equipment. The sounds of "MOTHERLODE - BERKELEY, CALIF. 5-20-68" came so clearly through the speakers that Jason nearly time-jumped back to the concert. It was like he could smell the pot and sweaty hooligans of the derelict sixties. The prelude was the sound of people milling around and it seemed the microphone had been on a person who roamed around the room. Voices came and went saying things like "brother-man" and "spooky" and the ubiquitous "far-out." There were male and female voices and they had funny American accents, as if the way in which they spoke was stirred up from that exact time and place and could never be replicated.

A man who was presumably on stage addressed the crowd in a deep voice, "Welcome earthlings!" The crowd cheered. "The Berkeley Consciousness Collaborative in association with President Lyndon Brother-Man Johnson," the crowd booed and laughed, "presents to you a far-out band straight outta No Man's Land. Ladies and gentleman, and even the FBI lurking tonight, put your hands together and let's hear it for MOTHERLODE!"

Fast drumming and bluesy keyboards filled the room and, much like the voices, the sound had a decidedly back-in-time ring to it. Uncle Stevie's electric guitar lead started slow and milky and with little distortion. Jason recognized the riff as that sound he'd been chasing lately, or maybe it was just a perspective. Whoever was singing had a lonesome, rambling voice and Jason hoped it was Stevie. He didn't think it sounded anything like his father's:

Feet, feet are kickin' down the door
Feet feet are taking us to war
Feet can bring you home from far away and long ago
Feet make you like a river, flowing, able to move
Water has feet, runs until the sea
People have feet and like to groove

* * *

The "Feet" song was by far the best of show. The rest of the concert was primarily an extended jam of blues tunes performed in the key of space. Robert made Jason a cassette copy which he took directly to band practice at Marty Bachmann's.

The boys listened to "Feet" on the hi-fi speakers and Jason strummed along on an unplugged Les Paul. He was amused that "Feet" was just a three chord deal and so easily figured out. Stevie's style, though, was harder to pin down, would need to work on that before the Fourth of July Band Battle.

"This is awesome!" Doug was impressed.

Marty seemed less impressed and Jason thought he was jealous over not having a derelict guitar man in his family. He quizzed Jason on the tape's origins and about what had happened to Stevie, which Jason didn't know. Other than not surviving, he and Robert hadn't been told what had happened to Stevie in Vietnam. Together they'd surmised that asking Curtis or Grandpa Krabb for details would be too uncomfortable.

"Well let's give it a whirl." Marty strapped on his gold-trimmed bass and played the "Feet" bass line perfectly from memory, even though he'd only just heard the song.

The boys played the song over and over and not because it required that kind of practice but because it was fun and sounded awesome. On the last go Jason and Marty were dancing around like sweaty hooligans and even Doug, their tick-tock steady Mormon metronome, nearly wobbled off his stool.

Afterwards, Jason tried to fist-bump-hand-slap Marty, but he didn't get it. "Relax Jason. Let's make some decisions. We only get three songs. If you want to play this, we'll have to drop something."

It was agreed that each of them would choose a song to play and Jason knew what was coming. Doug had conceded his vote to Jason so they could play his two originals, "Mighty High" and "Black Boots Woman." Marty wanted to cover something but hadn't chosen a song yet. They'd been rehearsing his favorite songs, primarily from Springsteen, Jethro Tull and John Lennon. These were fine songs but difficult to cover and they hadn't nailed any of them yet.

"There's this David Bowie song…" Marty picked up an acoustic guitar and sang "Oh! You Pretty Things."

Marty nailed the words, matched the guitar like a pro, and Jason and Doug were impressed. But it was also weird and they were unable to join in with any finesse. There were too many things wrong about Marty as a frontman, even though he was by far the best musician in the room. He was unassuming from head to toe and danced by twitching, but the most glaring element missing was simply that hard-to-pin-down thing that certain performers have. It occurred to Jason that whatever they played, he himself needed to be in the driver's seat. This was a humbling realization seeing as the concert was in five days and in front of a huge crowd. Gloating was the farthest thing from his mind.

Doug picked at a tiny mole on his cheek. "Yeah Marty, I think we should play Jason's songs and play this 'Feet' song as our cover."

Marty conceded. Jason felt guilty, the whole band thing had been Marty's idea from the start. Marty had shown him things and pushed him to play better. Marty had provided them with a full-on music studio and high-end instruments. Marty knew things about music but he couldn't flip his hair and swagger—the world just wasn't fair like that.

"I get it guys." Marty racked the guitar and once again donned his bass. "I don't think singing in front of a thousand people is ever going to be my thing."

A thousand people? Fuck! Jason hadn't anticipated having stage fright and it was worse than a punch in the nuts. How had he not seen *this* one coming?

"But Marty gets to pick our name." Doug was fair like that.

They'd tried naming themselves by matching random words from the dictionary, punning with their names and even inventing new words. Nothing stuck and Marty had labeled their demo submission as the Sunset Rangers just to have a name.

Marty liked this idea, "Then we're sticking with the Sunset Rangers."

This sounded soft to Jason. "You're naming us after your housing development?"

"MARTY?" Lindsay Bachmann interrupted on the intercom. "JASON'S MOM IS HERE TO PICK HIM UP."

Chapter 26

Leah drank fizzy water in Lindsay Bachmann's new kitchen and considered their flat golf course view. There wasn't much relief to Sunset Range, situated in the flat river valley. The Bachmann's home was the development's newest and reputedly had cost over a million dollars to build. Leah thought it was a shame to spend that kind of money for a view that could be had in anyplace, USA.

A stainless coffee machine sputtered on the counter and smelled heavenly, though Leah had declined a cup. "I'm down to two cups in the morning. Until the Coffee Bonanza opened up, I'd forgotten what good coffee tasted like. I went a little overboard." She hoped the smell would ease the withdrawal headaches she'd been having.

"Helen Springs is catching up." Lindsay leaned into her marble countertop, sipping an espresso blend. "I've reunited with wine, what with all these new labels at the supermarkets."

Short, with slowly graying, cropped hair, Lindsay seemed brassier than Leah remembered, must be all that chicken nugget money pouring in from the new plant. The Bachmanns had been in the food business ever since Lindsay's father, a Holocaust survivor, had moved to cattle country in order to raise chickens. Long in charge of marketing the family chickens, Lindsay loved describing her father as "plucky" and everyone in town just ate it up.

The two women were old friends who seldom talked anymore, mainly because life had gotten in the way and not because of any tension. Back in the day, Leah had carved out time for long country club lunches with Lindsay so Jason and Marty could swim together. Those were fondly remembered days, but she didn't miss the socializing all that much and preferred having a busy practice. They talked about the Fourth of July party at Diane and Dave Black's new pool. Dave

Black had built the Bachmann's new home but Lindsay said they wouldn't be attending, "Dave always mentions specific sums. I had no idea how rude he was regarding money when we hired him."

"I don't even own a swimsuit these days." Leah had wanted to skip the party, but Curtis surprised her by wanting to go. In fact, he was all jazzed up about it.

Jason's walking into the kitchen was a major distraction for Lindsay. "There's Mr. Rock Star. We're so excited for the boys."

Leah didn't know what this meant but played along so as not to appear uninformed about her son. Jason flipped his hair and Lindsay smiled like he was a big deal.

In the Lexus, Leah quizzed him and learned about the Z-93 Band Battle. "Why didn't you want to tell me? I've seen advertising for that concert all around town. That's great. Your father and I will try to go."

Jason squirmed. "No, don't. I don't want you there."

"Oh, come on Jason." She couldn't resist turning the screws. "It's going to be a packed show, you won't even notice us."

Pulling into Bill Krabb's storage units, she questioned Jason's wanting to work for his grandfather. "It doesn't look safe." Curtis had thought this was a good idea and she'd kept her mouth shut until now, seeing her father-in-law racing around on a tractor with a long-haired man riding in the bucket.

"Looks fun to me. Bye." Jason fled from her car.

At her office, she saw Jeannie from the blue jeans store—another round of vaccinations for her young ones. Her oldest son was leaving for Provo to be mission trained for the mean streets of L.A., where news of drug gangs with machine guns had been widely reported lately. "Oh Dr. Krabb, it's got me in a real tizzy."

Leah half-smiled and half-frowned. "The news exaggerates things. I've never been afraid there."

"Well, no offense, Dr. Krabb," Jeannie said politely, "but I don't suppose you were knocking on doors in the ghetto."

"Going hands-off is hard." Leah had always been uncomfortable giving out parenting advice, let alone to an old pro like Jeannie. "Say, how's the swim wear selection this spring at the mall?"

"It's okay. But that new outdoor store downtown, Eagle's Nest Outfitters, it's full of fun-looking activewear."

Along with kicking her all-day coffee habit, Leah had refrained making any mail order purchases and the urge to go shopping was strong. "Hopefully they have swimsuits."

She finished her final appointments and went home to fetch Robert, who desperately needed some shorts. While the temperature had soared in the last month, he'd dutifully been wearing the same khakis and button down shirts from her pre-college makeover. They rode silently and listened to *All Things Considered*, which reported on the booming sales of affordable and powerful home computers.

Leah was dubious. Her office had used IBM computers for insurance billing for years and the machines made her eyes tired. "I don't ever want a computer at home."

"We'll see about that." Robert acted like he had secret knowledge, but that was nothing new.

Eagle's Nest Outfitters was a tidy shop in a large space downtown. Leah was excited to find lots of low maintenance, expensive clothing from unfamiliar brands and with subtle colors. There were lots of sporty pullovers, quick-drying shorts and durable pants with many pockets and buckles. In a dressing room decorated with topographic maps, she tried on this garb and thought she looked ready for Doctors Without Borders. She pictured herself caring for the war-torn, impoverished masses with her many pockets full of trinkets for the children. Even the swimwear was subdued and flattered her body type, something she could wear at the Black's pool party.

With an armful of clothing she found Robert in the footwear section ogling, of all things, a pair of sandals. Helping him was the store's owner, and Leah got the sense he was new in town. He had a sandy beard, gray hair in a tiny ponytail and wore a southwest-motif button-down shirt with convertible pants and the same sandals that had mesmerized Robert.

"Mother, these use a very high-grade velcro. I knew this day would come."

The owner gave his pitch, "They were designed by grand canyon raft guides who were sick of getting their sandals torn off in rapids. I wear them every day. They're the most comfortable sandal on the planet."

Robert removed his shoes and put the sandals on over his white socks. He undid and refastened the velcro straps a couple of times for no good reason. He didn't bother to stand and walk around, just kept his feet squarely on the floor and marveled at the sandals.

The look on Robert's face sold Leah and she bought Teva sandals for the entire family. Getting Curtis into sandals might be a stretch, but he needed something to wear to the pool party. The owner rang Leah up at the counter and without batting an eye gave her the stunning total, "That'll be nineteen hundred eighty five and twenty three cents. I'm Denny Hudson, by the way."

Leah shook Denny's hard hand and thought him pretty smooth, acting like people commonly racked up thousands of dollars in outdoor wear. She gave him a credit card and pointed out to Robert a poster hailing the soon to be Sheepeater Wilderness. The shop was hosting a slideshow on the area and organizing day hikes and backpacking trips.

Denny pitched her again, "I'm trying to stir up interest. This wilderness designation could be huge, recreationally speaking."

"That's nice." Leah had never set foot in the wilderness and didn't plan to start now. "Are you new to town Denny?"

"I grew up nearby, but I've been living all over. You know, Santa Fe, Boulder, and Missoula, those kinds of places." Denny looked like he wanted to laugh at something.

Robert barely paid attention to any of this and Leah was pleased to see he'd lost interest in the matter. Whatever had happened, Herman Smith's big lawsuit over the Sheepeater Desert had fizzled out and Robert was spending less time at the firm and more time at home and with Curtis at the lab.

Proudly wearing his Tevas from the store, Robert marched soldier-like down the sidewalk. Leah's bags of clothing filled the car's trunk and spilled into the back seat. It felt good to splurge like this, especially when it benefited the rest of her family. Life was glamorous again and the occasion called for a daydream:

Leah knows her carload of safari wear is overkill for a Helen Springs pool party. She pictures herself abroad, in a somewhat civilized third world country, traveling from village to village in Tevas, a sun hat, and quick-drying khakis, serving up vaccinations by the truckload. She doesn't have the stomach for extreme diseases or heavy trauma, those doctors are real life superheroes and it would be an honor providing them with some preventative backup and cooking healthy meals, served in a thatch hut with some chilled wine. On the homefront, if only she could get Robert into some off-white shorts and a southwestern shirt like Denny, he might meet a nice girl at Princeton, pre-med and from a thoughtful New England family that hikes together and loves peanut butter and avocado sandwiches.

Chapter 27

The midday sun hit the black asphalt and the storage unit's I-beams were like a giant radiator. Riding in the tractor bucket with a rafter beam, sweat poured from Jason's body and his cargo shorts sopped it up like a sponge. Storage Unit Ted was perched like a crow atop the skeleton of a structure and accepted the beam from Jason, who steadied it for him to bolt down. Ted wore overalls and wasn't fazed by the heat, his creased skin and mangy hair staying amazingly dry. Grandpa Krabb was a maniacal foreman; once the beam was secured, he spun around to fetch another with Jason crouching and clinging to the bucket. This fevered pace went on for hours and Jason longed for a break. From up in the bucket, he could see the Black Elk River flowing gin-clear through its brushy tunnel and he longed for a dip. The cool water smelled like flowers after a rain, and it seemed like just the smell of it could quench his thirst.

Ted hadn't spoken a word all day, as if anything other than body language would lead to Jason over thinking his role, and this turned out to be quite efficient. The rafters weren't all that heavy at first, but by the time Grandpa Krabb killed the tractor they'd started to feel like wet logs. They headed over to the main building where Ted opened a vending machine with a key ring and motioned for Jason to help himself. Jason gulped an icy Mountain Dew in the shade while Ted pulled up the door to his private unit, which contained a cot, folding chairs, and overloaded bookshelves. The walls were covered in U.S. road atlases and highway maps that were lined with notes.

Bill Krabb removed his mesh hat, sat on a chair and gestured at the maps. "Ted fancies hitchhiking. He's been all over the country."

Jason studied the maps, careful not to read the scribbled thoughts of a crazy man.

Bill Krabb seemed unfazed by the heat and looked to have spent the day in air conditioning. "That's it for the framing Jason. We could use your help again, putting on the corrugated steel with a rivet gun."

"Okay." Jason tried to sound eager and nodded.

Ted couldn't stay still, grabbing a broom and sweeping his space. Grandpa Krabb acted like this was normal and made no effort to move while Ted swept around his feet. Jason jumped out of Ted's way and found himself staring at a New Mexico road map. Printed in blocky handwriting inside the Navajo Reservation Jason read, "Death is a Consciousness Upgrade!"

Jason immediately wished he hadn't read this and wanted to flee. That his grandpa seemed completely okay with Ted's strangeness didn't make it any easier to stomach.

"I should go look for my mom out front." Jason crumpled his Dew can and watched his grandpa pull bills from his shirt pocket. "Um, you don't have to pay me. I'm just happy to help. I need work experience anyways to get on my buddy Allen's pipeline crew."

Grandpa Krabb didn't protest. "How's that going?"

"Not so great." Jason frowned. There wasn't any call for sugarcoating things in this twilight zone of a storage unit. "See, Allen's older brother Stewart was into my girlfriend. Then Stewart choked me and her dad ran him off. Somehow I lost both my girlfriend and my friend Allen in the deal."

"Is that right?" Grandpa Krabb tucked the money back into his pocket.

"Yeah, um, there's more to the story, but I haven't exactly been available so maybe it's not that bad."

Grandpa Krabb squinted out at the new framing as if he'd already moved on. "Okay, thanks for working hard today."

"Yup. Oh and thanks for that old tape of Uncle Stevie, it's super cool."

Grandpa Krabb ignored this.

Ted stopped sweeping and came over to pat Jason on the back. "Yeah Jason, thanks for the help." Ted's voice was sturdy and confident. He didn't sound nearly as crazy as he looked. "I heard you're a guitar man. I'd like to play guitar. Maybe in another life though. This one keeps me busy."

"Cool." Jason was suddenly okay with Ted. There was something in his voice that was the most assuring thing ever, like knowing everything was possible. On his way out the door, Jason's eye landed on a map of Idaho where a quote surrounded Helen Springs, "What kills you makes you stronger!"

That night in Stone Bluff, Jason was at peace with everything that'd been nagging him. He felt close to Betsy, as if she was aware of his contentedness from way down in Nevada. For dinner, he ate seconds of his mother's avocado lentil salad and found it nourishing. Upstairs, he wasn't compelled to practice as his stage fright had disappeared. After a long shower in his en suite, he crawled into bed and slept with the dreamless intensity that was only possible when going through puberty.

* * *

The Blacks' pool party was Saturday, the third of July. There weren't any fences out in Sunset Range and Jason, Marty, and Doug just walked on the lawn around the Blacks' house to find a sparkling pool empty of swimmers. This was a shame as Jason felt like Aquaman in his new baggy swim trunks and navy-blue Teva sandals from the Eagle's Nest.

Diane Black greeted the boys in a two-piece red swimsuit with a built-in skirt. She looked impossibly tan and certainly hadn't been in the pool yet considering the poof and style of her hair. Her toenails were painted sapphire and her lipstick matched her firehouse suit. From under his bangs, Jason studied her body and saw it was the same sleek body that her daughter flaunted around school. He compared Diane and Becca to Alaska and California, different climates but both with great scenery.

Diane rested a bejeweled hand on Marty's arm. "Well, hello there, young man! Will your parents be joining us?"

Marty half-smiled and shook his head. "They work on Saturdays."

"Oh that's a shame. Dave wanted them to see the new backyard. He's really proud of it. Now you boys go see the girls. Okay!"

Sunning on the pool's edge, the girls were a mirage of oily, nubile skin. Becca Black rose to her elbows and studied Jason through white sunglasses. She fixed her skimpy white bikini top with far too much wiggling and then reclined next to Valerie Smith, whose bikini matched her golden curls and whose spiking breasts rose like mountains over the pool. Overloaded by female swimwear, Jason executed a dramatic cannonball before his boner rivaled the diving board. This soaked the shrieking girls and drew applause from big Dave Black, who flipped burgers at the grill in neon green Big Dog shorts and shouted, “About time someone used the pool!”

Jason stroked to the deep end, stalled on his back and listened to the sounds of tinny machinery and raspy pumps. He remembered that Betsy was afraid of underwater sounds, had said it was like something coming for her. Another splash. Marty Bachmann was in the pool, all grinning teeth and caved-in chest. Jason splashed him playfully. Water-bound Marty displayed no more grace than did terrestrial Marty and he acted as if swimming was the most exciting thing ever. Doug watched and peeled off his shirt, revealing a chest like rising dough. The same stringy black hair that sprouted from his upper lip also fanned from his nipples. He carefully entered the pool by the stairs and swam out to meet Jason and Marty in the deep end with a giddy expression on his face.

Jason had wanted to be with his fellow Sunset Rangers on the day before the show. It felt good messing around like this, like something the Beatles might’ve done in a spare moment. He splashed Marty again and then threw Doug across the water like a cat.

Becca came and dangled her russet-colored legs from the diving board. Jason chatted with her while Marty and Doug treaded water as if being circled by sharks. She talked about her summer: lots of shopping trips to Salt Lake malls and sunning poolside. “I was hoping to do more partying, but this town’s so lame. How’s your Mexican girlfriend?”

“She’s from Nevada and I haven’t seen her.”

“Why did you kiss Valerie if you had a girlfriend?”

“Um, it wasn’t like that. That kiss was just a joke. We’re always joking about something.”

“Valerie didn’t think it was a joke.”

“Oh.”

“You shouldn’t have done that.” Becca lightly kicked his head with her wet toe. “Don’t be a shithead Jason.”

More kids arrived at the party and Jason noticed that Becca's scene had changed over the summer. She'd recruited the next generation of jocks and top tier girls from the upcoming junior class. These kids seemed elated to have moved up a rung and they waited for Becca to come and show them how to act.

* * *

Leah had managed to get Curtis into some linen shorts and a short sleeve polo for the Blacks' pool party. He'd refused to wear the sandals, said the Velcro itched his feet, and instead went in sockless loafers. Robert had strapped on his new Tevas (over white socks) and wore a long sleeved Princeton T-shirt with an old pair of blue swim trunks (with Velcro pockets). Leah was done up from head to toe in synthetics from the Eagle's Nest. She wore a wide sun hat with mesh vents from which her fine hair poked through like grass. Beneath her moisture-wicking blouse and quick-dry safari shorts was a stoic one-piece beige swimsuit that she was excited to reveal, but only if the moment felt right.

The three Krabbs sat around a patio table, staring at a bowl of corn chips and not saying much. Curtis drank a Bud Light, Robert sipped water and Leah had a peach daiquiri, served up from Dave Black's weatherproof bar that was custom-built into the patio. There were plenty of Mormons in attendance, who didn't drink, but who were the most thrilled with this patio bar and lined up for virgin daiquiris. Leah figured every Mormon at the party would have a patio bar by the end of summer, stocked with decaffeinated Pepsi and juice boxes. She was always impressed by their lust for life, considering all their restrictions.

Dave Black also showed off his outdoor speakers. He played classic rock CDs from a disc-shuffling unit. Dave explained to Valerie Smith's father how the player held eight discs. Mr. Smith was enthused, "Honey, did you hear that? There's a disc slot for our whole family," and cackled over his own joke.

The Loverboy song "Turn Me Loose" came on and Leah tapped her Tevas on the patio. Music and daiquiris went well together and she hummed to the lyrics.

Dave Black was also inspired and spun over to Diane, who barely managed to set down her daiquiri before being danced away. With her dance moves suddenly on the spot, Diane kept her poise and demonstrated a stiff upper body style while letting her feet and legs switchblade across the newly stamped concrete. The kids laughed and the adults were entertained, save for Robert and Curtis, who seemed concerned. This was Diane's shining pool party moment and Leah was happy for her, liked seeing people excel at the things they loved. Dave danced like a goofball jock: open-mouthed, head jarring back and forth, bare feet clomping out of time and making it look like a ton of fun.

When the song was finished, Dave gave Diane an ogre-like kiss and then jackknifed into the pool with his sunglasses on and initiated a game of basketball on his poolside hoop. Teams formed: Jason, Doug, Marty, and Dave Black against Becca's junior jock squad. Jason swam circles around everybody, constantly scoring and high-fiving with Dave.

Leah watched the king of the jungle in action. When had he grown up? He looked so collegiate and manly, dominating the pool game like Poseidon—if only the school district hadn't axed the swim program he might've gone to the Olympics. Now if she could get him to cut his hair; he'd taken to wearing a ponytail, which gave Curtis fits, but at least Jason's hair was now out of his face. Then there was the matter of his heinous grade point average, but it was summer and she went and fetched another daiquiri from Diane at the bar.

She returned to her quiet men and went to work on Robert. "You should go join your brother's team."

Robert blinked and stirred forward; she knew how he hated to disappoint her.

"I'll just watch," he said. "Mindy will be arriving shortly with her family. I don't want to be wet when they show up."

"Honey it's a pool party. I'm sure they won't mind."

Mindy had been around too much lately and Leah suspected they were secretly engaged, a shame since Princeton must be full of interesting girls from interesting families and interesting places. Mindy was lovely, sweet, and righteous, but she was boring. For Leah, the culminating, fairytale event of parenthood was to dance with Curtis at their son's wedding, a celebratory ending to one of life's most daunting challenges. And now she feared Robert would be whisked off and wed in some secretive and exclusive temple ceremony that she wouldn't be allowed to attend. What was so secretive about a Mormon wedding? Did they gargle sheep blood or something? My goodness, she thought, remembering how alcohol made her melancholy, did the Blacks ever make a sporty daiquiri!

Leah realized her alcohol impairment just as Herman and Liz Smith walked up with their five children, Mindy and her younger brothers. Herman was a serious and fit-looking gray-haired man with bushy eyebrows and long, unusually pink fingernails that he habitually wiped clean while eating a messy burger. Lured from the pool by grilled meats, Jason joined their table and Dave Black bounced around him with tongs, filling his paper plate with dogs and brats. Dave was clearly smitten with Jason, who was after all the ultimate pool party guest—a guy who loved to eat and swim.

"Over eighty percent of Idaho is federally owned," Herman Smith said. "That's wildly out of balance. Much of that is already restricted and there's more wilderness on the way. I understand the need for protected public lands, but that's millions of acres totally out of the picture and forever off limits to any kind of revenue or industry."

Herman immediately got on Leah's nerves, so self-assured and staid with his meek wife mindlessly nodding agreement; she was probably mulling over the furtive details of Robert and Mindy's wedding.

"What's wrong with wilderness?" Leah knew some things here, had belonged to the Sierra Club back in college. "California is full of wilderness areas and it's the seventh largest economy in the world. Unless you stand to directly profit from some kind of land raping, then I don't see the harm in having wilderness." My goodness, she thought, that had sounded a little raw.

Herman wasn't fazed in the least. "And it would be even bigger if all those natural resources weren't off limits!" He smiled and licked his small teeth. "All joking aside Leah, this is about fairness on public lands. Wilderness designation affects an inordinate amount of space relative to the small number of people willing to walk for miles only to get nowhere. And now we have a heavy-handed president, making up rules and regulations by executive order, which is totally against the constitution. The more rules the government comes up with, the more people it hires to manage these rules and we're just piling on our debt."

"What about the wildlife?" Leah was getting tired. "The fish and the birds have a right to thrive."

"Assigning intrinsic value to wilderness is a murky proposition, Mother," Robert said softly, clearly torn between defending her and disagreeing with her. "That's too teleological a consideration for me, as if wilderness is ethically good just because it represents the natural order of things. This leads into intelligent design and divine origins. I believe ecosystems are evolved and open-ended and that they have no final cause, which isn't to say that natural processes aren't seeking toward certain end conditions, but that they are more than likely independent from anything supernaturally external."

Mindy proudly grabbed Robert's hand and Herman watched his future son-in-law with rock-groupie eyes.

"Yeah," Jason said, smirking. "What he said."

Everybody but Curtis laughed at this.

Chapter 28

Curtis drained his Bud Light and crushed the can, disgusted to learn that a year's worth of Princeton tuition had gone right down the drain. He excused himself to the restroom before Robert spewed anymore of that ivory tower mumbo jumbo. If only he could go back to some other time or place when the world wasn't so murky, before corrupt politicians, huge militaries, clandestine agencies, and all these asshole contractors running things from behind the curtains. But he knew there'd never been such a time and, anyways, somebody had to live through these strange days, that's just the way the world worked. The only good thing to come out of his knowing things was the revelation that the universe was full of infinite possibilities and this greatly helped his depression. And now the drilling companies, their lawyers, and their politicians were blaming this wilderness deal on the new presidency. Yup, that goddamned tree-hugging president had thrown the environmentalists another bone and good luck finding out otherwise.

The Sheepeater Basin was better left alone anyways, it was barely suitable for cattle grazing. The few ranchers that held Sheepeater grazing allotments were a resilient bunch. It usually took those guys a full day from the pavement to even reach their stock, crawling along four-wheel drive paths overgrown with sage and riddled with crumbly, jagged rock. The thin soil out there was full of bentonite and the roads became an impassible clay for weeks after a rain. The ranchers told stories of getting pickups mired in milkshake mud after the tiniest of showers and having to walk back to the pavement for days. Nowadays, they all brought ATVs as backup, but a few held on to the old ways and worked the place on horseback. These guys were some of the last cowboys and Curtis was sorry to lose them.

Just before dark, Curtis raided the desserts. He filled up on cookies and brownies and went to sit with Leah on the edge of the golf course for the Sunset Range fireworks, held on the eve of the Fourth and smaller than the city's display, planned for tomorrow night after the Z-93 concert. A sunset haze rose above squat brown mountains that were dotted with stumpy junipers and in jagged contrast with the sea of placid green fairways. The evening was warm and the kids, still in their swimsuits, fanned out across the golf course for a taste of freedom.

When the fireworks commenced, Dave Black pumped the nation's greatest hits on the outdoor speakers, the "Star-Spangled Banner" followed by "The Ballad of the Green Berets." BOOM! The fireworks started.

Leah leaned her head against Curtis's shoulder and swayed to the music. Curtis thought about his dead brother Stevie who'd boldly carried his guitar into war, trying to make a difference. Curtis laughed and proudly considered that Stevie had been much braver than his big brother. Still, Curtis was thankful for how lucky he'd been and imagined, for the umpteenth time, blowing the whistle on the shit he knew. Jesus, they'd probably kill him and then start another war. He didn't want to start any wars.

BOOM! The fireworks finale coincided with Lee Greenwood's "God Bless the U.S.A."

BOOM!

BOOM!

BOOM!

The adults clapped and commented on how impressive the fireworks were for a homeowner association.

"Bachmann Foods was an extremely generous sponsor this year," Dave Black said, laughing. "All that chicken nugget money!"

Leah stood and steadied herself on Curtis. "Still so hot. I'm jumping in the pool."

She stripped down to her swimsuit, right there on the edge of the golf course. Curtis didn't even know she owned one anymore. "Right now hon?"

"It's the perfect moment."

Robert and Mindy walked up holding hands. Mindy had always brightened Curtis's mood, so much optimism and a smile that could melt a reactor wall. Robert would do well to marry Mindy, much better than some entitled girl from Princeton with some mumbo jumbo major. Robert was a good boy who'd make all the important cuts. His working with computers was certainly a positive turn and wasn't it funny how this whole World Wide Web thing had just snuck up out of nowhere?

They all watched Leah clumsily gathering up her clothes.

"Don't let Mom drive you home Dad." Robert snickered and Mindy made the mistake of joining him.

"Mindy," Leah said. "Are you going on a mission anytime soon?"

Curtis grabbed Leah's arm to steer her away. Of course Mindy sensed nothing malicious and informed her cheerily that girls, if they went at all, waited until their twenties. "It's totally not required for girls. I may not go, with nursing I..."

"Oh but maybe you should," Leah interrupted, "Imagine the places..."

"Come on honey," Curtis interrupted, "You kids have fun to-night."

Mindy smiled at Curtis and Robert frowned.

Dave and Diane both wolf whistled as Leah sauntered onto the diving board. She tip-toed to the edge and gave a little hip shake to the pool party before plugging her nose like a schoolgirl and jumping in. Curtis hadn't seen this coming. Had anyone in the history of the world ever really seen anything coming?

* * *

The high schoolers were gathered in a dark grove of evergreens on the edge of the fairway, passing around a plastic vodka jug that Becca had stolen from a case in her garage. Jason watched her sip from the bottle, wince, and then quickly wash it down with warm cola. It seemed that Becca was trying on a new persona and he figured she hadn't done much drinking. Jason made a show of taking a strong pull but secretly swallowed a tiny amount, taking a move from Ron's playbook.

The other junior recruits made an effort and were repulsed by the taste. Even Marty took a swig, but Doug declined and stood resolutely aside with his fellow Mormons, Valerie and Brad Smith.

Mindy's teenaged brother Brad, was a big-eyed, wholesome lad who, as a freshman, had been cruelly nicknamed Bambi, simply for being too adorable. Over the summer, however, it seemed that Brad's nuts had dropped with spectacular results: six feet tall, shiny brown hair, glowing blue eyes, powder-white teeth, and a giant Mindy smile. Most astonishing was the gritty stubble on his face and puffs of golden chest hair poking out his collar. He was the top recruit in Becca's new scene and seemed to have partnered with Valerie. This didn't surprise Jason at all—the world, working on Valerie's behalf, had simply sent Brad Smith through a double round of puberty and turned him into George Michael.

Becca took a second, deeper pull and soon her face was hanging and she laughed at everything. In a snap, she was drunk and Valerie was mad at her. "Really Bec? Our parents are like right over there."

"So?" Becca giggled. "My parents had daiquiris with breakfast."

Marty spoke up, "She's right. There are some drunk parents here. Jason's mom just jumped in the pool."

"Huh?" Jason had missed this and couldn't picture his mom swimming.

Brad was tense and looked like he wanted to go tattle. "Come on guys, let's do something else." His deep voice sounded like something off the nightly news.

There were three other juniors, Kate, Kim, and a boy called Rafferty who appeared to be vying for Becca. Shirtless and obviously strong, Rafferty had shaved his head as part of a baseball team pact, North Helen was going to state.

Rafferty took a long drink. "No way man, I've fucking earned this."

Kate and Kim also seemed new to drinking. They were game and seemed a little scared.

"You're a big guy," Rafferty told Jason. "How come you don't play football?

"My mom doesn't want me to. I don't know the first thing about football."

Rafferty had no response for this. He drank more vodka and shouted at Becca, "Let's go steal some beers already. Straight vodka? Really Becca? Jesus Fucking Christ."

Brad squirmed in his topsiders. "Enough, okay! That kind of

talking just isn't necessary."

Becca clung to her vodka. "Suit yourself. There's all kinds of beer in the garage."

Armed with beer, the kids roamed the golf course in their swimsuits. Rafferty chugged warm beer like Gatorade in the dugout and tried to sing Garth's "Friends in Low Places." He flubbed the lyrics until Valerie jumped in and saved the song, pegging the high register and raising the hair on Jason's neck.

Wielding her vodka bottle like a torch, Becca swaggered over to Jason, trying to sing along. She couldn't sing at all, but she was seventeen, beautiful and drunk in a bikini.

Becca whispered close in his ear, "I got some pot back in my room." Her arm went around his waist.

"From who?" Jason immediately feared Stewart's role in this.

"One of my dad's carpenters. Let's sneak off and smoke some together. Then I'm going to kiss you. Valerie said you're good at it."

What did the world have in store for him tonight? Recent experience had taught him that life wasn't that simple, that he couldn't wander off with the hottest girl in school, get high and make out like it was no big deal. He wanted Betsy here, wanted to wander off and go whole hog with her, not start a new roller coaster ride with a whole other hog. Still, Becca's white bikini had its own magnetic field, and her touching and soft whispers had him gun-barrel hard.

"Hurry up, let's go," Becca warned, "before the sprinklers turn on." She made a sultry laugh.

Brad was entirely fed up with this scene. "I don't like this. I'm leaving, maybe I can still get a ride home with Mindy." He seemed to be waiting for Valerie to offer him a minivan ride.

"We should stay, Bradley." Valerie watched concerned as Kate and Kim staggered off leaning against Rafferty.

"I know Val, but my dad would have a flipping fit if he knew I was around drinking. I could get kicked out of Scouts for this!"

Rafferty blew up cursing, "Fuck! Watch it! Shit!"

Kate and Kim were vomiting in unison and mostly on Rafferty. Kate collapsed to the grass with a gurgling burp. Kim said she felt much better but then threw up again. Rafferty was horrified and gagged.

Marty suggested that he roll in the grass. "Stop, drop, and roll dude."

Rafferty did this and dredged himself in pukey grass clippings.

"Fuck!" Rafferty burped and then puked. The smell of vodka vomit rose from the fairway and made everybody squeamish. Kate and Kim tried to stand but couldn't. Valerie activated her health class skills and made an assessment, "We should take them home."

Kim and Kate hated this idea. They promised to sober up but couldn't walk anywhere. The sprinklers turned on and there was screaming and running for Becca's house, though Rafferty stayed behind to power wash himself in the sprinkler jets. Jason went to help Valerie with her patients. Kim was tiny and Jason tossed her across his shoulders like a bag of dog food. Her skin was cold and she shivered against him. Brad followed his lead and carried Kate, his topsiders slipping on the wet grass. Valerie walked between them and Jason felt her watching him. It was like he carried her too.

The party was over at the Blacks and they snuck the drunk girls into Becca's walk out basement. Valerie dried them off with pool towels and vowed to watch them. Doug offered Jason a ride home but Becca intervened, "He stays."

The alcohol had caught up with Jason and he suddenly felt drunk. "Yeah, Becca, I don't want to be a shithead."

Becca pretended she didn't hear this and marched upstairs.

Valerie stopped Jason at the slider door. "Good luck at the concert. I hope you guys win."

He stared into her doll eyes and was overcome with a realm-jumping intensity, much like during their minivan kiss. Valerie was the least wayward person he knew. She'd avoided the worldly paths that he'd taken, but she knew things just the same. Jason knew she felt sad for him and he didn't like this. Brad walked over, acting much too fatherly, and this clearly aggravated Valerie.

Jason suddenly wanted to help them. "You know guys," he flipped his hair and they were rapt upon him. "I got mixed up with a South Helen girl. I fell hard for her, like I can't stop thinking about her. But she also scares the crap out of me."

Brad looked confused. Valerie looked like she wanted to be kissed.

Jason kept playing with his hair. "You guys are like the cutest couple in the history of Idaho. Just know that love really pops when it gets frightening."

Brad puffed up, "Well I don't like the sound of that!"

This was Jason's drunken goodbye with Valerie. He wouldn't be seeing much of her if things went his way and he wanted to make sure Brad was up to snuff.

"Chill out Brad. Grow your hair out and start mouthing off in church. Don't be such a dad. Otherwise you'll lose her. That'd be a shame because you two could really burn the house down, once you get that Mormon Kama Sutra."

Valerie was still a sucker for his jokes. Her golden curls jiggled with laughter. "Oh Jason. Don't ever stop joking."

Brad poked Jason in the chest. "What the flip are you talking about? You're just drunk and acting stupid."

Brad obviously knew something about the secret sex book, otherwise why get so aggressive? At least he'd showed some backbone and Jason was pleased to finish with Valerie on a funny note.

Chapter 29

On Sunday, the Fourth of July, Jason watched the morning from the kitchen's picture windows. A few cottony-white clouds floated around the Black Elks and the gash of river through town looked like it was being hugged by Helen Springs. Strange how the world seemed so peaceful on what promised to be the most hectic day of his life.

His mother came downstairs, wearing a robe and looking rather spent. She made him a surprise breakfast of fried eggs with spicy breakfast sausage from the deli counter. Leah sat down with him and shocked him by eating a sausage. "Are you nervous?"

"No."

"What kind of music should I expect to hear? I don't like how you kept me in the dark about this."

"You're still coming?" Jason frowned. "Now I'm nervous."

"Well don't be. It'd be a shame to worry. Life only hands you a few special moments."

"Thanks for the sausage."

"I bought hot dogs too, but don't expect me to cook them."

Jason said he already knew how. "Betsy's mom just boils 'em up like eggs."

Leah looked like she might be sick. "That's lovely. Are you still seeing Betsy?"

Jason shrugged. He couldn't explain to his mom that while he hadn't seen Betsy, she was still with him, because they were tapped into an atmospheric teen line.

Leah half-frowned and half-smiled. "I still feel that the situation at her house was entirely inappropriate. Otherwise, I might apologize for my behavior that morning."

"That's okay. I got some, uh, feedback that opened my eyes to the situation. So I know you were just being a mom."

"Are you dropping out of school?"

"Um, I dunno. Things have been pretty cool around here lately. Might not be so bad, being a senior with a really cool band. I still hate North Helen but for some reason I'm gonna miss it."

"I certainly hope you'll stick around. Dropping out of school would also be entirely inappropriate."

Upstairs, Jason relaxed with a chaw in his bean bag. There was nothing better than a big chaw after a good feeding and his lower lip vibrated with pleasure. It was another hot day, but he didn't want to wear cargo shorts on stage. The fancy jeans he'd worn at the shitkicker bonfire were now faded enough to be suitable for rock and roll. He slipped on his Vans, which hadn't smelled right since the flume, and a plain white T-shirt. Being called the Sunset Rangers would downwardly affect their cool factor and he couldn't go on stage looking like a rich kid. It was surreal thinking about playing on a stage. His only experience playing in public had been late night up at the shitkicker bonfire, when he'd realized he wasn't any good. What if tonight resulted in a similar realization only in front of a crowd? What consoled him this late in the game was that Marty and Doug thought he was up to snuff and also some other force that he couldn't pin down, except that it was calming and seemed to come from deep within himself.

The band gathered for a quick rehearsal at Marty's before heading to the concert. Marty wore slacks, loafers, and a polo shirt, and Jason almost barfed. "Dude, we're not a jazz band. Can't you wear something else?"

Marty obviously hadn't considered his outfit and studied himself. "Like what? These are my clothes."

Doug looked more agreeable in black jeans, black sneakers and an old T-shirt, heat stamped with Garth Brooks's likeness. They played their three songs on autopilot and sounded good. Marty cased up his gold-trimmed black bass and the purple-sunset Les Paul that Jason always played. Doug would be stuck using the drum kit provided by Z-93.

* * *

The concert was at Riverside Park, a sprawling expanse of green grass, naturally occurring boulders, cottonwoods, and scrub oaks. The park separated downtown from the river and its main attraction was a large white bandshell facing the city's low-slung skyline. The Band Battle Blowout was the culmination of Z-93's well-funded campaign to dominate south Idaho's rock-and-roll airwaves. So much hoopla seemed like overkill since the station had already won a huge following with its commercial-free, classic rock blocks (with trivia) every weekend for the entire year of 1993. During the work week, the station played all kinds of random stuff, good and bad, old and new, and everybody just tuned in out of habit.

People were out in force for the Band Battle. Girls in jean shorts, cheap sunglasses, and tank tops walked around drinking soda. Sweaty boys in cargo shorts and T-shirts stood in line for hot dogs and cheese pretzels. A giant beer garden overflowed with noisy college kids and happy Mormon couples strolled wide-eyed around the park, tickled to have a huge party in their sleepy town.

The Sunset Rangers were the only band from Helen Springs and the boys were shocked to find the other bands were mostly from out of state, even Portland and Seattle. These bands had cooler names like The Grundys and Slowcooker and The Munchies and they'd come for the cash prize and studio time offered to the winner. These other bands hung around the backstage area, sporting facial hair and tattoos, looking totally out of place in south Idaho. There was an all girl band called Sanscock and they were fierce-looking girls with dark red hair and piercings.

A cool guy gave Jason the stink eye but complimented Doug on his Garth T-shirt, "Rad shirt man!"

Doug was intimidated, "Was he being ironic?"

Marty nodded, "I think so. Garth must be cooler than we realize."

Jason didn't exactly know what ironic meant and figured it was just like aesthetics. Sizing up the other bands felt weird, as he'd never approached music like sports, but that was the backstage vibe. "Yeah, um, we're actually going to battle these bands?"

Marty nodded, "Music as a zero-sum game. At least we have the home field advantage."

A man carrying a clipboard approached the boys and introduced himself. "I'm Craig, the host." Craig had a square face, snazzy shoes, and gelled, black hair.

"Are you a DJ?" Jason had never met a DJ.

"No." Craig kept his eyes on his clipboard. "We're a voiceover station, we don't use DJs. I work for marketing. Sunset Rangers, you guys go on at eight. You get five minutes for set up and twelve minutes to play, no exceptions." Craig finally looked up at them and jabbed a thumb against his chest. "If you have any questions, I'm your man."

"We're the local act," Marty said proudly.

"I know," Craig said. "Tell your friends to dance."

The battle started at five and the boys watched the bands from right below the stage. The large crowd that had gathered for the concert remained on the park's outskirts, more concerned with the snack bars than dancing to live music. The acts were polished and experienced on the stage, but they were far from explosive and innovative. What stood out to Jason was how they all sounded alike, even Sanscock sounded like Nirvana. But it also seemed they weren't letting their hair down and he blamed this on Craig, for going around backstage acting like an asshole—helluva way to set the stage.

Backstage, Marty tuned Jason's guitar for him and gave a pep talk. "We can win this thing. I haven't heard anything memorable."

Doug nodded, "And we got the cheese going for us. None of those bands seemed cheesy enough for Helen Springs. You guys plug in, and I'll start 'Mighty High' with a drum solo, to get the crowd going for us."

Jason liked this idea. Walking onstage, that jackpot feeling swept over him and boosted the easygoing confidence he'd been feeling all day.

After a three second pre-flight inspection, Doug unleashed a fury upon Z-93's tom-toms. This took everybody by surprise, the crowd stopped milling and headed over in a swarm. Even Jason and Marty were shocked at Doug's level of intensity. Their Mormon Metronome had gone nuclear. Doug's jumping the gun somehow helped to close the circuit between the boys and Jason felt the current like a change in the weather. This shifting of forces induced a great roar in the crowd but Jason could barely hear it. He was a part of the sound now, like how running with the wind cancels its speed. Everything was delightfully slowed down and there was no fear anymore.

Did what I had to do
Wanted to do what I had to do
But when I had to
And I didn't want to
I got high, so high
Mighty high

Doug didn't have a mic and Marty nailed the backup vocals solo, sounding just like a grown woman:

We come to play
Ever-y-day
Sunshine or Moon
Midnight or Noon
Gotta plan to fly
So mighty high

Jason was astonished by how easy it was to sing the right notes, they seemed to bubble up from his stomach into his throat:

When I was done
With what I wanted to do
I didn't think
It'd matter to you
I got high, so high
Mighty high

Backup Vocals:

We come to play
Ever-y-day
Sunshine or Moon
Midnight or Noon
Gonna stay so mighty high

Now I'm done
With what I did
I'm getting high
So high
Mighty high ...

Fans screamed and pushed up against the bandshell, looking up at them with awe. The snack bars were deserted. The band looked around at each other, confused but ecstatic over what was happening. Letting his hair fall around his face, Jason addressed the crowd, "Howdy Helen Springs!"

ROAR!

"Well Alright! We're the Sunset Rangers!"

ROAR!

"Let's hear it for those other bands too." ROAR! "You know they came all the way from Portland and Seattle, that's so awesome isn't it?"

ROAR!

"This next song goes out to a special person. I know she's listening somewhere out there."

Singing 'bout our scene, those American liquid dreams
Long hair and sneakers, blues riffin' on the speakers
Moby Dick met Mary Jane and we were on our way
Gettin' messed up on the range

Isn't it grand when you can hardly stand?
Soaking it up till it feels just right
Keeping one on through the burning night
Drinking down your perfect potion
Whatever suits your best emotion

A familiar voice screamed up to him and Jason looked down at Isabel Perkins. Standing beside her was the Black Boots Woman, or was Betsy an illusion? No she was real, in a red tank top and jean shorts, watching him with groupie eyes and dancing.

"Fuck yeah dude! You Rock!" This came from Allen who danced with Krissy on his serape-covered shoulders. Wearing a bikini top and jean shorts, Krissy swayed to the music and raised up her hands, a glowing lighter in one and a joint in the other. The pipeliners were down there too, Sean Patt, Bruce Simpkins, and Ross Early, throbbing with the crowd and trying to dance like hippies.

Singing in the choir at the shitkicker bonfire
Rock on Black Boots Woman, dancin' in my dreams
Breaking the rules and beating the fools ain't easy like it seems
What you do or don't you do
It's only up to me and you

The atmospheric teen line was real. It had reached Betsy across the deserts and mountains and brought her back.

Shiver and shake
Like a lemon squeezing earthquake!
Ahhh—aaa-AA—AA—A LEMON SQUEEZING EARTHQUAKE!

Marty pointed at his watch and held up seven fingers to Jason. Seven minutes left for "Feet." This left plenty of time for another speech and some derelict jamming.

"Thanks Helen Springs! You rock!"

ROAR!

"I didn't write this next song, but I think it's about assholes. The world's full of 'em. Don't let them get you down! Peace!"

ROAR!

Feet feet are kickin' down the door
Feet feet are taking us to war
Feet can bring you home from far away and long ago
Feet make you like a river, flowing, able to move
Water has feet, runs until the sea
People have feet and like to groove...

ROAR!

Chapter 30

The Munchies followed the boys and benefited from the warmed-up crowd. While not as cheesy as The Sunset Rangers, they were cheesy enough and Helen Springs boogied. Velcro sneakers stomped the grass, keys jingled in cargo shorts pockets and denim-clad hips were shaking it. The boys listened to the show from one of the snack bars. Doug bought a round of colas and they slurped in a daze.

Marty was thrilled, "That was amazing. I can't wait for the results."

Jason scanned the crowd for Betsy, couldn't wait to see her. It had been hard not staring at her during his final song. He was about to dive into the crowd when his parents strolled up wearing sandals. Leah especially looked dressed for a desert trek. "I had no idea you played *that* kind of music. Who wrote those songs?" She sounded wildly happy for him.

"Jason did," Doug said. "He's got a knack for the cheese."

Jason thought to mention Uncle Stevie's role but didn't.

Curtis crossed his arms and acted stern, but the sandals seriously cut into his honcho-ness. "Good job boys. I didn't know you could play guitar like that Jason."

Jason let his mom hug him and fist bumped with Curtis, obviously his first time—since nobody ever fist bumped for physics.

A classic purple sunset faded in the desert sky as Jason squirmed up to the front row. The concert smelled of stale hairspray, sweat, and snack bar popcorn. Strange how his first concert was the one he played. He found Betsy dancing up front, black boots and all. It was too loud to talk and without missing a beat or any kind of greeting she started dancing with him. She'd changed in Nevada, wasn't quite as scrappy and hard-edged, or maybe Jason had again forgotten how wonderful she looked, especially while dancing.

The Munchies finished to roaring applause and Z-93 classic rock came lightly over the speakers, ZZ Top with a gravelly voiceover: "STAY TUNED FOR THE CROWNING OF THE BAND BATTLE CHAMPION. ZEEEE-NINETY-THREEE IDAHO ROCKS!"

Allen's tree trunk arms encircled Jason from behind. "*Amigo!* You guys rocked! I had no idea you were a guitar man."

Sweat soaked through Allen's serape, his hair was lighter and his tan darker. Krissy was wasted but her complexion was clear and her ribs weren't showing beneath her bikini top. Isabel and the pipeliners circled around Jason, clearly in support of how awesome he was. Isabel's hair was messy and the outfit was still early fifties, Idaho male. She was obviously now a part of this crew, independent of Ben Stone. Betsy kept dancing, which was fine since Jason didn't know what to say to her.

Craig appeared on the stage with his clipboard and two flashy blond girls, presumably also from marketing. The girls held an oversized check for the winner, two thousand bucks, and they watched Craig looking at his clipboard. Craig tapped the mic and addressed the crowd, "Okay, here we go with the Band Battle results."

"Who's that guy?" Betsy asked. "He don't belong up there."

Jason unsuccessfully tried making eye contact with Betsy. "That's Z-93's man, Craig."

"Okay, first let's get all the bands up here." Craig turned and made small talk with the blond girls while the bands emerged from backstage. Jason climbed up the front of the bandshell stage. The crowd saw him and roared, Allen was especially loud. The Sunset Rangers were a shoo-in and Jason again felt bad for the other bands.

The boys listened nervously as Craig named each band, starting with those at the bottom who'd least impressed the judges, all the way up to Sanscock at number three. The boys excitedly realized they were in the top two. Marty and Doug grabbed hands. Jason watched Betsy, finally making successful eye contact, and she tried to hide her smile by pouting.

"Okay, we ready for the winner?" Craig finally looked out at the noisy crowd. "Okay, number two, The Grundys. Let's hear it for your Battle champions, The Munchies!"

The crowd settled down for a moment but then roared anyways for The Munchies.

Marty dropped Doug's hand. "What about us?"

Doug frowned, "Maybe he forgot."

Knowing things about how the world worked, Jason knew better and felt sad for Doug and Marty, and anybody else who hadn't learned about the world.

The Munchies were quickly presented the check and the stage cleared out. Marty confronted Craig backstage, flanked by his rangers. "What about us?"

"What about what?"

"Where'd we place? Every other band got mentioned."

"Huh. Sorry about that."

"So where'd we place?"

Craig flipped a page on his clipboard, acting bothered. "Okay, here's the problem. You guys were dead last, you weren't on the front page. That's why I missed you. Honest mistake."

Craig didn't stick around for Marty's tantrum.

Doug tried calming Marty, "Forget it man. We sounded awesome."

Jason felt guilty. "Sorry, Marty, I must have upset the judges, talking about assholes and stuff on the mic."

"What judges?" Marty's face was pinched and red. "It was just Craig, the asshole."

* * *

The heartbreak was all over Allen's face. "The Munchies were good, but you guys owned it. What the hell *amigo?*"

"I know what happened." Betsy came and stood by Jason. "You got shut down by the man."

The pipeliners knew all about the man and nodded their agreement. Ross Early was their music guy, "You guys had your own sound, can't put my finger on it, but it was custom."

"Yeah," Jason said, "We call it cheese."

Having Betsy and the pipeliners lined up behind him was better than any grand prize. Jason learned that Allen and the girls were skipping the fireworks to go camping at the Black Elk Reservoir. He walked Betsy out to the parking lot.

"My dad's at his camping spot, right down by the water."

Her braid had a hexagonal pattern that looked wildly complicated. Jason wondered if her grandmother, or some cousin or aunt had twisted up this masterpiece, sitting behind her on a spacious porch with a grand view of Nevada.

"I called your teen line. Some god awful noise kept answering."

"Sorry about that. My brother hijacked the teen line with his computers."

"Huh? Whatever, I hate soppy phone calls anyways."

"Are you coming back to town?"

"No." Betsy bit her lips. "I saw Isabel this morning at the truck stop. She told me about your concert. I think you'll do just fine out in Portland and Seattle."

"I don't know what's in store for me anymore."

"Nobody's seen Stewart around, if you wanted to come camping."

She made this sound like a bad idea, but then why the offer? It seemed that the higher the stakes were between them, the harder to get she played. When they'd met at the shitkicker bonfire, with the whole world before them, she'd gone after him with wolflike fervor. Now, with the future uncertain and much stronger feelings between them, she acted like she might barely tolerate his company.

Still, it wasn't a hard decision for Jason. He loaded up into Betsy's Ford with Allen, Krissy, and Isabel and made the drive out to the reservoir. Betsy turned down an unmarked path that coursed through the sage and onto the hardpan sediment of the receding reservoir, drawn down by another prosperous growing season. Camper trucks and tents were lined up on a flat beach and a campfire reflected across the choppy, darkened water.

Betsy killed the engine and briefed Jason, "My Dad's buddy Mahlon and his girlfriend came up from Vegas. Mahlon was with dad in Vietnam."

Aaron Aarsdrager held court around the campfire. He sat in a lawn chair with his legs crossed, wearing blue jeans, Velcro sneakers, and a snap-button shirt, drinking Busch and engaged in conversation with a heavyset black man. A small woman with a massive, hair-sprayed perm stared at the campfire and looked bored. Donna wasn't around and Jason wasn't surprised.

Aaron nodded at Jason, "How ya doing Country Club?" He sounded anything but hostile.

"Good. How's it going?"

"I'm okay." Aaron's tone confirmed that Donna had left him. "Meet Mahlon, he's a casino rent-a-cop." Aaron chuckled at this.

Mahlon harrumphed at this, "Country Club? And you're hanging out with Aaron?"

Jason had never met a black person and certainly hadn't planned on it happening at a campfire in the Black Elks with Aaron Aarsdrager.

"He's with Betsy," Krissy answered, sounding dumb. "She took his..."

"No more a that talk!" Aaron was annoyed. "We already dragged Country Club through the mud. Get that boy a cold beer and leave him be."

Trying to be well-mannered, Jason eyeballed the woman and waited to be introduced.

Mahlon took the hint, "This is Angie, she hates camping."

Jason wondered if Angie was Vietnamese. It suddenly felt like Vietnam had everything to do with him; his family, Betsy's family, high school, and his awakening as a musician were all somehow tied together by a war that he knew very little about—probably should've actually read some of that war literature assigned by Mr. Ebbett.

The evening was cool up there, the perfect night for a fire and the Las Vegas visitors sat a foot closer to the fire than the locals. Krissy chain smoked, drank beer and twitched a lot, as if she couldn't get comfortable. She wasn't totally strung-out like the last time Jason had seen her, but like Isabel's hair, permanent damage had been done and she wasn't the same person he'd met at the shitkicker bonfire. Her coffin complexion had cleared but scars remained on her cheeks and probably on her soul.

Angie wrapped herself in a blanket and Mahlon addressed Aaron calling him a rent-a-cop, "I wear pleated pants and button downs, get my shoes polished on the job."

"I'm sorry to hear that." Aaron seemed disgusted by this.

"Nah, man you don't get it. We're high tech, everything's a system now. Alarm systems and sensor systems, and a camera system you wouldn't believe. We got an army of security cameras. I watch the people running these systems, make sure there's no funny business. Get my drift?"

"So you're a spy?" Aaron still sounded disgusted.

"In-house intelligence."

"He's a spy," Angie spoke up. "Big brother really is a big brother."

"Yeah, you card dealers get my drift." Mahlon turned to Angie and pointed two fingers at his eyes, "I'm watching you, too."

Mahlon's giant laugh vibrated the frame of Jason's lawn chair.

"You're a card dealer?" Allen was suddenly interested in Angie. "Always wondered how you get that job. You grow up playing cards or something?"

Angie laughed at him. "I was raised in a strict Baptist family. I was just a waitress who they decided to train. That's it." She had a trace accent and eyes that joked with everybody all at once, as if the whole world was a big joke.

"We like to promote from within," Mahlon said. "Had my eyes on Angie from the get-go." Mahlon laughed and pointed two fingers at his eyes again.

Angie explained her situation to the kids, "I was fooled. You'd think someone with shiny shoes and pleated pants would take a girl on a fancy trip. But no, the big brother takes me camping in Idaho. I didn't sleep last night, fucking werewolf or something howled all night long while Mahlon snored."

Betsy shook her head, "These mountains are full of scary things."

Aaron's mustache wiggled with laughter, Krissy smirked, and Betsy looked ready to get teased about something.

Jason wondered what in the woods could scare Betsy.

Krissy fought off another mini-seizure and laughed. "Go ahead Betsy, tell us how you saw the bogeyman."

"I've been thinking about that a lot lately." Betsy kept her eyes on the fire and everybody waited silently for her to continue. "The week before I started sixth grade we camped here during a heat wave. I was swimming by myself, not very far out, where it was still shallow. The mountains flooded that spring and the beach was full of washed up timber. Mom and Dad were sitting right here in their chairs watching me, but they couldn't see down the shoreline because the camper was in the way. Out the corner of my eye, I kept seeing something down the beach, moving through the logs. When I watched close, there'd be nothing there, I only caught the movement when I wasn't looking directly down the beach. I knew something was coming for me but I couldn't move or yell or do anything about it."

From the look on her father and sister's faces, it seemed to Jason that they hadn't heard this version before. Krissy looked sorry for bringing it up and Aaron sat forward, gripping his chair and frowning. Everybody else was all ears.

"It went on like that, knowing something was there but I was paralyzed. I was confused, like when you wake up from a deep sleep and you don't recognize where you are. This was like that, I looked for him but couldn't recognize anything. I knew it was a he from the get-go. Suddenly I saw his head and shoulders above a log. His head was about the size of a stop sign and his eyes were big as apples. He had perfect teeth and all kinds of hair, but the worst part was he was smiling at me."

Betsy's story had charged the atmosphere. She looked scared and Jason cringed, imagining her as a sixth grader, cowering on the beach, crippled with fear.

"What the hell was it?" Angie said from the edge of her seat. "What did you do?"

"Still sounds like a cow to me," Krissy said. "Range is full of them."

"It wasn't a cow and he wasn't just any old creep," Betsy said. "He was a ghost, or something. A motorboat came speeding by and he vanished. I was able to move again and I ran and shut myself in the camper."

"Goddamn perverts are everywhere!" Mahlon sounded nervous. "Even out here in the middle of nowhere. Too bad Aaron didn't catch that son of a bitch and shoot his balls off."

"Trust me Mahlon," Betsy said. "Seeing that creep just paralyzed me. Wasn't anything a gun could've done."

Aaron shot a stern look at Mahlon. "Whatever happened changed Betsy. She started having nightmares, came to sleep in our room that whole year."

"You saw a cow!" Krissy stayed with that.

"You know," Isabel said. "Creepy archetypes are a common theme in the women's lit I read. They're larger than life and capable of putting a curse on you."

Mahlon made a big deal of rolling his eyes at Aaron, like this was some serious mumbo jumbo. Betsy nodded at Isabel, as if this was common knowledge.

"Well he was the first creep to put a spell over me." Betsy rocked back in her chair, pulling her knees up and resting her black boots on the seat, revelation spreading across her pouty face. "Feels like I bucked his curse though. Seems he only had his power long as I kept quiet."

Mahlon was scared straight up in his chair, "No more talking about ghosts, Angie's gonna have a hard time sleeping again."

Aaron's mustache quivered. "You believe in ghosts, Mahlon?"

Mahlon shook his head, "Nah, don't go there Aaron. We were just boys, that jungle was playing tricks on us."

"That's not true Mahlon. Betsy's right, keeping quiet makes it worse. I'm sick of pretending this world ain't full of ghosts."

Mahlon erupted with sadness, shaking and whimpering out mumbo jumbo. Aaron cried peacefully.

Seeing grown men overcome by emotion was scarier to Jason than any ghost. The girls acted like they'd seen it coming.

* * *

Betsy led Jason to her tent, zipped them up inside and invited him down onto the air mattress beside her. It was chilly away from the fire and they snuggled under her sleeping bag.

Entirely contented, he kissed her cheek and nuzzled her ear. "Just so you know, I'm not gonna do it with you tonight." He was so tired.

"Showing off is tiring. I know that better than anyone." Betsy gave him the softest kiss in their history.

Closing his eyes brought visions of ghosts and alien bogeymen, though anymore it was hard to be scared by something that'd been there all along. Not exactly knowing *how* they were real had been the scariest part of them. It seemed they weren't real like he'd imagined them to be, more likely they shared bandwidth with atmospheric teen lines and derelict guitar riffs, hard things to pin down but present, nonetheless.

After a solid night of dreamless sleep, Jason awoke the next morning overloaded with affection for Betsy. What started as snuggling quickly turned to making out. She was unbelievably warm and at first shy—possibly due to morning breath—but they forged on, each craving the experience. In a flash, they stripped off their underwear and he was on top of her. She grabbed his boner and inserted it with no maneuvering, in fact the speed at which it went in surprised them both. Compared to their last try, the difference he felt was nothing less than spiritual. He watched her eyes close and her mouth open; she seemed to float up into space, carrying him with her. There was no cursing, hip thrusting, panting, sweating or any of the theatrics that had marked their first coupling. This was slow, effortless, and totally incapacitating. That he was in a live socket became of increasing concern to Jason. In an act of herculean self-control, he overrode his autopilot and pulled out just in time, diverting his river across her sleeping bag.

Gravity slowly returned to the tent and their bodies ticked like shutting down engines. Betsy looked more stunning than ever: sparkling brown eyes, midnight-black hair, rippling skin and a regal face cast in the filtered tent light. It still amazed him how her appearance kept shifting on him, but now the difference was that she was totally there. This was the whole picture and he wouldn't want it any other way.

Betsy played with his hair. "Come visit me in Nevada."

"Can I ride Molly on the playa?"

"If she'll let you." Betsy looked sad and forty years old. "Living down there has ruined it for me. It was better when I knew I had to come home. Now it's the same every day. I never thought I'd get bored there."

Jason felt old. "Things never turn out like you think they should. The world has rules about this."

"I was just showing off when I met you. Never thought I'd fall in love."

Betsy looked shocked to have admitted this, but happy too.

Jason smiled at her and blushed. "I never saw it coming either."

Epilogue

In August, Curtis grilled up a mess of hot dogs on the back patio for Jason's eighteenth birthday celebration. As a countermeasure, Leah had sliced up a freighter's worth of fruit and tossed a jungle of a salad.

Grandpa Krabb, Mindy, and Jason sat in patio chairs, facing town and listening to Robert explain his plans for returning to Princeton. "I've conceptualized server software that will make it super easy for anyone to have a Web account. Grandpa, you'll be able to send and receive messages, to anyone, anywhere in the world."

"Is that right?" Bill Krabb looked amused. "Does the government have a position on this Web stuff? It's got to be all over their radar."

Robert looked like he hadn't considered this. "I would hope so. I mean they helped invent it." Robert thought some more. "But I don't suppose they're aware of how easy I plan to make it."

Bill Krabb considered something for a moment and then laughed.

Curtis walked up, "What's so funny over here?"

"Nothing Dad." Robert sounded nervous. "Computer stuff."

Curtis pointed the hot dog tongs at Robert, "You talkin' software?" He sounded extra cocky. "I don't get all the fuss. Sure, everything depends upon it, but where's the excitement? I'd rather be in the lab with my sleeves rolled up, telling the programmers what I need from them. The firms we contract with have armies of software guys, locked away in suburban office parks, far from the action and mostly without a clue of the bigger picture."

Robert frowned at his father. Curtis rambled on about "algorithmic modeling" and this sounded to Jason like his Aunt Judy saying something like "aesthetic malaise." A month ago he would've rudely pointed this out to his father, but Curtis had mellowed on him ever since the Z-93 concert. Jason wasn't sure if he'd finally earned the respect of his father or if Curtis had just given up on him. Whatever the case, they got along now and here he was cooking hot dogs!

The high slopes of the Black Elks were brown as grocery bags and a portion of the lower slopes were charred from a recent wildfire. The fire had almost been that summer's biggest news, if not for the drug bust in the Sheepeater Desert. Federal agents had arrested a Helen Springs man they claimed had been receiving Mexican contraband flown into a makeshift air strip on an abandoned ranch. They hadn't named their suspect, but the agents bragged of confiscating a huge pile of drugs and cash, a high-end Enduro motorcycle equipped with oversized gas tanks and a wardrobe "worthy of several kingpins" from one of Grandpa Krabb's storage units.

Leah was still appalled by the news and couldn't stop talking about it. "You expect drugs in big cities. I can't believe there was a huge demand around here, not until this guy showed up and created it. It's pure evil."

"That's No Man's Land out there," Bill Krabb said. "Wonder what tipped them off."

Jason was convinced that the culprit was Stewart Heber, and more and more he found himself in the odd position of knowing things. His mom seemed to know he knew something, she kept bringing it up and looking expectantly at him.

Robert smirked. "Funny how it coincided with the wilderness designation. They should designate a smuggler's hiking trail, to honor the historical land use."

Only Curtis laughed at this.

The family gathered around the patio table. Curtis poured a bag of potato chips into a bowl and slid it over to Jason. Then, most astonishingly, he handed him an icy Bud Light from a cooler. Jason couldn't hide his excitement and opened it before Leah could protest.

"Here's to manhood Jason. Enjoy it." Curtis tapped cans with Jason and the whole family toasted him, Leah wiping away tears.

But later in his room, upon his bean bag, under his swim meet ribbons and with his Fender Catalina in his arms, he felt like a boy. He longed for Betsy but calling the Nevada number she'd given him hadn't worked, as nobody would answer the phone. What kind of ranchers didn't answer the phone? The situation wasn't exactly dire as he had plans to go visit her next week with Allen, Krissy, and Isabel—before heading to the high desert of east Oregon to join Allen's pipeline crew. On the fifth of July, on the way back from the reservoir campsite, this opportunity had fallen into his lap. Allen had complained how hard it'd been replacing Ben Stone, all the new hires had clashed with the crew and left for greener pastures. Out of nowhere, Krissy asked Jason if he was up for the job. Without hesitation he'd said yes, and not so much because he wanted a crack at the pipeliner persona, but more because he didn't want to lose his connection to Allen and the Aarsdragers. Allen squinted at him for a second in the rearview mirror, as if hiring another privileged kid might not be a good idea, but then his eyes slacked back to their normal state and he smiled. "I think that's a *primavera* idea *amigo*. Consider it done. Hell, if you play guitar for us like you did last night, then you can even sleep on the job!"

But Jason had no intentions of slacking and he'd returned to help finish his Grandpa Krabb's storage unit with a vengeance. He was quite proud of his new callouses and aching back and was ready to keep the lights on in Portland and Seattle.

The doorbell rang and quick footsteps bounded up the staircase. Ron entered without knocking, packing a can of chaw and gloating over having been in Wisconsin all summer. His brand new concert T-shirt shined like a neon light, his pale goatee was more pointed—or maybe his teeth had grown—and Jason noticed a new pair of Teva sandals, but quickly averted his eyes because Ron had strange feet with long nails and goatee hair on his toes.

Jason was happy to see his friend and was excited to catch him up on everything, the Z-93 concert, his work and love life, his father giving him a beer! Of course he couldn't get a word in because Ron dominated the conversation. His Wisconsin friends were more epic than ever, the shows were all stunning and paradigm-shifting, and then there was the Milwaukee honeymoon with Shelly, where he'd watched her rock out on the mats and win most every event.

"It was sweet," Ron licked his teeth, "I stayed in her room at the downtown Hilton that whole week, mini-bar, HBO, the whole package."

This was by far the most Ron had ever shared about his relationship with Shelly and Jason was wracked with envy, but not for Shelly.

A whole week living like adults? What he wouldn't give for one night with Betsy in some high-rise hotel, sexing up the sheets, eating room service hot dogs, and falling asleep to VH1. Instead, he imagined his upcoming adventure to Nevada, Betsy's grandma making him sleep in the hay barn like a wayward bull where some jilted cousin would probably try to snip off his balls. That Ron's love life went easy while Jason's was paved with roadblocks was perhaps the world's most persistent mystery.

Robert knocked on the door and waited to be invited in. Jason introduced him to Ron and, aside from their wardrobes and grooming habits, he was struck by the similarities between the two. They were both gaunt-faced and bespectacled, their personalities emitted the same overconfident intelligence, and now they studied each other like brothers from other mothers.

"Mom's on the phone from the hospital," Robert said, keeping a close eye on Ron. "She asked for you. Your phone should work now."

Jason hadn't known anything was wrong with his phone—again—and he guessed Robert was behind the unanswered phone calls to Nevada.

"Jason, I just saw Mr. Ebbett," Leah said in her doctor's voice. Jason could tell she was half-frowning and half-smiling. "He's had a serious heart attack and asked to see you."

Why the hell did Mr. Ebbett want to see him? Jason wasn't in the mood to explain himself to Ron. "Catch you later man. Let's go for a cruise before I leave next week."

Ron was confused. "Where the hell are you going?"

"Nevada and then Oregon." Jason handed Robert a thick manilla envelope that had come from the energy company. "Um, I think this is my pipeliner's contract. I don't really understand it. Can you read it for me?"

Robert nodded and cautiously accepted the envelope. "What's going on Jason? Is Mom alright?"

"She's fine. A patient wants to see me."

"Pipeliner's contract?" Ron was pissed. "Dude! You're not doing senior year?"

"Nope." This shouldn't have surprised Ron, had he been paying attention to anyone but himself.

Jason wasn't in the mood for Z-93 classic rock on his way to the hospital. Since the Band Battle, the station had stopped its uninterrupted weekend rock blocks, even though they'd promised them the whole year of 1993. This was obviously because the Sunset Rangers had pissed off the man and Jason took great pride in this. He slipped in his Bobby Womack tape and hummed along to "Lookin' For a Love" with the volume low, not entirely sure what was in store for him at the hospital.

Leah had never taken Robert to the hospital much, but Jason's childhood had been full of hospital visits. The hospital was a familiar place to him, one he associated not with illness but novelty wheelchair rides and free snacks in the doctors' lounge. He rode the elevator with a melancholy ranch couple, a man in smudgy bib coveralls and a tattered baseball cap and a woman in black jeans, cowboy boots, and a flowery blouse. He realized they were the same couple that had rudely vibed him at the train tracks on the way to the shitkicker bonfire last spring. They looked fried with emotional stress and he wondered if their imagined daughter at the state college had been injured or fallen ill.

There was nothing he could say so he sang the "Lookin' for a Love" chorus in his highly-tuned, rock-star voice, jumping around the octaves for fun. The man didn't seem to notice, but the woman closed her eyes and smiled with relief. They stepped off on what Jason knew to be the cancer floor and he sang louder, one last gust for their sails. Next stop was the cardiac care unit where Leah, wearing quick-dry clothing and a stethoscope, met him at the elevator and guided him past rooms of sick men.

"What are you doing up here?" Jason didn't see any kids in the rooms.

"I always visit the patients I know. Talking is good for them. Being hospitalized is very boring."

Jason's idea of his mom's practice had been her jabbing kids with vaccines and prescribing antibiotics. But this sounded vaguely spiritual to Jason, which must have something to do with souls, whatever they were. "Why does he want to see me?"

"He likes you."

Mr. Ebbett was propped up in bed watching a cable news show, surrounded by piles of newspapers and news magazines. Leah skillfully used her pager to divert herself, and teacher and student were alone. Mr. Ebbett was in a hospital gown and hooked up to much apparati. His face was unshaven and pale, his eyes red and shrunken, but he smiled when he saw Jason.

"Mr. Krabb," he bellowed, "I hope you like Mexican beef."

"Sounds good to me." The hospital was full of beefy cafeteria smells that had Jason craving a squishy pile of Swiss steak—though Mexican would work fine.

"No, you fool!" Mr Ebbett jabbed his thumbs at the TV. "That's what this NAFTA deal means for your dinner plate. All those juicy Idaho steaks? They'll sell those to fat cats in New York, London, and probably now Beijing. Meanwhile we'll be gnawing on the rubbery scraps of free trade. Do you know what they feed cows in Mexico?"

"No."

"Well, I don't either, really." Mr. Ebbett disarmed somewhat, as if he needed a rest from blustering on like his old self. "But I suppose it's a mix of thistles and cactus. I read in the paper today they're gonna scrap our beef plant here, the one I worked at after Vietnam, and ship our cows to Arkansas where they'll be slaughtered by Mexicans!"

Jason thought maybe this was ironic, but he didn't want to say so and be wrong in front of his ailing English teacher.

"This country's had its share of money grabs, but at least we knew who we were facing. But your generation, Mr. Krabb, yours will have to face the faceless. These new corporations, they aren't of men anymore. I'm not sure what they are, but I'm sure the house is haunted."

Jason nodded. "Ghosts."

Mr. Ebbett tried to relax but he couldn't slow his breathing. Jason grabbed the clicker and switched the news over to VH1, hoping for some fleshy bottoms or some K.d. lang to soothe his teacher. "My mom gets her news from public radio. She thinks cable news is bad for you, says it kills you slowly, like hot dogs."

"Your mother's an angel. Don't ever forget that Krabb."

"Okay."

They didn't speak for a while, just watched a Black Crowes video, "Remedy."

"This song's not so bad. By the way I caught your performance on the Fourth of July. That was quite the show. I never knew you were a musician."

Jason wasn't surprised, all kinds of people had been complimenting him on the show. "Funny thing about that, I could hardly play until I was thrown into some heavy fire. You were right about that, sometimes people learn best under fire."

"Except it didn't work for you with algebra. Did it?"

"No."

"I'm a pushy old fart, huh?"

"Yes."

"That's how I ended up in here. See I wasn't about to stay off the Sheepeater Desert and thought I'd start scouting elk on foot again. I didn't get very far before it felt like I had a boulder in my chest. I could hardly breathe and sat down, that's when the pain set in. I crawled back to my truck and barely drove it back to the pavement. And wouldn't you know it, there were a bunch of hippies parked at the intersection. They'd heard about the new wilderness and came out to watch the sunset with flowers in their hair, doing pot and everything.

"These kids put me in their van and drove me straight to the hospital. Of course I lectured them the whole way, said they should go invent something and told them there's no such thing as a free ride. At the emergency room I offered them money but they wouldn't take it. Turns out that ride *was* free."

"That's gotta be ironic?" Jason was riveted.

"Yeah, it woke me up. Then I went into emergency surgery and I feel pretty damn good considering. But today the doctors told me I need a bigger, more expensive surgery that I might not survive. I'm okay with that. Know why?"

"Why?"

"The best part of nearly dying is knowing things. Crawling through the Sheepeater with a busted heart, I realized that lies never cancel out. Unless you own up to them there's always a little remainder to deal with. That remainder is what's coming for all the bullshitters, these NAFTA royalists and those wilderness-designating, asshole bureaucrat-politicians. When they finally see what's coming for them, like I have, that's when all hell breaks loose."

Jason was pleased to see the familiar ranter's glaze had returned to

Mr. Ebbett's eyes, though this latest tangent was difficult to follow. It reminded him of when Doug got stoned at the shitkicker bonfire. Was this why he'd wanted to see him, to have another tangent?

Mr. Ebbett needed to catch his breath. Jason heard him ask for the oversized hospital water jug. He handed it to his teacher and then realized, with a chill, that Mr. Ebbett hadn't actually asked for it, not by speaking anyway.

"Thanks. How'd you know I was thirsty?" Mr. Ebbett winked at him. "You're wondering why I wanted to see you. I didn't expect to lecture you. Okay of course I did, but mainly I wanted to compliment you on your concert. Where'd you come up with those riffs?"

Jason shrugged. "I'd like to think they came through the atmosphere, but I heard them on an old tape."

"They were beautiful. I believe that riffs are the purest and strongest signal an individual can send. Also, your mom tells me you're not doing senior year?"

"Yeah, I got a pipeliner's job out in Oregon. I figure it'll give me a leg up on the music scene out in Portland and Seattle."

"What have I wrought?"

"You had nothing to do with it."

"I doubt that, Krabb. I threw you into heavy fire every chance I had." Mr. Ebbett shook his head and winked again. "Kind of like throwing pine needles on a shitkicker bonfire."

Author's Note:

The tangible inspiration for this novel came in 2011, when I did a whitewater kayak trip down 150 miles of the Owyhee River. This trip started on the Duck Valley Indian Reservation in Nevada, and ended near Rome, Oregon, passing mostly through the remote desert of southwest Idaho. The first rapids on this stretch occur where a ghostly looking pipeline spans the river gorge, and I decided that this zone would make a good setting for my novel. Since the Owyhee desert lacks any real population, I needed to create a town for it, which ended up as Helen Springs.

I love to hear from readers, so please drop me a note at pipelinernovel@gmail.com. I'm also happy to talk with book clubs.

Amazon reviews are greatly appreciated—if you enjoyed the novel, or disliked it, please let the world know your thoughts.

I've also written a short story book, Feather Falls which may be purchased for a nominal fee in the Kindle Store or downloaded for free on Smashwords.

My Bio: I was raised in Sioux City, Iowa and have lived for stints in Idaho, Colorado, and West Virginia. Northern California has been my home since 2002. I enjoy the outdoors; paddling wild rivers and hiking in rural zones, and skateboarding with my kids in urban zones. To stay current with my writing projects, send me an email, visit www.shawnhartje.com, or join me on Twitter: @pipelinernovel.

Thanks for reading!

—Shawn Hartje